Sound of fury—voice of Death . . .

To withstand such a terrible bombardment, a man needed nerves of beryllium and blood vessels of tungsten. *Or he had to be Richard Camellion!* Every third or fourth vehicle was either destroyed, turned over, or knocked off the twisting route that lay between giant mushrooms and other strange kinds of trees and shrubbery. Turned into blazing bundles of agony, men ran in circles, only to collapse from shock or die when they inhaled fire that ate their lungs the way a blowtorch eats tissue paper. Scores of Reds, toward the rear of the disrupted column, stopped firing at the flying platform, jumped from the carriers, and sought sanctuary under the canopies of the mushroom plants.

The explosions did not lessen. More carriers were shattered, the twisted, burning metal and pieces of things that had once been human beings vomiting upward, much of it coming back down on top of the mushrooms. There was one final explosion at the end of the line. Men screamed, and then were silent.

Flying back over the blasted Red column, the Death Merchant saw that he had not miscalculated. The black smoke floated almost straight up. The smell was not pleasant. He inhaled the nauseating stink of burnt oil, and the odor of leather and fire-blackened flesh.

The Death Merchant Series:

#30 in the incredible adventures of the

DEATH MERCHANT
THE SHAMBHALA STRIKE
by Joseph Rosenberger

PINNACLE BOOKS • LOS ANGELES

DEATH MERCHANT #30:
THE SHAMBHALA STRIKE

An original Pinnacle Books edition, published
for the first time anywhere.

First printing, October 1978

ISBN: 0-523-40385-2

Cover illustration by Dean Cate

Printed in the United States of America

PINNACLE BOOKS, INC.
2029 Century Park East
Los Angeles, California 90067

This book is dedicated to
The Krauses—
Bob, Marilyn, Barbara, and Nancy
of Buffalo Grove, Illinois

*For there is nothing covered,
that shall not be revealed;
neither hidden, that shall
not be known.*

—Luke 12:2

Deep within the unconscious of every human being there are dark impulses of savagery that should be let alone, that should not be uncovered, brought to the surface, and probed; correlatively, there are fantastic secrets to man's primohistory* which, if revealed, could destroy the stability of the civilized world. . . .

—Richard J. Camellion

*Primohistory: parallel to prehistory but differs from it in that it presupposes the existence of advanced civilization.

THE SHAMBHALA STRIKE

Chapter One

Wind! Cold! And death creeping down from the hills! Comfortable in his one-piece snowmobile suit, Arctic cap, and Sno-Mo boots, Richard Camellion stood only a few feet from the southeast corner of Thimphu monastery, his back flat against the ancient stones of the five-story building. The Death Merchant waited, letting his eyes accustom themselves to the darkness of this Roof-of-the-World night. Although there wasn't any moon, the ground snow would hasten the adjustment.

The Death Merchant was positive the figures creeping down from the hills had to be Red Chinese. Who else? The Tibetan border was only forty-two miles to the north. And the "autonomous region" of Tibet was part of the People's Republic of China. At least the Chinese, coming down toward the monastery, furnished an answer to a question that had been bothering Camellion: now he knew for sure that Chinese Intelligence had been watching him and his people. He wasn't surprised. On the contrary, he would have been flabbergasted if they had not been aware of the tiny Posten Expedition. No doubt the Reds always learned about any foreigners who entered the mountainous little kingdom of Druk-yul, or Bhutan as it was called by the Western world.

"The forgotten navel of the world!" That's what Vallie West had called the spit-on-a-map nation. *An apt description!* reflected Camellion. Nestled in the eastern Himalayas, Bhutan was only 90 miles in breadth; extreme length from east to west, 190 miles. Population? A bit over a million. The official language was Dzongkha, which belonged to the Tibeto-Burman group of languages. The majority of people were Mahayana Buddhists of the

1

Drukpa subsect of the Karyud School, which was first introduced from Tibet during the twelfth century.

Well now, into each mission some rain must fall, Camellion thought with amusement, *and we're about to get a cloudburst. I should suppose it's about time. . . .*

The flight from the States to Calcutta had been—as they say in books and movies—"uneventful." The flight from Calcutta to Thimphu, the capital of Bhutan, had been without complications. The Indian government, which administered to the external affairs of Bhutan, had done its part. The plane, a four-engine prop job, had been met by Ugen Wangchuk, a member of the National Assembly (or *Tsogdu*) of Bhutan, and General Sigye Penlop, the commander of the four thousand-man Bhutanese army.

How unfortunate. The audience with King Jigme Singye Wangchuk had to be postponed. His Majesty was ill. A day later, Camellion and his people had driven north in three enclosed jeeplike vehicles and a truck. With the addition of the four Bhutanese soldiers, the entire party numbered thirteen.

Finally they parked the four vehicles, which would later be driven back to Thimphu by Butanese army men. Under a sky that was a deep Holland blue, and a bright but cold sun, Camellion and his party had begun the trek into the mountains. They saw very few people, for the Bhutanese (or Bhutia) were mountain dwellers, living in small villages and isolated homesteads separated by almost impassable terrain.

During the afternoon of the second day, they had reached the monastery, a cluster of tremendous buildings perched on a massive plateau protruding from the slopes of the mountains. The Buddhist monks had made them welcome, Karni Padme Hum, the *Tulku*, or head lama, informing them in British-accented English that they were welcome to stay as long as they wished.

In honor of their visit, two rows of bamboo poles had been planted in the large courtyard, in the form of an avenue. Flags flew from each pole, with the inscription AUM MANI PADME HUM ("horse of the air"), surrounded by magic formulas.

Every part of the welcome was in accordance with social and religious customs. There was the blessing by the

2

Tulku of the *gompa* (monastery), then a meal of tea, roast lamb, and mixed vegetables, with the Tulku and a dozen other ecclesiastical dignitaries, each of whom was a lama.[1] Only Karni Padme Hum and Dumvar Gatze-Ding, another lama, spoke English; yet the conversation did not lag, mainly because Foster Cross and Loren Eaton, two of the Black Berets who were conversant with Dzongkha, talked, not only with the lamas but with the four Bhutanese soldiers, after which Cross and Eaton translated to Camellion and the others.

There had been religious music, the small orchestra consisting of two *gyalings* (a kind of hautboy, or oboe), two *ragdongs* (huge Bhutanese trumpets), and two kettledrums. A bell striking a special rhythm peculiar to Eastern temples was sounded as a prelude. After a few moments' silence the deep-toned *ragdongs* rumbled for a while, then the *gyalings* by themselves sang a slow musical phrase supremely moving in its simplicity. They repeated it with variations, supported by the bass notes of the *ragdongs*, which finally joined the kettledrums that imitated rolling thunder in the distance. The melody flowed as smoothly as the water of a deep river, without interruption, emphasis, or passion, yet producing a strange, acute sense of distress, as if all the suffering of the beings wandering from world to world since the beginning of the ages was breathed out in this weary, desperate lamentation.

At the time, the Death Merchant had felt very uneasy, his intuition in high gear. Hostile forces had seemed to gather around him, and he had had the feeling of being possessed by invisible beings who urged him to leave the country, who warned him that he would not be able to advance any farther, that his search for the fabled Shambhala would only result in dismal failure. By a sort of clairvoyance, he saw those unknown enemies laughing

[1] Written as *blama*, which means "superior"—"excellent." The only monks who have a right to the title of lama are the dignitaries such as the tulkus, the heads of the great monastic colleges, and monks who hold high university degrees. All other monks are called *trapas*—"students." Nevertheless, it is usual to give the courtesy title of lama to aged and learned monks when addressing them.

and rejoicing, then sneering: *We will nullify your agreement with the Cosmic Lord of Death!*

You will try, as you have tried many times before, but you will not succeed! a certain, specific part of the Death Merchant had replied.

An hour earlier, after the Tulku had greeted him and the others, Camellion had asked him for permission to post a lookout at the top of the sixty-foot-high stone bell tower in the center of the courtyard. The Tulku had granted permission, and Camellion had sent Norbert Shireling to the tower, telling him that if he spotted anything unusual, he could contact them with his AN/PRC radio set and that he would be relieved in two hours.

With the approach of twilight, Albert "Red" Degenhardt had crawled to the top of the tower, taking with him a nightsight scope, the best that modern science had to offer. The Mimerex G6, built like an enormous pair of binoculars, and had an 82,000/1 minimum gain, and was refractive and catadioptric. In short, the M-G6 turned the darkest night into the brightest day. Degenhardt would not have any trouble spotting anyone approaching the monastery—unless the enemy had the power to make himself invisible.

Degenhardt's two hours had ended, and Foster Cross had taken his turn in the tower, in the sort of cup above the enormous beam supporting the brass bell. Slowly, he had moved the M-G6 in a circle, sweeping the landscape. At 9:41 P.M. Cross had contacted Camellion on the AN/PRC Electro-5 radio and had calmly informed him, "I've spotted figures coming down from the hills on the north slope. Maybe forty of them. I can't be sure. Maybe a mile away."

"How about weapons?" Camellion had asked.

"Affirmative. Automatic weapons. They're not close enough yet for me to be sure. But they're dressed in white cam suits. They've got to be chinnies. Orders?"

"Stay in the tower and keep watch. Keep your set open. We're coming out."

"We can ambush them," Vallie West had said matter-of-factly.

Before Camellion had been able to reply, Karni Padme Hum had said in his soft voice, "We anticipated that the

4

Chinese Communists would attempt to terminate your existence. We cannot assist you in any way. We consider all life sacred and cannot kill."

Vallie West had spoken up. "Can we assume then that you won't interfere with us and what we have to do?" He had regarded the Tulku with a steady gaze, one that was both demanding and a warning. "We can kill and intend to. Our lives depend upon it."

"*Kushog*[2] *Tulku*, there isn't any guarantee that the Chinese won't harm you and your people," Camellion said evenly, "or do you have some special protection?"

Karni Padme Hum's wrinkled old face had not changed expression. He had continued to stand with his folded arms hidden inside the wide sleeves of his green and orange brocade robe.

"We will not hinder you in any way," he had replied. "It would be immoral if we did not permit you to defend yourselves." He then had smiled, before adding, "We realize that your business is a peculiar one, and we know that you conduct your affairs on the premise that it is not how you play the game that counts, but whether you win or lose."

"As the Buddha once said, 'It is far easier to be wise for others than to be so for oneself,'" commented the Death Merchant. "In the games we play, we dare not lose. We are never permitted a rematch."

"The Buddha also said that 'Advice is like snow; the softer it falls, the longer it dwells upon, and the deeper it sinks into the mind,'" the Tulku had replied softly.

Dumvar Gatze-Ding had interposed in a sly voice, "One might say our 'special protection' is political. The Red Chinese are aware that if they harmed us, or members of the priesthood in other gompas, our tiny nation would rise in indignation. The government in Peking does not want the world to condemn it for killing innocent monks."

The Death Merchant, Vallie West, and Red Degenhardt had then left the hall and had gone outside. Camellion armed with two .44 Alaskan Auto Mags, an eight-inch long Jurras Sionics suppressor attached to each twelve-and-a-half-inch Mag-Na-Ported barrel; West and Degen-

---

[2] The equivalent of "Sir" in Bhutanese.

5

hardt carrying M10 Ingram submachine guns, similarly equipped with silencers.

The three other Black Berets had taken positions around the west and north side doors of the building in which the lamas lived. The four Bhutanese soldiers would watch the south side and east end. As for the lamas, they had departed to one of the upper floors. Paul Gemz, the archaeoastronomist[3] who was also working for the Central Intelligence Agency, would stand guard over Professor Lauterjung and Helena Banya. The three had gone to the second floor of the building.

The Death Merchant blinked several times. Good. He could see twice as well as five minutes ago. His body concealed by the dark shadows, he looked up at the edge of the high roof which projected outward, first downward, then upward, in a graceful five-foot curve.

Holding one of the Auto Mags with both hands—he had no choice because of the over-all length of the weapon and the silencer—Camellion checked to make sure that the other AMP was snug in the breakaway spring-clip holster on his left hip. He felt good about the temophene gloves; they were as thin as silk, yet as warm as goosedown mittens. The gloves were electrically heated, a wire running from each glove to a celsian battery strapped to each of Camellion's wrists.

Camellion cradled the AMP in one arm, then reached down and pulled the AN/PRC radio from its case on his belt. He flipped the Ext-Off-Int switch with his little finger, held the telephone-shaped set close to his face, and pushed the Push-To-Talk button. "Cross, where are they?"

"Damned close," Cross's voice floated back. "They're coming in from both the north and the west. I estimate the ones to the north are a little over ninety meters away. The ones to the west—maybe fifteen or twenty of the cruds—are closer, maybe sixty meters from the end of the building that's farthest to the south."

"All right. Keep your set open. Roger."

[3] Archaeoastronomy: a discipline that combines the method of archaeology and astronomy, to discover what primitive civilizations saw in the skies and how they interpreted their sightings.

"Wilco."

The Death Merchant switched off the radio and shoved it back into its case while he shifted his memory into second gear, focusing on the diagram of the monastery complex that General Sigye Penlop had given him.

To the north, on the other side of the courtyard, was a long building whose middle length could be compared to the connecting section of the letter H. The ends of the building formed the perpendicular sections of the H. Due west, from the center side of the courtyard, was a two-story rectangular building built with one end pointing east, the other west. This building was the infirmary. South of the infirmary was the storage house, its north end so close to the south side of the infirmary that there was only an eight-foot passage between the two buildings. Likewise, the south end of the storage house was only ten to twelve feet from a part of the north side of the library building. The east end of the library was directly in front—to the west—of the Death Merchant.

Camellion had calculated that the Chinese—*Or could it possibly be the Ruskies?*— would try an ice-tong movement and send in teams from the west. The east side was too open: there was only open ground for several hundred feet. then a straight-down drop a few hundred feet more.

Vallie and Degenhardt can handle the creeps coming in from the north. They were positioned at either end of the H-shaped dormitory housing the *trapas,* or student monks. *I'll take care of the rice-and-chopstick boys on this side of the monastery.*

The Death Merchant toyed with the idea of moving to the south side of the library. He quickly changed his mind. Too much uneven land, too many big rocks to the south. His eyes darting from south to north, he scurried across the thirty-foot space to the northeast corner of the storage house and once again looked all around him. He could see fairly clearly for a radius of several hundred feet. Nothing! Only the darkness and patches of yellow light behind the narrow windows of the lama's building, and the *trapas'* dormitory to the north. Plus the background of starlight reflected from the snow, although the courtyard had been cleaned to the bare stones.

Silence! Except for the constantly wailing wind, which

7

at times sounded like the far, far, far away whistle of an old-time steam locomotive. It was apparent to Camellion that the Commies to the north had not yet gotten close enough for Vallie and Red to open fire. Then again, maybe the Oriental Marxists had. *I wouldn't be able to hear Red and Vallie's Ingrams, since they're silenced. On the other hand, I'd hear the chatter of the enemies' weapons. Or could they have sound suppressors? Yeah, it's possible but not probable.*

Camellion strained to hear something. All he got for his effort was the moaning of the cold wind. He didn't like the setup. The trouble with this kind of night fighting was that to survive, one had to have more than know-how based on experience. One had to have sheer luck. Without the vital element of Good Fortune, one could not survive—no way. *But I can't just stand here and wait for them to come to me. Everything is too open. I must catch them off guard. So get on with it.*

Richard carefully looked around the corner of the building.

Jackpot! Good fortune! Four white-hooded figures, each carrying a machine gun, were in the passage between the north end of the storage house and part of the south side of the infirmary. The first two Chinese commandos were only twenty feet away; the second pair was ten feet behind the first two Commie jokers. *A risk! But the odds are definitely on my side.*

The fingers of his left hand around the three-inch diameter sound suppressor, his right hand around the butt of the AMP, the Death Merchant stepped out from the corner and fired.

A .44 AMP jacketed soft-point bullet can go through both shoulders of a bull moose at forty yards. What the 265-grain slug did to two Chinese was ordinarily done only in a slaughterhouse, even if the two men weren't bull moose.

The bullet hit one man full in the stomach, the cannonball impact folding him like an accordion and knocking him back toward the man in back of him. The second Chinese, Wang Wei Chang, couldn't have cared less; he had trouble of his own. The .44 projectile had bored through the body of the first man and had struck Wei

8

Chang in the right side of his belly, shattering the pelvic bone before boring out his lower back. Shocked into unconsciousness, he crumpled and went down, joining the first corpse on the stones.

It took a moment or two for the last two commandos to fully comprehend what had happened. The first man was trying to swing up his machine gun, when the whispering death in Camellion's hands murmured again, the .44 JSP punching the man in the chest, exploding his heart, and taking bits of bone with it as it tore through his back and headed in the direction of India.

Cho Ke-min, the last man, was as quick thinking as he was fast. He ducked low, brought up the machine gun and, as he dodged to his right, snapped off a short burst. He was suddenly terrified when he saw that every one of his 7.62mm slugs had missed Camellion by several feet. He was as good as dead—and knew it! And then he was, his head flying apart from the Death Merchant's next bullet.

Camellion gave the fallen Ke-min a brief glance, thinking that getting shot in the head was a good way to go. *You're dead before you know it, before the brain can register any pain.* "You came close to wasting me, you Chinese chump," Richard muttered. "But you don't win a cigar."

Camellion darted forward, picked up one of the submachine guns—a Type 54, 7.62mm job with a forty-round magazine—and raced to the southeast corner of the infirmary. He had shoved the Auto Mag into the open-sided holster and was checking the Chinese T-54—it was identical to the Soviet designed Sudarev PPs-43—when he heard harsh sounds he didn't like: more 54s roaring to the north. The Chinese could only be firing at West and Degenhardt.

The Death Merchant realized that in his present position the odds were against him. *They can come at me from four different angles, from between the buildings, and from the southeast and northeast corners.*

The T-54 ready to fire, he sprinted to the northeast corner of the infirmary, leaned around the huge stones, and checked the long north side of the building. Richard's eyes narrowed in thought. *Cross said "fifteen or twenty." I've terminated only four of them. The rest of them have to be to the west and the southwest. They haven't re-*

9

*treated. They're just being their usual Oriental selves
. . . very very sneaky.*

He ran back to the southeast corner of the infirmary,
looked toward the south, saw that none of the Chinese
were in sight, then headed out and streaked down the
passage between the infirmary and the north end of the
storage house, dodging around the four Chinese he had
smoked five minutes earlier. Glancing around him before
darting to the southwest corner of the storage house, he
heard a short, high scream of agony far to the north. A
moment later the chattering of Chinese machine guns
stopped. Contact Red and Vallie by radio? Too risky. He
couldn't take the time. His position was too vulnerable.

He moved closer to the edge, every muscle tense and
ready to spring into action. As unruffled as a crocodile, he
poked his head around the corner and looked toward the
south.

Damn! Camellion inhaled sharply with surprise. Five
feet away, a Chinese commando standing by the wall
stared back at him. To the fellow's left was a second
Chinese, carrying a 56-1 assault rifle. Behind them were
two more American-hating termites. All four were garbed
in overwhites—white pants and white parkas with hoods.
Even their insulated boots were white.

The Death Merchant felt like a man with one foot on
the gas and the other on the brake. If he moved back,
they could spread out and paste him to the wall with
slugs. He might get two of them, but not all four.
Camellion took the only possible course of action open to
him: he attacked! He leaped out at the four Chinese, who
were just as startled as he and almost as fast.

The man closest to the Death Merchant, employing the
same strategy, jumped forward, evidently thinking that he
would kill Camellion before Richard could open fire. The
result was that Li Feng-lan and Camellion almost crashed
into each other, each man so close to the other that neither could fire. No Einstein in the think department,
Feng-lan hesitated, his mind gripped with indecision. In
contrast, the Death Merchant was not hindered by such
hesitancy. While he didn't have time to step back and
swing the machine gun horizontally toward Li Feng-lan,
he was still far from helpless. With both hands on the

10

chatterbox, he brought up the weapon the way a farmer would use a pitchfork while pitching hay, the end of the barrel stabbing solidly underneath Feng-lan's chin. A loud grunt came from Feng-lan and his eyes snapped shut as blood and broken teeth dropped from his mouth. He had been knocked out as effectively as if he'd been hit by an ax.

Since there wasn't time for either the Chinese or Camellion to plan any moves, all they could do was react by instinct. As the barrel of Richard's machine gun glanced off Feng-lan's broken chin and moved sideways, Chi Mo Ting, the man who had been to the left of Feng-lan, reached out with his left hand and grabbed the center of the barrel. With his right hand he attempted to ram the muzzle of his own T-54 into Camellion's stomach, screaming *"Un-haeng t'ong dae-bu* (White foreign devil)!"

At the same time, Fim Tien-Shong and Ji Hoklong, the third and fourth men, pressing in close, were unable to fire because Chi Mo Ting and Li Feng-lan, who was falling, were between them and the despised foreigner.

A man with less experience than the Death Merchant would have tried to keep his machine gun. Camellion had more sense; he had to end this and fast. Envying an octopus, he let go of his machine gun, grabbed the barrel of Chi Mo Ting's T-54 with his left hand, shoved the muzzle away from his body, and, with all his strength, leaped as high as he could. With his right hand, which was now free, he chopped Chi Mo Ting above the bridge of the nose with a terrible *Shuto Uke* chop. In the same lightning motion, his left leg shot out, his foot twisting in a *Goju-Ryu* karate sword-foot kick. Ji Hoklong saw the battering-ram blow coming, but he was moving forward and couldn't check his own momentum. The heel of the Death Merchant's booted foot crashed into Hoklong's groin with such force that, in spite of the man's heavy clothing, Camellion could feel the pubic bones shatter and turn to jelly. Hoklong dropped his machine gun, screamed like a banshee touched with the tip of a hot poker, and tried to put his hands over his groin. But all he could do was gasp in agony and stagger in shock.

Fim Tien-Shong, the fourth Chinese commando, jumped back and attempted to swing his machine gun in line with

11

Camellion, who grabbed the sagging Hoklong by the cross-straps of his ammo belts and pitched him into Tien-Shong, who tried in desperation to move out of the way. Those few seconds were all that Camellion needed. Before Tien-Shong could reorganize his moves, the Death Merchant was on him.

In two very fast movements, Richard grabbed the barrel of the machine gun with his right hand, shoved the muzzle to one side, and, with his left hand, used a *Ura Uchi Ken* smash against Tien-Shong's upper lip. While Tien-Shong was feeling his mouth fill with blood and broken teeth, the Death Merchant switched from a back-knuckle fist to a *Tettsui* hammer fist. His first blow smashed into Tien-Shong's left temple, an explosion of force that, had it not been for the fur-lined hood, would have cracked Tien-Shong's temporal bone. As it was, the blow only dazed Tien-Shong. Camellion's next *Tettsui*, to the chin, knocked him out. The Chinese's fingers went limp on the machine gun and he wilted to the ground, blood flowing from his mouth.

Now that the four Chinese were down and Camellion had Tien-Shong's T-54, he didn't waste time. He sent the four Chinese to their most honorable ancestors with a long burst of 7.65mm slugs. He then tossed aside the half-empty weapon, picked up the machine gun he had previously dropped, and ran back to the space between the infirmary and the storage house—just in time to avoid a hail of semi-spitzer projectiles from a T-54 sub-gun and a 56-1 assault rifle. He couldn't be sure, but from the sound of the firing, the Chinese were positioned west of the library.

He ran to the northeast corner of the storage building and quickly surveyed the courtyard. Except for Foster Cross hidden at the top of the bell tower, the courtyard was devoid of life—and so was the east end of the library. Not one of the rice-and-noodle nitwits was in sight.

Very well. They have to be behind the buildings to the west.

Keeping as low a profile as possible, Camellion tore across the east side of the storage house, skidded to a halt at the southeast corner, poked his head around the side, and looked west, at the space between the south end of the storage house and the north side of the library.

Well, throw hot grease on my grits! Five or six or maybe seven Mao Tse-tung morons were at the opposite end of the passage. Seeing him, several of them pulled up short, steadied their machine guns, and fired short bursts, the dozen slugs cutting off a cloud of chips from the corner of the building. But the slugs completely missed Camellion, who had ducked back, dropped to one knee, and now thrust his machine gun around the corner and triggered off a short burst—*That will hold them for a while!*

He jumped up, raced north, turned at the northeast corner of the storage house, and again ran between the corpses of the first commandos he had permanently neutralized. This time he did not put on the brakes when he came to the corner. Instead, he darted straight to the west side, knowing that the Chinese who had just fired at him would either be spread out on either side of the space between the storage house and the library, or else, in an effort to trap him, they would be creeping north along the west side of the storage house. There was always the possibility that they could have moved to the south side of the library, but Camellion didn't think so. Why should they? He was only one man!

Camellion saw at once that the Chinese had chosen to move north. All six of the chopstick stupids were creeping along the west side of the storage house, several of them walking backward as a precautionary measure, in case he would have elected to come at them from the south.

The Chinese jerked to a stop and tried to fire. But the Death Merchant, catching them by surprise, had had a few seconds' head start. His chatterbox chattered, the flashes from the hot muzzle keeping time with the streams of slugs that stabbed into the Chinese. The first two died without a single sound. The third and fourth men cried out as chunks of gilded lead tore through their parkas and peppered their chests. Both of them pitched backward into the last two men who were spinning around in an effort to get their own weapons into action. One did manage to get off a brief, frantic burst, but his slugs went wild. Camellion was in constant motion and the chain of projectiles missed him by several feet. His own slugs blew the man away a moment later, the burst knocking the

13

Chinese against the last man, who died in practically the same instant, from solid-based bullets that cut across his middle and made his stomach think that it had been caught in a meat grinder.

Camellion spun to his left and dashed back the way he had come, his thoughts revolving around the two Chinese who, farther to the south, had fired at him. He was also concerned about the machine guns roaring to the north. New notes had entered the melody of firing—9mm Berthier Bren sub-guns. The Chinese would hardly be using old style British weapons! The Bhutanese soldiers would. They carried Bren guns furnished by the government of India.

But if one of the Bhutanese boys iced the Commie Red, what is he doing outside the lamas' house? And I know it's Brens firing to the north! Dammit! What's going on?

Once again, Camellion paused by the northeast corner of the storage house. He looked to the north, then to the south.

Hammer my hamhocks! A white-clad body lay face down between the east end of the library and the west end of the huge building housing the lamas. How about that? Either one of the Bhutanese boys had wasted the joker, or else Cross, in the bell tower, had zapped him. Cross had gone up into the tower with a NATO M14 rifle fitted with a silencer and a nightscope. Then again, a Black Beret inside the lamas' building, by the west end could have terminated the single Chinese.

I can't continue to stand here! Camellion moved around the northeast corner, alert to any sudden movement from ahead. He had no intention of moving north until he was positive that there weren't any Chinese commandos west of the library, the storage house, and the infirmary. He was taking a chance, but no more so than if he had stayed in one spot and waited.

Camellion had moved halfway up the east side of the storage building when Peng Wo looked out from the southeast corner of the Library. If the Chinese Red commando had ducked back and stayed there, he would have remained alive, at least a little longer. But he was overconfident. Thinking that the figure ahead had not seen him, he stepped out and squeezed the trigger, firing so fast that he did not take time to even aim.

14

Even so, it wouldn't have done him any good. The Death Merchant had seen him the first time. Camellion, knowing that he did not have time to retreat, did the only thing he could do: watching the corner of the library, he darted to the southeast, at an angle that took him toward the huge building which housed the lamas. He was sixty feet out into the courtyard when Peng Wo jumped around the corner of the library and fired like a wild man, triggering off a dozen rounds.

Peng Wo did not have time for his brain to tell him that he had fired at empty space. Even if he had realized his fatal mistake, he would not have had the opportunity to correct his aim and swing his machine gun to the right.

You poor dumb slave! Camellion fired a short burst of six rounds, and all six slugs stabbed into Peng Wo's right side, the projectiles ripping through cloth, fur, and flesh, each one less than an inch from its predecessor. His side shot away, the dead Peng Wo fell back against the corner and slid to the stones. He had drunk from the cup of life and the last drop was gone.

Camellion raced straight to the library, jumped over the body of Peng Wo, ran up the south side of the building, and charged around to the west end. He stopped at the northwest corner and surveyed the entire area to the north. Empty. He turned and looked at the rocks and uneven rubble on the incline to the west. As bleak and quiet as the moon.

Quiet to the north, too. The machine guns had stopped firing.

Camellion pulled the radio from its case and switched it on.

"Val, what's the situation up there, and who's with you and Degenhardt?"

Vallie West's deep voice, coming through the Electro-5 speaker, was touched with faint amusement. "I figured you'd notice the Brens. Two of the Bhutanese showed up. Don't ask me who sent them. I only know they're fighting fools and saved the day. Maybe I should have said 'the night.' The Commies are piled up in front of us as thick as dead branches in a forest."

"Any more around?"

15

"Half a dozen or so. They ran back into the hills. I don't think they'll come back."

The cool voice of Paul Gemz broke into the conversation. "I had Eaton tell two of the Bhutanese to go out and help West and Degenhardt. I hope you don't mind, Camellion?"

"Hope again!" Camellion said coldly. "Fortunately, it worked out. The next time we might not be so lucky."

"But this time it worked," Gemz said smoothly. "You're all alive and safe."

You idiot! Camellion thought. *From the instant of our birth, we exist on the brink of death. Getting into Shambhala is one thing!*

But how will we get out?

16

Chapter Two

The sun is always welcome in Bhutan which, lying in the eastern Himalayas, is more remote than any other Himalayan state, since it is away from the routes leading from the Indian subcontinent into Tibet. The mountain system, with peaks rising above twenty-one thousand feet, and at a mean distance of from four hundred to five hundred miles from the sea, forms a barrier against the warm winds from the south. Even during the rainy season, when the monsoons bring rain from the Bay of Bengal to the hill section in the south, the air is cold.

Now, in the brightness of the morning sun, the beautiful but inhospitable region around the lamasery stood out in stark and lonely contrast. In the southern part of the tiny nation were rugged mountains and dense semitropical vegetation. Higher up, toward the center of Bhutan, there were oaks, varieties of ash, tree rhododendrons, and maples. However, at this height the region was covered with conifers and other trees. Farther up, as the region rose higher and higher, there were only shrubs and herbaceous growth—and bears, dangerous only if bothered.

The bright sunshine reflected more than sparkling jewels in the snow. There was another sight, as gruesome as the distant mountain peaks were resplendent: the corpses of the Chinese commandos. The Death Merchant, the night before, had had Troju Gyud, one of the Bhutanese, contact army headquarters on the URC-17 radio. An hour later, the B.A.H. had radioed back: Do not touch the bodies of the dead Red Chinese commandos. General Sigye Penlop would fly to the gompa the next morning. His helicopter would arrive at ten o'clock the next morning.

At ten twenty-seven General Penlop's helicopter, a

troop-carrying British De Havilland C-94, landed in the courtyard of the gompa. With Penlop was a squad of Bhutanese soldiers and a tall, pointy-chinned man whom General Penlop introduced as Major Kor Sidkeong, explaining that Major Sidkeong, who spoke excellent English, would be going along with the Posten Expedition, in the capacity of an "official representative of the Bhutanese government."

Whether or not Penlop or Sidkeong thought they were fooling the Americans, was a moot question. They hadn't. Richard Camellion, Vallie West, and Paul Gemz were well aware that both General Penlop and Major Sidkeong were in the pay of Indian Intelligence. Still another problem for the Death Merchant because the intelligence service of India was as useless as snowshoes on an Arab. The I.I.S. was riddled with agents in the pay of both the Soviet Union's KGB and Red China's Social Affairs Department, the latter of which, referred to as SAD in the intelligence communities of the world, was the Red Chinese espionage apparatus. Some of the Indian agents were even "triples," selling information not only to the Russians and the Chinese but also to the American CIA.

Accompanied by Camellion, West, and Gemz, General Penlop and Major Sidkeong visually inspected the bodies of the Red Chinese commandos. Captain Norbert Shireling, the senior Black Beret officer, and Phob Dotong, the Bhutanese sergeant in charge of the squad that had been on the chopper, trailed behind the five men.

General Penlop then gave orders to Sergeant Dotong: remove the uniforms and the equipment of the dead Chinese and have the squad throw the bodies off the east side of the plateau. There was a deep ravine to the east, and . . . "the bears will make short work of them down there," General Penlop said. "The bones will never be found."

As the group walked toward the great hall of the lamas' house, the Death Merchant concluded that he really couldn't blame General Penlop and Major Sidkeong for being double agents. Their army pay couldn't have been very much. Bhutan was a very poor country. Because of its isolation, the nation had a culture that had not changed in hundreds of years, the economy based on the

18

age-old elements of agriculture, the raising of stock, and the gathering of timber. Rice was the staple, but it did not grow above seven thousand feet. At about that altitude the staple was buckwheat. Rice was grown in small irrigated fields in the valley bottoms. In winter the fields were left fallow. Higher up the slopes, cattle grazed in the scrub and forest. Red pepper was the main vegetable, liberally used to spice the rice dishes. In the high altitudes, the Bhutanese kept yak—used mainly for transport—and goats, but not many sheep. All over the country, wild foods from the forests were collected to supplement the diet, a diet that was good by Asian standards, consisting mainly of pork, eggs, rice, and vegetables. Tea and Tibetan beer were the main drinks.

Religion dominated the nation, as it once had in Tibet, to the north, before Tibet had been absorbed by Communist China. The oldest of the Buddhist orders in Bhutan was the *Nyingmapas*, an order in which there were several different kinds of practitioners. There were the celibate monks who either lived in monasteries or had their own houses; all followed a strict discipline derived from the traditional Indian Buddhist rules; all aimed at an ascetic way of life. Belonging to the same order were nuns and local priests. The priests, who were allowed to marry, performed rituals and magic ceremonies for villagers . . . driving away hail, chasing demons, and guiding the souls of dead people into new bodies.

The most important order was the *Drukpa Kargyupa*, one of the so-called "red hat" sects, which gave the little nation its Tibetan and Bhutanese name—*Druk*. Monks of the *Drukpa Kargyupa* could either marry or take a vow of celibacy, such as Lama Karni Padme Hum and his monks at the Thimphu gompa. If a monk was married, he had to live outside the monastery, unless he was a full-fledged lama, in which case he could also have a dwelling place inside the gompa. However, married *gelongs* had to live outside the gompa.

Buddhism has its paradoxes, Camellion thought, entering the great hall with the other men. Lamaseries are meant, just as the *viharas* of Ceylon or the monasteries of any Buddhist country are, to house people who pursue a spiritual aim. *But in Buddhism that aim is neither strictly defined nor imposed, and common to all the dwellers in any gompa!*

In a slow walk, the Death Merchant and his party, General Penlop and Major Sidkeong, followed Karni Padme Hum and Dumvar Gatze-Ding up the wide stone stairs to the second floor. Preceding the two lamas were two gelongs, chanting *"Aum vajra sattva"* over and over, and swinging to incense burners on long bronze chains. In the rear, and last of all, were two more gelongs, they too chanting *"Aum vajra sattva"* and swinging incense burners filled with sandalwood, *kyabdo* spice, and prepared resin from the miraculous Kum-Bum tree.

Reaching the second floor, the entire party proceeded down the wide corridor and finally entered the long *dihdka* room. Here, Karni Padme Hum and Dumvar Gatze-Ding—both were mighty *Gyud Pas*—would perform the magic ceremony that would protect Camellion and his expedition from the demons of death, failure, misery, and destruction. This protective ceremony was a must and a vital part of Bhutanese social custom.

In every lamaist monastery there exists a temple, or a room, reserved as a dwelling place for the ancient deities of the aborigines and those imported from India, the latter having lost considerable rank in entering the Land of the Snows. Unconscious of their irreverence, the Bhutanese (like the Tibetans) have turned them into mere demons. *Which only proves that other people's gods eventually become our demons!* mused Camellion.

Mahakala is the most terrible and the most famous among the exiled Hindu deities, his original personality being in the form of Siva in his function of Destroyer of the World. It was from the vindictive wrath of Mahakala that the Death Merchant and the rest of the *philings* ("foreigners") had to be protected.

Lighted with torches set in the walls, the long *dihdka* room did not have an abundance of furniture. Two wooden chests were against one wall. At one end of the room was a low wooden table. Toward the front, before an image of Mahakala—made of stone and painted a dull black, the hideous green face containing enormous red eyes and a gigantic red tongue—was a stone altar on

20

which were butter bowls and copper lamps filled with grain and water. Scrolls of religious paintings covered the stone walls; under one of these was hidden a small cabinet in which female devils, called *mkah hgroma* (pronounced "kandoma"), were imprisoned.

All the scrolls pictured hideous scenes of torment. For example, in the middle of one panel, lust was undergoing punishment. A naked man, abnormally thin, faced an unclothed woman. Her enormous, disproportionate belly gave this "beauty" the appearance of an Easter egg mounted on two feet and topped with a doll head. The lecherous sinner, incorrigible slave of his passions, forgot where he was and how he had been led there, and hugged the infernal creature in his arms, while flames, springing out of her mouth and from a secret recess between her legs, scorched him.

A short distance from this hellish couple, a sinful woman suffered her chastisement. Bound, in a reversed position, to a triangle pointing downward, she was compelled to accept the caresses inflicted upon her by an orange devil with teeth like a saw and a large tail like a monkey. In the background, other demons, variously colored, were seen running forward to take their turn.

Karni Padme Hum and Dumvar Gatze-Ding wore identical clothing that was Chinese in style: the snow-white skirts of the *Respas*, who were adept in *tumo* (the art of keeping warm without fire in even the coldest weather), and garnet-colored waistcoats. But these, as well as the voluminous sleeves of yellow shirts that could be seen through wide armholes, were insignificant when compared to the tall red hat each man wore, the five-sided crimson hat of the tantric mystics. For both Hum and Ding were the highest of adepts. They were not only *ngagspas;* they were also *Gyud pas* and *doubtobs,* the latter being sages and wonder workers.

While the four gelongs, two at each end of the altar, stood chanting and facing the two lamas, Karni Padme Hum and Dumvar Gatze-Ding reached underneath their waistcoats and pulled out their *phurbas,* ritual daggers made of bronze, the handles inlaid with gold and ivory.

With his magical dagger pointed toward the terrible image of Mahakala, Karni Padme Hum took out two *tor-*

mas—ritual cakes—from beneath his waistcoat and placed them on the altar. At the same time, Dumvar Gatze-Ding drew an invisible circle on the floor with the point of his *phurba*. His old brown face a mask of concentration, Karni Padme Hum moved backward to Gatze-Ding and the two lamas began to jerk their bodies, as though on the verge of an epileptic fit, and to make stabbing motions with their *phurbas* in the direction of Mahakala. The chanting of the four gelongs, becoming much louder, changed to *"Tsi chig lus chig sangyais."*

The group stood some distance back from the two lamas, the Death Merchant against a wall, in a position that enabled him to study the faces of the other people who were perpendicular to him. Vallie West looked uncomfortable. He was! And Camellion knew why. In an effort to break the vicious cigarette habit, the big CIA agent—he was over six feet tall, with 240 pounds of solid muscle—was almost constantly sucking on a lollipop. But West could hardly make like "Kojak" while a Buddhist religious ceremony was taking place. Knowing that West was miserable, Camellion felt sorry for him. He and West had worked on numerous missions together, and the big man was not just another Company yo-yo. He was a good friend, one of the few people the Death Merchant would trust with his life.

Next to West was Emil Lauterjung, who seemed to be perpetually amazed, somewhat like a man who had bought a pair of water skis and was disappointed because he could not find a lake with a hill. With his fluffed out red hair, gold-rimmed glasses, and round, cherubic face, the soft-spoken professor of anthropology reminded the Death Merchant of a lean and lanky grown-up "Howdy Doody" who had reached a comfortable middle-age.

At least I don't have to worry about Red Degenhardt and his three boys. The four Black Berets—none was over thirty—stood with their arms folded and their legs spread, their faces hard and expressionless. Trained to deal with the grim reality of this world, they weren't the least bit concerned with the unreality of the next. The only devils they believed in were the enemies of the United States, especially hellish terrorists.

And then there was Paul Gemz, who peered at the two

22

twisting and turning lamas with intense interest. Gemz had once taught archaeology at a private college in Pennsylvania, and had been trying to start a Department of Archaeoastronomy at the University of Chicago when the CIA had tapped him for Arrowhead-6, the cover-name for the Shambhala mission. West had also confided to Camellion that Gemz had worked for the Company several years before and had a C-6y rating, which meant he was dependable and had taken part in violent action. Of medium height, Gemz had a coarse salt-and-pepper mustache, a fine remembrance of hair, and keen, combative eyes; and, while he had a sense of priorities, he also had a tendency to disregard orders.

Camellion appraised Major Kor Sidkeong and the four Bhutanese soldiers. The soldiers—they were all young—looked like average Bhutanese males—black hair cut short, black eyes, dark brown skin, and a perpetual expression of cunning. They weren't amateurs in the kill department either. West and Degenhardt had reported to Camellion that the two Bhutanese who had helped them had fought very professionally. Nor were they trigger-happy. "They fired only when they had a clear target," Vallie had said, sucking on a lemon-flavored lollipop.

The circuits in Camellion's mind clicked. *The Bhutanese call themselves the* Drukpa—*the "Thunder People." An apt name that reflects the harshness of the country. It's certainly not a paradise for the women. They do as much, if not more, manual work as the men. Combine that with years spent in pregnancy and they're old by the time they reach thirty.*

The Death Merchant let his eyes tiptoe to Major Sidkeong, who was tall for a Bhutanese, and was lighter-skinned than either General Penlop or the four Bhutanese soldiers. It was difficult for Camellion to assign the general run of Bhutanese to any one Mongolian type; yet, the Indo-Aryan and the Southeast Asian types were discernible. The Southeast Asian strain was predominant in Major Sidkeong, who, like most Bhutanese males, had little hair on his face. He did have a thin drooping mustache growing from the outer edges of his upper lip. And from the expression of disdain in his eyes, he was not much of a

23

believer in Buddhism—or at least in any ceremony that professed to scare off devils.

But how would the Major react under pressure?

The last member of the expedition, and the one the Death Merchant trusted the least, was also the best-looking. Beyond any doubt, Helena Banya was the best-looking woman in Bhutan . . . for that matter, all of Southeast Asia. Anyhow, one of the best.

The Russian girl's attraction was that she was a true blond. The radiant gleam of her hair had not come out of a bottle. She had a delicate roseate skin, blue eyes, narrow temples, a fairly high forehead, and long, shapely legs. Her breasts tended to be round, rather than pointed, and she accentuated these natural assets by wearing blouses and sweaters that were so tight as to reveal the full extent of her mammaries. When she walked, the ample bounce revealed that her main attraction had not originally come from a rubber plant. Below her ample lacteal endowments, Helena evinced a narrow waist and buttocks so frankly suggestive that Camellion found himself resisting the temptation of pinching her—*But I'd need an arm fifteen feet long! I'm here. She's way over there.*

A Russian proverb popped into the Death Merchant's mind—*An ape in silk is always an ape.* The corners of his mouth became hard. *And a KGB Sparrow doesn't have clipped wings merely because she flies to the West—not in my way of thinking. One a Commie pig farmer, always a Commie pig farmer. . . .*

Camellion knew quite a bit about the good-looking Helena Banya, who was on the uphill side of thirty and who, for four years, had been a member of the KGB's "sex service." *Which means she was in the KGB's Second Chief Directorate. . . .*

The main function of the KGB's Second Chief Directorate is to control the lives of Soviet citizens and to subvert foreign visitors. The Second Chief Directorate also recruits and trains sex-spies. In this area of intelligence, the KGB excels.[4] While all intelligence services use sex as a matter

4 Since 1945 the Soviets have used sex-spying to obtain a wide range of top-secret information from the West. The KBG has used sexpionage to infiltrate NATO—the North

of course, it is the KGB that has turned sexpionage into a fine art, even more so than the CIA. Beginning with the reality of sexual attraction, the KGB has combined specially trained prostitute-spies—both male and female—with photography, sophisticated electronic bugging, and computer technology, so that the total result is a very elaborate method that is constantly being employed to gather intelligence and to subvert and/or blackmail diplomats and officials of nations all over the world.

Sex-spies—the women are called Sparrows (or Swallows), the men Ravens—are well trained. Besides politics, economics, codes and ciphers, photography, and various methods for making and cultivating contacts, students are taught many other things. They are taught how to drug victims, using drinks, candy, cigarettes, and various kinds of food . . . and how different drugs are used for different effects; and in case they are drugged, what symptoms to expect and what to do about them.

During training, instructors make no pretense about the sinister nature of the *gryaznaya robota*—the "dirty work." Since sex is the main weapon used to accomplish bribery, extortion, and blackmail, emphasis is not so much on theory but on practice—on physical techniques. Female students go to bed with hundreds of Red Army men, and take part in sexual deviations that would leave Alfred Kinsey shaking his head in astonishment (and make Krafft-Ebing turn over half a dozen times in his grave). The girls indulge in homosexual relations with one another and in groups. This is not intended to turn them into homosexuals—a psychological impossibility—but to broaden their sexual experiences. All the while, cameras grind away, photographing every details of every act, be it homosexual or heterosexual. The films are later shown to the entire class, with instructors commenting on the students' performances, explaining what they did wrong and how their technique could be improved.

Male students—the Ravens—are instructed not only in

Atlantic Treaty Organization—to disgrace and discredit enemies of the Soviet Union abroad, and to preempt counter-intelligence strikes against their own agents. It is estimated that there are over 4,000 sex-spies in the KGB.

homosexual practices but in how to make love to middle-aged women, especially middle-aged women who are unattractive. Any man can have sex with a pretty girl, unless he's homosexual or a fanatical misogynist. Being passionate and getting the juices to flow with a frigid spinster is an entirely different matter, one that requires the skill of an expert.

Helena Banya was a good student. She was even better as an agent. After several years of seducing foreign visitors who came to the Soviet Union, she was sent to the European area of operations, where she used her body in scores of sexpionage entrapments. Among her victims was a junior diplomat in the United States Embassy in Brussels. The poor fool didn't reveal any secrets after he was approached by Russian agents and shown a dozen eight-by-ten-inch glossy photographs, and threatened with exposure. Instead, the man committed suicide.

Finally, Helena Banya, who spoke excellent English, was sent to the United States. Ostensibly she was a secretary in the Soviet Embassy in Washington, D.C. However, her real job was to entice important men into the bedroom of an apartment that was equipped with ultrasensitive microphones and a hidden miniature television camera focused on the bed. The camera was hidden in the wall. When pictures needed to be taken, a molding automatically opened and the lens would shoot through a one-inch-diameter opening. Should Helena's victim feel guilty and prefer to make love in the dark, that was all right, too. The KGB had thought of everything. The lens was fitted with a brightness-intensifying unit that increased background light up to 168,000 times. The lens captured every lustful twist and turn of the two bodies on the bed, just as the hidden mikes would pick up every gasp and whisper of passion. The TV pictures were transmitted by closed circuit to a room in the apartment next door. Here a KGB agent monitored the recorder and snapped pictures from the television screen, using a special still camera loaded with fine-grain emulsion film.

After ten months in the United States, Helena Banya did the totally unexpected. She surprised the CIA, whose agents were watching her, and both shocked and incurred the wrath of the KGB by going to the U.S. Department of

Justice building, on Pennsylvania Avenue in Washington, and defecting to the West, bringing with her—"as proof of my sincerity"—an attaché case of stolen documents from the Soviet Embassy.

The Death Merchant thumbed through the files of his mind, his almost-total recall picking out what he had been told about Helena Banya at Company headquarters, while being briefed about Arrowhead-6.

The Russian spy-prostitute had defected—so she had told CIA interrogators—because she could no longer stand the work she was doing and because she had lost all faith in the Soviet system. Now she realized that she and everyone else in the Soviet Union were being brainwashed with lies about the West. Her dissatisfaction had begun in Europe, where she had personally seen the freedom and the prosperity of the people. There was even more freedom and more of the good life in the United States. Why, an ordinary factory worker lived better than professional people in the U.S.S.R. She had been astonished at how the American press could openly criticize the United States Government, not only the Office of the President, but even the FBI and the CIA! *Snarivu-zhivu!* Unbelievable! In the Soviet Union, people didn't even criticize the KGB in private. Even among close friends who trusted one another there was a reluctance to discuss the secret police.

Helena Banya was granted political asylum, but only after she had been put through a battery of tests to ascertain her true motives and intentions. She was also injected with sodium pentobarbitalinium, a tremendously powerful truth drug. Conclusion: Helena Banya was telling the truth. Or was she? CIA specialists were convinced that she was. Richard Camellion had not been convinced. He still wasn't. He knew of two methods by which one could beat a polygraph, or lie detector. There were Yoga techniques of concentration that locked the unconscious mind to the probings of truth drugs. Uh-huh . . . so how many people knew of these techniques, both of which required years and years of training? Helena Banya couldn't be using any of these mystical methods. She wasn't old enough to have studied such techniques. At the time, weeks ago, Camellion had done some hard, rock-bottom thinking. There was behavior modification. Was it possible that Helena Banya had been programmed to do a specific job—without her being aware of it? *"No, it was not possible,"* said the CIA. *"We can't make a 'Manchurian Candidate.' Neither can the Russians—not yet. It's all fiction."*

The Death Merchant's suspicions continued to simmer. He analyzed the problem objectively, taking into consideration his intense abhorrence of anything or any person connected with Marxism. He continued to suspect the KGB in general and Helena Banya in particular. He had his reasons. For one thing, the documents she had stolen from the Soviet Embassy were not exactly earth-shaking—reports on U.S. soybean sales, analyses of American consumerism, and such nonsense and irrelevant material—i.e., from a military standpoint—as the different brands of lipstick used by American women.

However, there was one folder of papers that experts of the CIA's Office of Science and Technology considered to be very important: a twenty-page report on what American writers had to say about the legend of Agharta, the fabled system of caves that supposedly lies under Tibet, Bhutan, Manchuria, Mongolia, Kurdistan, and Afghanistan. Only those who worshipped evil were ever admitted to the underground complex.

Another part of the legend, whose origin was lost in the mists of antiquity, was that the ruler of Agharta had his palace in the fantastic subterranean metropolis of Shambhala. This ruler was known as Rigden-Jyo-Po or "King of the World." He was also called the *"Brahytma"* and *"Metatron,"* and was served by high priests known as "Goros." Another part of the incredible saga was that Shambhala contained all sorts of marvelous inventions, as well as a library in which was a true history of the human race, a recording of events that went back seventeen million years!

The Russian research paper (containing numerous quotes from American parapsychologists and writers on the occult and the mysterious) and the CIA had not told the Death Merchant anything he had not heard or read. He had always had a keen interest in subjects out of the ordinary—but Shambhala? Very well! So, more than cultists and crackpots believed in Shambhala. Ferdinand Ossendowski, the Polish explorer, Nicholas Roervich, the white Russian painter, and the Baron Roman Ungern von Sternberg the World War I German general, all were convinced that the underground world existed; and so did the enigmatic Professor Karl Haushofer, the geopolitical adviser to Adolf Hitler and a ranking member of the Thule group, a mystical society in Germany. In fact, it was Haushofer who had gotten Hitler to adopt the swastika as the Nazi symbol!

The CIA had then dropped the bombshell on the Death Merchant! The Agency was planning to investigate the legend of Shambhala. For several years the Agency had been toying with the idea of running down the legend about Shambhala. Now that the Company knew the Soviet Union was interested in the secret city, speed was essential, for more reasons than one. If the Soviets were interested in the underground cavern complex—and they were—then so were the Red Chinese. Still another reason for acceleration of effort, was Helena Banya's contention that the Soviet Union had already attempted to penetrate Shambhala.

How did she know? Helena Banya had once been a "secretary" in the Soviet embassy in Paris. During that time, her boyfriend had been one Major Nikolai Suda of the KGB's Directorate *T*, the Scientific and Technical Directorate. Major Suda had also been stationed at the embassy in Paris. Suda confided to Helena Banya that the KGB had sent thirty-one men and nine women to Bhutan in 1975 to search for one of the entrances to the mysterious Shambhala. The other two entrances were in Tibet and Mongolia, territory firmly controlled by the Red Chinese.

For a time, all had gone well with the Soviet expedition. There had not been any difficult mountain-climbing, the supposed entrance to the underground city being on the lower slopes of the mighty Himalayas. The Himalayas are so vast that in many regions the slopes are more than a hundred miles long and cannot be thought of as mountain inclines, not in the conventional sense.

Disaster had struck the Russian scientific expedition. One by one the Russians began dying, dropping dead from apparent heart failure! Finally, the Russians had turned back in panic, their number having been whittled down to twenty-two men and three women.

Major Suda had been a member of the expedition—so he had confided to Helena Banya. He had also revealed to the prostitute-spy that the KGB force had been within seven miles of the principle landmark pointing to Shambhala: two tall, needlelike peaks resting side by side. Several thousand feet to the right of the peak on the right—or a few thousand feet to the east of the peak on the east side, as one moved north—there was a tremendous cliff wall. The entrance to Shambhala[5] was behind one of the huge boulders close to the wall. This boulder was shaped like a giant egg.

Helena Banya had told the CIA that she had not believed Major Suda and that she had chided him for telling her a tall tale. Several days later, Suda had shown her photographs of the twin peaks to prove that he had been telling the truth. He had taken the pictures himself. He had further confided to Helena Banya that part of his duties in Paris was to search old newspaper records and scientific journals, in an effort to discover if some French mountain-climbing expedition might have stumbled onto another entrance to Shambhala without realizing it. Such expeditions kept very accurate records of each day's activities. It was possible that some newpaper or magazine might mention an "endless cavern" or a "bottomless hole" that an expedition might have come across. Suda had explained that other Directorate *T* agents were searching magazines and newspapers in other nations—countries in Europe, South America, and the United States.

A curious Richard Camellion had asked the CIA if Helena Banya had revealed how the KGB had first learned of the supposed entrance in Bhutan. Yes, she had given the CIA the same information that Suda had given her. The KGB had obtained the location of the entrance from a Buddhist monk in Kathmandu, the capital of Nepal. Furthermore, Helena Banya had told the identical story, over and over, while under the influence of sodium pentobarbitalinium.

[5] The legend of Shambhala is genuine; we did not invent it for the sake of this story.

The Death Merchant had not been impressed. In the first place, none of the Russians had actually seen the entrance to the mythical city. *Provided she was telling the truth! Or hasn't been programmed!* In the second place, there was the factor of parallelism, of sheer coincidence. For years the Agency had been making plans to run down the rumors about Agharta and its capital, Shambhala. And now here was Helena Banya, a KGB slut, with all the information about the location of the subterranean complex!

Camellion had retained his doubt. He had not stayed alive all these years by trusting in nebulous assumptions. He had kept his health by using super-caution, by trusting no one—with few exceptions—and by plain old-fashioned common sense. The hell with the CIA and its foolish putations and assumptions.

And the hell with Richard J. Camellion! The D.D.O.[6] didn't give a damn what Camellion thought. The Company wasn't paying him a tax-free hundred grand to give opinions, but to get the job done.

The D.D.O. had explained to Camellion that there was another reason why the United States Government was interested in Shambhala: if the underground kingdom existed, and if it had a library that did contain a true history of the Earth, then perhaps the riddle about an ancient atomic war could be solved. There was a large body of evidence that such a world-wide holocaust had occurred in the past. When nuclear weapons were tested in the New Mexico desert, the sand was vitrified—i.e., fused into glass by the heat of millions of degrees. Yet the Gobi Desert has enormous areas of vitreous sand that have been there for untold thousands of years. There are identical glassy sands in parts of the California desert, and in Peru and Bolivia. Mysterious, glassy tektites have also been found in the Middle East and in North Africa. Volcanic action? Indeed not. Volcanic action will not produce this effect, nor will ordinary explosives, nor fires. The heat of thermonuclear reactions is necessary.

Very ancient writings describe radiation sickness in clinical detail. The *Mahabharata*, a very old Sanskrit text,

6 Deputy Director of Operations. Also called the Clandestine Services and/or "The Dirty Tricks Department" in slang.

31

tells of the explosion of great fireballs, the terrible gales, and storms which they created, and the aftereffects—hair loss, vomiting, weakness, and eventual death. All classic symptoms of radiation poisoning!

The Death Merchant had not laughed at the D.D.O., who had then wanted to know if the man from Texas would lead a small expedition into Bhutan to search for the entrance to Shambhala, say a small force that would leave without the usual fanfare and wouldn't attract any attention? Yes, Camellion would, but only if he could have an assistant of his own choosing. Agreed. Camellion chose Vallie West, a man he knew he could depend on.

There was just one more thing, the D.D.O. said. Helena Banya would be going along. She could identify the twin peaks.

"If she's playing a double-game, don't look for her to come back," the Death Merchant had told the D.D.O., who had replied, *"We've pumped her dry about Russian sex-spy methods. We wouldn't have any regrets if that Russian whore fell off a mountain. . . ."*

The CIA had immediately swung into high gear. Arrangements were made through the Office of Proprietary Operations, which controls Agency "front" companies and organizations. Orders were sent from the F.E.D. (the Far East Division of the D.D.O. Division) to CI (counterintelligence) agents in India and in Nepal: Report any unusual Soviet and Chinese Intelligence activity in those areas.

Arrowhead-6 was put into operation by means of the Posten Expedition, which would go to the tiny nation of Bhutan "to study Ural-Altaic Mongolian body types." Emil Theodoric Lauterjung, who headed the Department of Anthropology at Posten College, a small private college in Colorado, had been tapped as the "front" man. Having lost two sons in Vietnam, Professor Lauterjung had readily agreed to help the Agency.

To pull the wool over the eyes of Posten's president and the Board of Regents, the usual smoke screen was set up, in that the money for the expedition was given to the Department of Anthropology as a grant from the Bannerman Foundation; a humanitarian group based in Boston, and controlled by Bannerman, Fuseey, and Krims, Ltd., a

32

public relations firm, which was in turn a company "front."

Helena Banya had not left the Denver airport with Professor Lauterjung, Camellion, West (the Death Merchant and West were listed as "guides"), and Paul Gemz, who was going along as the "representative of the Bannerman Foundation." Nor had the four Black Berets left.

Banya's defection, months earlier, had created a sensation in the press. The Soviet Union had angrily demanded her return, the Soviet ambassador in Washington stating that Helena Banya was suffering from a nervous breakdown and that she was a liar. The Union of Soviet Socialist Republics did not use such despicable methods as sex-spying! A lie! An invention of the Central Intelligence Agency.

The United States State Department politely told the Russian ambassador that Helena Banya was free to return to the Russian Embassy. If she wanted to! But she didn't want to! Sorry . . .

The CIA flew Helena Banya and the four Black Berets to India in a very surreptitious manner, and in a roundabout route, the five of them making contact with the Posten Expedition in the middle of the night at a private airfield outside of Barasat, a town fifteen kilometers northeast of Calcutta. Everything had gone smoothly. God Almighty couldn't have done better. . . .

Camellion coldly studied Helena Banya, who was dressed in a gray goosedown sweater, gray Cargo jeans, and insulated mountain boots. Her long blonde hair was twisted into braids coiled on top of her head. Trained to notice anyone who might be watching her, Helena turned her head slightly and caught Camellion's eye. She didn't smile. For a moment she stared haughtily at the Death Merchant. Then a quick flicker of fear flashed over her pretty face, and she swung her gaze back to the two lamaist monks whose ritual dance steps were forming precise geometric figures. All the while, Karni Padme Hum and Dumvar Gatze-Ding continued to wave their *phurbas*, pausing every so often to jab the points of the magic daggers at the ugly face of Mahakala.

Helena Banya shifted uncomfortably. She could feel Camellion's razor-sharp stare but she pretended not to notice. Although he had not spoken one cross word to her, she sensed that his manner was always deadly. She compared him to a cobra watching its victim a moment before it strikes. Her training and intuition warned her that, whoever he was, he was not an ordinary human being. The majority of people always turned away when one stared directly into their eyes. This man called Camellion did not. Several times she had looked straight into the icy-blue depths of his eyes—the second time to test the reality of the first experience. Each time she had felt something akin to an electric shock flow through her body. For half the time it takes a bolt of lightning to strike, she had experienced ultimate panic—the kind of horrible dread that strangles a dreamer having a nightmare just before he screams himself awake. Never again had Helena Banya, who was afraid of Camellion, stared fully into Camellion's eyes.

The Death Merchant folded his arms and resumed watching the two gyrating lamas continue with the magic ceremony of protection against the demon Mahakala. Camellion wasn't worried about devils. Nor was he concerned about Helena Banya. There was nothing she could do, nowhere she could go. The Red Chinese were a definite problem. They would attack again. He couldn't ignore the possibility of a Russian force putting in an appearance. He thought of the Russian force of which Major Suda had been a member. Nine men and six women had been struck dead. Suda had told Helena that the KGB had never unraveled the mystery. The theory was that a quick-killing virus was responsible for the deaths. That's what had gone down on the report to the fat old men in the Kremlin. Suda had also confided to Helena that the KGB had not believed its own story about a virus. The KGB simply did not have an answer.

Neither did the Death Merchant.

The silent death had struck once. Why shouldn't it strike again?

Question: How do you fight something you don't know what it is, something you can't see?

You don't!

Camellion was still pondering the problem many hours later, after he and the rest of the expedition had left the monastery and, in the bright sunlight, were moving northward on the slope that led to the uplands of the region.

If Shambhala existed. they were about eight days away from the entrance. . . .

If . . .

Chapter Three

At times the wind blew furiously, its raging voice a sixty-knots[7] roar. There were those other times when the wind was meek, its whisper down to a timid B-S Zero.[8] But always, day and night, the wind was a constant companion.

Progress was slow, on a route that was deceptive, misleading because, while Richard Camellion and his people were constantly moving upward, the over-all grade was such a gradual decline that they had to remind themselves that, with each step, they were moving into a higher altitude. It was difficult even to imagine that they were in the Himalayas, the most rugged mountains on earth.

The Himalayas are so unbelievably vast—over fourteen hundred miles long—that its lower slopes comprise thousands of square miles. To the northwest, the Himalayas meet the Hindu Kush in Afghanistan, and the southwest section of the Tien Shan range, which extends deep into northwestern China. Entire nations rest on the southern slopes of the Himalayas—Nepal, Sikkim, and Bhutan.

One thing in favor of the Posten Expedition was that its members would not have to climb any dangerous mountains. Other than *couloirs*, steep gullies of snow, and

---

[7] *One knot*, as a unit of speed, equals one nautical or geographical mile per hour. An international nautical mile is 6,076.115 feet, or 1852 meters. However, the British nautical mile—or Admiralty mile—is equal to 6,080 feet, or 1853.2 meters.

[8] *Wind forces* are logged according to the Beaufort Scale. This scale ranges from 0 to 17, with a maximum wind velocity of 136 miles per hour.

névés, packed hard-frozen snow, there were only rock-studded hills and hundreds of minute ravines to contend with. Not that the way wasn't dangerous and the trek torturous. The snowcovered hills dotted with *findop* shrubs, scrub pine, and cypress trees, were often precipitous and slashed with twenty-foot-deep gullies, from the sides of which jutted sharp rocks. One slip, one fall, could result in a broken arm or leg . . . or, worse, a broken back.

Moving over such unfriendly terrain was not pleasant, nor easy, especially since each person carried a heavy backpack system and, with the exception of Helena Banya, arms and ammunition. In addition, every member of the Posten Expedition carried a two-man Quinault Snow-Line tent, all except Helena Banya and Professor Emil Lauterjung, both of whom had all they could handle with their heavy packs. The going was especially rough for Lauterjung, who had a slight case of emphysema and at times had to suck air from an oxygen bottle. He was another reminder that the force was more than seven thousand feet above sea level.

Days earlier, in Barasat, India, Paul Gemz had questioned the wisdom of taking seven two-man tents. Four tents could accommodate eight people and could be arranged to form one large tent. Helena Banya would have a tent to herself.

"The last I heard, five from seven still leaves two," Gemz had said. "What are we going to do with the two extra tents? And what are you and West going to do with those two large squares of green nylon that you're packing?"

"You'll see," was all the Death Merchant had said.

Gemz saw—during the late afternoon of the expedition's first day on the trail, when they were on a fairly large *thang.*[9] Toward dusk, the Death Merchant called a halt and cheerfully announced that here they would camp for the night.

The four Black Berets glanced uneasily at one another. Major Kor Sidkeong jabbered in his native tongue to the four Bhutanese soldiers and they chattered back, their

[9] A Bhutanese word meaning a tableland of level ground between hill ranges or a very wide valley.

37

loud singsong-ese indicating that they were very upset. Podku Kalimpong, the more vociferous of the four, waved a hand toward all the open space of the *thang*, jabbered some more, and pointed upward at the tallest hill to the north.

"Camellion, this is no place to put our butts down for the night," Red Degenhardt said in his rather nasal voice, with the trace of a lisp. The Black Beret officer stepped closer to Camellion, the dying sun reflecting from the smoke-gray lens of his Tasco sportglasses. "Down here we're grade-A targets," he said boldly, "and only several heartbeats from catastrophe, if the chopsticks decide to pay us another visit."

Major Sidkeong joined in, his voice steady, his eyes on Camellion.

"We should pitch our tents behind the last rim of rocks on the largest hill. There would be ample room for us behind the rocks. Our tents would be concealed, and the Chinese would have to creep up to us."

"We are going to camp up there in the rocks," drawled Camellion. "But not yet. It's still light enough for spotters in the distance to see us through binoculars, if they're there. Major, explain all that to your men. I don't want them to get the idea that I might get us all killed."

"Yeah," joked Vallie West, shifting the lollipop in his mouth. "If we get scratched, it would upset the civilians over their morning coffee and look bad in the newspapers."

"Up in the rocks is more like it!" Degenhardt turned the corners of his mouth upward in a zippered smile, and glanced from Camellion to Major Sidkeong. All five Bhutanese carried one-man tents of Indian manufacture, and each wore a long *Bakhu*, the volumnious robe-like coat common in Bhutan and Tibet.

"That's the name of the game, Red," Camellion said, his breath turning to frost as he spoke. "We move up there after dark and hope the Chinese attack down here. It will be like shooting fish in a barrel—using a shotgun!"

"Do you think it will work?" Degenhardt asked thoughtfully, stroking the end of his chin.

Camellion, who had slipped out of his backpack, placed it on the ground and got down on one knee beside it.

"Why not? We'll set up the tents right here, all except two. Or rather, we'll take all of them down except two. The moon won't rise until seven forty-five. We'll have plenty of time to sneak up to the rocks in the dark."

"We can use the nightsight scopes to see by," Loren Eaton said.

"I think you're underestimating the Chinese," Paul Gemz said solemnly, directing his words at the Death Merchant. "They were using trigonometry when our ancestors were still trying to figure out what comes after ten. I don't think you're going to convince them that fourteen people can fit into two two-man tents!"

For several moments Camellion didn't answer. He had opened one compartment of his backpack and was removing a dozen round objects made of metal, each slightly larger than a thimble. Richard put the objects into a pocket of his parka, stood up, and gave Gemz a slight smile.

"Don't worry. Those two tents are going to look like one big one when we move out," he said. "What you should have asked is how we're going to protect ourselves after dark, before we get up to the rocks. The Chinese could show up before we get up there."

"I was going to ask, but I assumed you would have some impudent and contumelious answer."

Camellion's expression became one of mock surprise. "I probably would have," he said innocently, "but only because I feel that a man shouldn't sit down to a gourmet dinner when he's not even ready for McDonald's."

The Death Merchant turned to Vallie West who was smiling at Gemz, whose face was quickening with a red flush. "Val, let's go and check out the hills. We can find a place to move to after dark while we're at it."

Gemz, Degenhardt, and the rest of the force, watched as Camellion and West moved off to the north.

"Red, do you figure Camellion knows what he's doing?" posed Foster Cross. "I guess he does or he wouldn't be here."

"He knows," Degenhardt replied firmly. "The way he whacked out the Commies last night, all by himself—only an expert could do that and not even get a scratch."

Norbert Shireling said, "I think the Red SOBs had better pray to whatever god they believe in that they don't tangle with him."

"Have you forgotten?" said Loren Eaton, laughing. "Those savages are Communists. They don't have enough sense to believe in God."

"They might not believe in God, but they'll damn sure believe in hell if they tangle with that doomsday machine," Degenhardt growled. He looked at the faces of the three Black Berets. "Let's get the tents up." He glanced at Helena Banya, who was a short distance away, applying a Chapstick to her lips.

"Keep an eye on that Russian whore," Degenhardt whispered to Eaton, who was closest to him. "I trust her the way I would trust the plague."

"She could be on the level," Eaton said.

"Sure she could. And I could run for President of the U.S. next year!"

The wind blowing tiny swirls of snow around their insulated boots, Camellion and West climbed the side of the steep hill, first digging in their feet, then taking a step upward, reaching out for large rocks to use as handholds, whenever possible.

From the base to the top of the hill in the center of the "wall" to the north, the distance was a good 30.5 meters, (approximately 100 feet). A rock-filled ridge was 30 feet from the summit, which was flattened out and filled with rocks and scrub pine.

Reaching the top, the two men looked around. The next nearest range of hills to the north was more than two hundred forty meters away. Good. Too far away for effective firing. To the east, there was an eighteen-meter-wide gap between the hill on which they stood and the next hill, and the slopes of both were steep and dangerous. To the west, the space between the top of the hills was not quite as large; yet it was wide enough. The north slopes of the hills were just as steep and as long as the southern slants.

"It all reminds me of a golf course in Poland," Vallie said. "It's just what we want. There's plenty of room between the rocks for our tents, and no way the Chinese can reach us without our being warned in plenty of time. I'm almost hoping the Red trash shows up after dark."

The Death Merchant hooked a gloved thumb over one of the straps across his chest. "Chinese Intelligence isn't stupid. The Social Affairs Department knows what we're up to, knows we're looking for Shambhala." He turned slightly and looked at Vallie. "I suppose K'ang Sheng is dead by now?"

"You're six miles behind the times." Vallie took the lollipop stick from his mouth and dropped it on the snow. "Sheng died of cancer in 1966. The present head of the Ministry of Public Affairs[10] is a fat idiot named Chan K'o-nung. He's the number-four ant at the top of the ant-hill, which makes him the most powerful intelligence chief in the world. On the other hand, KGB influence in pig-land is greater now than at any time in the last twenty-five years, and Andropov's[11] star is rising like a rocket. But he's not as powerful as K'o-nung."

"I don't think I'd want to buy a used car from either one of them," Camellion said. He slipped four of the thimblelike Model E.As. into a side pocket of Vallie's hooded parka. "But the Agency still has the edge on both the KGB and SAD."

"Sure, but what about five years from now?" Vallie's voice was bitter. "What with more and more Commie agents coming into the U.S.,[12] while the left-wing liberals keep cutting away at the Company, who knows what the situation will be even a few years from now?"

---

10 SAD is part of the Ministry of Social Affairs. The Ministry is headquartered at 15 Bow String Alley in Peking. Foreign Intelligence is handled by Department-Y-C5, and the Red China News Agency, the latter of which, has directing correspondents—all Chinese espionage agents—in sixty countries.

11 Yuri Andropov is head of the KGB.

12 Communist agents are becoming more numerous in the U.S.A. Since détente began in 1972, the number of Communist-bloc agents in the U.S. has increased fifty percent, to some eight hundred. The total number of "legal" Soviet spies in the West—using press or trade or diplomatic cover—is estimated at ten thousand.

41

"Tell you what, old buddy," Camellion said, "You take the right side. I'll handle the left. You have only four. But they'll do the job. Each station has a pickup of two hundred feet, a sweep radius."

"Don't confuse me with Gemz," said Vallie, chuckling. "I've done this sort of thing before, y'know." He stuck another four-hour sucker into his mouth.

"How many of those a day do you consume?" Camellion asked.

"A dozen or more. I find myself eating the damn things. I'll probably get cancer of the gut from the sugar. There's no way we little people can win."

They moved out, the Death Merchant going to the west, Vallie to the east. They could easily have tossed each M-4 E.A. into place, but if they had, and the Red Chinese were watching from some high place of concealment, the Commies would become suspicious. To fool any enemy, Camellion climbed down on the west side and, when he reached the bottom of the hill, stealthily dropped one of the units on the ground, stopped, pretended to look around, and pressed the unit into the snow wtih the end of his foot.

It's all relative, he thought with irony. *A bit over thirty years ago the Chinese were the guys in white hats and the Japanese were the heavies. Now we're playing the game the other way. . . .*

He made his way around the large hill to the bottom of the north side slope. This time he bent down and pretended to adjust his boot while he pushed a unit into the snow. He stood up, looked around him, walked another thirty meters, and, as he stumbled along, dropped another warning device into a *findop* bush. Fifty feet ahead was West, who had come from the east side of the hill. Together, they made their way back to the summit—a shorter distance than walking all the way around the base—and surveyed the entire area with 15X Zeiss binoculars. In the little light of day that remained, there was no sign of life, of man or beast. Very quiet. A low wind. As if nature had become speechless. Many, many miles to the north, the tips of tall peaks, tinged blood red, rose majestically into the darkening sky.

To the south, sixty meters from the bottom of the center hill, the Bhutanese and the members of the Posten Expedition had set up the tents, ten in all, and were going through the motions of preparing to settle down for the night.

Camellion and West stared down the south grade of the minimountain, careful not to slip on any snow-coated rocks.

"When we get to the bottom, you or me?" Vallie asked.

"I'll do it," Richard said. "You should have one or two left."

"I have—one."

"Place it center-south of the camp, about twenty meters from the tents."

"Right." Vallie glanced up at the twilight sky, sighed loudly in disgust, and pulled the lollipop from his mouth. "I hate any operation in cold weather. It's so damned cold here that if you see a bird and think it's a robin, it turns out to be only a sparrow with a chapped chest." He laughed slyly. "If they had robins and sparrows in this part of Asia, which they don't."

"I prefer the warm air of the Caribbean myself," Camellion said.

"Speaking of the Caribbean—remember the time we saved Fidel Castro's hind end? We should have let the KGB murder him.[13] I tell you, Rick, this business we're in is so incredible that if we put any certain mission into a book, everyone would think it was fiction. I just wonder if all the risks are worth it!"

"Why ponder intangibles? You've lived a 'good clean life,'" joked Camellion. "You can expect the Big Reward when you go to that wonderful world of spirit."

"Yeah, but I'd prefer to stay alive to dirty up that 'clean' life a little. The way things are now, that's not too likely. It would seem that we're going to have to take on the entire Red Army, or maybe drop dead three or four days from now. How do we protect ourselves against that?"

"We don't," Camellion said. "I don't think we'll have to. I don't think any of the Russians died up here. I think

[13] See *Death Merchant* #7: *The Castro File.*

43

they tangled with the Red Chinese but didn't want to admit to the Kremlin that they lost the battle. The Russian officer didn't tell Banya the truth."

Vallie's expression grew serious. "In another way, you're saying that the China boys may have already found the cavern complex. I doubt if they have, or they wouldn't be trying to stop us."

"You've got the idea," agreed Camellion. "I'm afraid we're in a race with the Chinese . . . unfortunately."

"Suppose you're wrong about the Russians dropping dead?"

"In that case, we might be dead within a few days. We've no choice but to risk it."

They came to the bottom of the hill. The Death Merchant let the M-4 E.A. unit slip from his hand, then paused and pressed the rounded metal object into the snow with his foot. He quickened his pace and caught up with West, after which he reached into one of his parka pockets and turned on the E.A. receiver.

In the deep twilight they made their way to the encampment, both confident that the area where they would really spend the night was well protected. It was. The Model-4 Emergency Alarms were basically simple devices, the system consisting of broadcast pickup units and a main receiver. Operating on the Doppler principle, each thimble-sized station—a masterpiece of electronic miniaturization—sent out a sweep radar beam. Without movement in any of the sweep areas, the transmission between sender and receiver would remain constant. But, should any object disturb any of the very high frequency waves, there would be a loud buzzing from the receiver and a red light would begin flashing. There was one flaw: any large animal, such as a bear, could also trigger an alarm.

The members of the Posten Expedition and the Bhutanese Army men ate supper: local fare—*chura*, fried rice heated in tea until it has swollen; *churpi*, cheese beaten and dried; and *tsampa*, small cakes of barley and eggs, all of it washed down with strong tea. While eating, the Death Merchant kept the M-4 E.A. receiver in front of him, both the buzzer and the light system switched on.

Supper over, everyone went to work in the darkness.

44

Gear was packed, and tents were quickly and quietly taken down. All except two. These two were placed together, end to end. West and Camellion now went to work with the large squares of nylon they carried, attaching them to the raised side flaps of the two tents, then raising each side with metal telescoping tent poles. Once their task was completed, there was, to all appearances, one huge tent.

Just as quickly, Camellion and West led the others to the top of the hill, the way spearheaded by Norbert Shireling and Loren Eaton, using nightsight scopes.

The tents were set up on the hilltop, around a tall cedar, in an area surrounded by boulders and piled slabrock. The side flaps of the tents were raised and locked together, so that each individual tent was a unit of the final, much larger one. The only tents that were not part of the general effort belonged to Helena Banya and to the five Bhutanese. There was some grumbling, mostly from the Bhutan Army men, when they learned that just before dawn all the tents would be taken down and that the entire force would recamp on the *thang*. By all the demons in the purgatories, the white-faced *philing* was crazy! Putting up the tents three separate times and taking them down three separate times all in one night was too much work. The four stopped muttering when a clever Major Sidkeong told them that because Camellion was actually a *Rishi*,[14] he knew exactly what he was doing. Such an explanation made more sense to the highly superstitious soldiers than telling them the blunt truth: that a move back to the original camp site was necessary to fool any Chinese who might be spying on them.

Provided the Reds didn't attack during the night!
They didn't. . . .

---

[14] A sage possessed of supernatural powers.

Chapter Four

The following morning, the sun climbed into the sky with a quiet splash of light. As usual, the air was clear and crisp and the wind cantankerous, as if trying to make up its mind. Far to the west, the sky was stained with dirty streaks of gray-black clouds.

The force ate breakfast. Tents were taken down and packed. The Death Merchant and Vallie West spent an hour and a half collecting the Emergency Alarm stations. There was a chip override circuit in each thimble transmitter. When activated by a control on the receiver, each transmitter emitted a low-level amplitude modulation that manifested itself in the central receiving station, but beginning only when one was within thirty-two feet of each thimble. The louder the buzzing, the closer the station-transmitter.

Once more the search for the mysterious Shambhala began; and even Helena Banya, despite her KGB training to always remain calm, had the uneasy feeling that unseen eyes were secretly measuring her for a casket.

Nonetheless, the morning passed without incident—no one even slipped in the snow. The only break in the monotony was a bear. The large animal, standing in the distance, gave them a long, curious look, then slowly lumbered away in the opposite direction.

The afternoon crawled peacefully by. . . .

Toward the end of daylight, Camellion spotted a chain of hills, half a kilometer to the northeast, that offered excellent refuge for the night, inspection through binoculars revealing that the tops of the huge humps were adequate for a camp site.

Upon reaching the area, Troju Gyud, one of the Bhutanese soldiers, discovered a large cave in the base of

46

one of the hills, which prompted Major Kor Sidkeong to suggest that they use the cave to camp in for the night. But Camellion vetoed the idea on the grounds that a cave was too much like a prison, that there was too much danger of being trapped inside. "The Chinese could set up a cross-fire from the sides of other hills and keep us bottled up indefinitely."

"They could use explosives," Helena Banya pointed out. Ignoring Camellion, she looked at Major Sidkeong. "They could seal the mouth and bury us alive."

The Death Merchant pointed to a large, ragged elevation twenty-five meters or so to the northwest. "We'll camp at the base of that hill," he said. "After dark, we'll climb to the top for the night."

"And back down again before daylight," said Red Degenhardt, laughing.

"You act like you're not too fond of your job," mused Camellion. "I know that moving back and forth is monotonous, but it's necessary."

"I like my job all right," Degenhardt said, with pseudoseriousness. "It's the work that I hate."

The night passed peacefully enough—except for one disturbance. According to the prints in the snow, a bear had wandered into one of the E.A. beams and had set off a alarm. By the time Camellion and his people had decided that the alarm was false, several hours without sleep had slipped into the past.

Weatherwise, the next day was a repetition of the previous two, the only difference being that now the sky was cloud-covered and threatening. Toward midmorning they spotted, through binoculars, a stark-naked ascetic, several miles straight west. The man was standing ramrod straight on a ledge protruding from the slope of a hill, his face turned up to the sky, his arms straight above his head.

"He is a *Jowo gomchen*, a Lord Contemplative mystic," explained Major Sidkeong, sounding slightly embarrassed. "He is seeking his own personal salvation. I suppose that such practices are difficult for Westerners to understand."

"Not at all," Professor Lauterjung said gently, as the party resumed the strenuous march over the uneven

47

ground. "It's simply that different people use different methods in their search for God."

"Very true," Richard Camellion said. "In the case of the *Jowo gomchen,* it is *Aum mani puzim hok.*"

Major Sidkeong, both pleased and surprised, gave the Death Merchant a respectful look. "Yes, that is so. The *Jowo gomchen* has found the jewel in the lotus."

It was Vallie West who said, "I've heard that expression before, but what does 'jewel in the lotus' actually mean?"

"It's symbolism," Camellion said. Slowing down he adjusted his vermillion-tinted sunglasses. "The simplest interpretation is: In the lotus—which is the world—exists the precious jewel of Buddha's teaching. Another explanation takes the lotus as the mind. In the depth of it, by introspective meditation, one is able to find the jewel of knowledge, truth, reality, liberation, or nirvana, these being terms for one and the same thing."

"It's slightly different in the doctrine of the Mahayanist Buddhists," said Paul Gemz. "According to them, nirvana, the supreme salvation, is not separated from *samsara,* which is the world; but the mystic finds the first in the heart of the second, just as the jewel may be found in the lotus. Nirvana, the 'jewel,' exists when enlightenment exists. *Samsara,* the 'lotus,' exists when delusion exists, which veils nirvana, just as the many petals of the lotus conceal the jewel nestled among them."

Vallie West, who liked to conceal the fact that he was highly intelligent, chuckled. "It's all Greek to me," he said with fake indifference. "I suppose there are different roads that lead to heaven."

During the early afternoon the sky cleared and the wind rose, the increased intensity swirling more snow from the rugged terrain. The members of the expedition increased their efforts; yet, their progress declined. The wind was simply too strong.

The middle of the afternoon brought them to a wide, fairly level *thang.* To the left, several hundred meters from the route, was the dwelling of a *Dopka,*[15] made of stone and wood, its architecture resembling a Swiss chalet. The

[15] Dopka: "man of the solitudes," or "herdsman."

house had two stories, with the Dopka quartering his yaks on the first floor where the walls were four feet thick and made of earth between sections of stones. The second floor contained the living quarters: one large living room, in which was a hearth, or stove. There was never a chimney, and because of the smoke, many herdsmen suffered from inflamed eyes and eyelids.

The upper story was made of wood and painted white. The roof was flat. On top of the flat roof was a second widely pitched roof supported on a heavy wooden frame, leaving underneath an open-sided loft. This loft contained dried yak dung which was used for fuel.

"Think we should stop by for a bit of chitchat?" joked Vallie.

The Death Merchant shook his head. "We can't afford the time required for the Bhutanese ritual of hospitality. We'll move ahead a few more miles, then stop for the night."

"Yeah; if the Chinese caught us in there, they could completely surround the house," Vallie commented in all seriousness. He gave the house a long, suspicious look, his rugged features tense with caution.

Major Kor Sidkeong nodded toward the wind-beaten dwelling of the Dopka and pulled the heavy hood of his *Bakhu* closer around his face.

"It is best that we do not stop," he said loudly, his voice fighting the wind. "The herdsman and his family would have to offer us food, the best they have. Not to do so would be an offense against the gods. And to feed us at this time of the year would seriously deplete their own food supply."

About then, a man and two women stepped from the front door of the house. The Dopka was dressed in a fur hat, a knee-length sheepskin coat, and high felt boots; the women were clothed in a similar manner, but with their faces smeared with *cutch*, a greasy red substance that prevented their skins from becoming desiccated by the wind.

"We have an audience," Norbert Shireling said. "I guess they're wondering who we are and what we're doing up here."

"They're warmly dressed, that's for sure," called out Red

49

Degenhardt. "I suppose that's the latest style in these parts."

Degenhardt's remark prompted Camellion to think that the Black Beret fighter wasn't altogether wrong. Although clothes varied slightly from region to region, all Bhutanese wore the same kind of garment—a long, loose-sleeved coat tied tightly at the waist, worn long by women and shorter by men. A loose fold in the coat is used as a pocket in which betel nuts and often a heavy straight knife are carried. The wealthier members of Bhutanese society usually wore long leather boots or modern Western shoes, although in warm weather in the south many people would go barefoot.

A very efficient people, both the nomads and the farmers were experts at the domestic arts of spinning, weaving, and dyeing. They made all their own household goods and clothing, including the cotton trousers that, worn under the long coat, were tucked into either felt or leather boots.

Being excellent weavers, Bhutanese women produced a wide variety of cloth patterns from wool, cotton, and rough silk on their simple back-strap looms, making their clothes from striped, checked, and embroidered materials, often in bright colors and of complex design. The usual-style dress was pinned at the shoulders with large silver brooches joined by a chain.

But no doubt those two women in the distance are wearing thick woolen dresses under their coats. Another thought bloomed in Camellion's mind: that women had always held a high position in Bhutanese society, being free, both economically and sexually.

I've been in a lot of countries, but when it comes to marriage customs, the Bhutanese are a paradox! Monagamy existed as in most other nations. Promiscuity was almost unheard of and was considered a terrible sin. Be that as it may, polygamy was very common, with a man being allowed to have as many wives as he wanted, that is, as many as he could afford. *It would seem that what's a good deal for the gander is also a prize for the goose!* Polyandry was also normal, with any woman free to take as many husbands as she wanted.

An American sociologist would have a double nervous breakdown trying to figure out who's married to whom!

The Dopka and his two wives, more than a quarter of a mile away, stood solemnly and watched as the Death Merchant's party trudged by. They did not smile. They did not wave. They merely stood there and stared.

On the north side of the stone-and-wood house was a pen of half a dozen *dzomo*—a crossbreed between the yak and domestic lowland cattle. These hardy animals added butter, curd, and dried cheese to the diet of the Dopka and his family.

Soon the Dopka, his wives, and his house lay behind and were only a memory. Ahead lay miles and miles of scree, small loose stones, in a partially dun-colored moonscape marred by enormous patches of glistening snow. More than fifty miles to the north were the first peaks of the vast Himalayas.

In the immediate vicinity—for at least half a day's march—there were no suitable hills whose summits could be used for the night's camping. Instead there were only scattered chains of hummocks—small but rough ridges of rock, formed by pressure millions of years ago. With the wind whipping the snow from the chopped-up rocks, the hummocks looked as inviting as hell frozen over.

Professor Lauterjung cleared his throat and rubbed one side of his round face, now red from the wind. "I'm not an authority in matters of security, but I should think we will not have much natural protection tonight."

"What gave you the first clue, Professor?" asked Foster Cross, grinning. Removing the NATO M14 rifle from his shoulder, he squatted down on his haunches and, along with Loren Eaton, lit a cigarette.

"We still have several hours of daylight left," Paul Gemz ventured. He turned and looked at the Death Merchant, who was studying the jagged ramparts through binoculars. "But if we moved ahead, we wouldn't be any better off than we are now."

"We don't really know that the Chinese are in this area," Helena Banya said to no one in particular. She did smile when Vallie West gave her an interested glance.

The Death Merchant removed the binoculars from his

51

eyes, put them into their case, closed the cover, and let his eyes wander over the group. As usual, the Black Berets were watching all directions, each man ready for instant trouble. The four Bhutanese soldiers, their teeth stained brown from chewing betel nuts,[16] wore their usual noncommital expressions. *They'll probably die with the same unenterprising look on their brown faces!* Then there was Major Sidkeong. A slight smile on his face, the Bhutanese Army officer reminded Camellion of a huge gilded Buddha he had once seen in northern India, a Buddha that had worn a "smile of enlightenment."

"The Russian doll has a point, Rick," Vallie West said forcefully. "This is the fourth day and we haven't seen one riceball." He let his voice drift off into the wind, a clear indication to Camellion that the big CIA troubleshooter was worried.

The Death Merchant sighed. "You're right, Val. You have a good point." He nodded at the Russian woman. "So have you, Helena. We don't have any proof that the Chinese are breathing down our backs."

Red Degenhardt pulled a long face and gave the Death Merchant a hostile look. "What do you want for proof? A bellyful of slugs made in Peking? We must assume that those Chinese bastards are eating their rice not too far away."

"Quit spitting out razor blades, and let me finish," cracked the Death Merchant. "Theory is the flower, not the root of experience. That means simply this: either the Chinese aren't around, or else they're obviously keeping at a very safe distance. They'd have to stay far, far away in the daytime, or risk open conflict, and that's not their style. So they have to be keeping track of us through high-powered scopes."

"Then why haven't they tried to hit us at night?" Paul Gemz stepped closer to Camellion, West, and Degenhardt. "What better time could they have? My own belief is that

16   Betel chewing is a habit of an estimated one-tenth of the world's population. Chewing results in a copious flow of brick-red saliva, which may temporarily dye the mouth, lips, and gums orange brown. But, contrary to general belief in the West, the teeth of habitual chewers do not remain blackened by the betel juice.

52

they're watching us, in the hope that we'll lead them to the Shambhala entrance—assuming it exists, which I doubt!"

"You might be right; I can't prove that you're wrong," Camellion said slowly. "I'm more inclined to think that the Chinese are using infrared nightscopes and are wise to the nightly traps we've been setting for them. The only thing wrong with that concept is that, if that is the case, they could have attacked just before dawn, right after we moved back down to the decoy camp."

Vallie West pursed his lips speculatively. "Listen, Rick. If you're saying that you think the Commies have given it all up as a bum deal, I'll have to say that your brain cells are misfiring. You know as well as I do that the Mao morons have infinite patience and fanatical persistence. They're crazier than even the Ivans!"

Camellion's lips parted in amusement. "I'll spell it out very clearly. I'm convinced that the Chinese have been keeping track of us, but haven't attacked because they want the odds to be overwhelmingly on their side. They don't want another defeat like the one we gave them at Thimphu gompa."

"Which adds up to what?" asked Gemz.

"The Chinese know that the waiting is bad for us but good for them because there isn't any way we can smoke them out. Like you said, Val, they have plenty of patience. I've come to the conclusion that they'll attack when they feel they have us set up for a massacre that can't fail."

"In that case, they should be positively ecstatic over our present position," Gemz said glumly. He frowned with frustration and his eyes shot to Camellion. "Maybe we should have stayed overnight at the herdsman's house a few miles back?"

"No. We don't involve innocent people!" Although loud, because of the wind, Camellion's voice was firm. "Anyhow, we're in a better position here. There aren't any ridges around the house."

Gemz pushed up his sunglasses and stared in amazement at the Death Merchant. Helena Banya's mouth fell open.

"I see!" Gemz said in disgust. He waved a hand toward

the dismal countryside. "So we're 'safer' here among these rocks and ridges! If we had been riding camels, I'd say your brain had been shaken loose."

"The idea is to shake the Chinese," said the Death Merchant, laughing, "which is what we'll do if they attack this night." Tilting his head, he looked up at the sky. The broken clouds—big balls of ragged cotton—raced by as if blown along by a giant fan. There would be a clear sky and a bright moon. *That's not good. But I can't control the weather.*

Camellion lowered his eyes, looked around the chopped up landscape, and heard Vallie West say, "Even with the E.A. gismos and our remote control big bangs, we're going to have to be like the crosseyed cat who worked overtime watching both ratholes."

"Do you have any special ideas?" asked Camellion, fixing an eye on West. "I believe that advice is much more than what you take for a cold."

West shook his head in the negative. "And I believe that the business of the future is living dangerously. We might as well camp in this general area, and take what comes—as if we had a choice!"

Major Sidkeong pointed ahead. "Over there would be an ideal place for our camp, in that place partially surrounded by those four ridges. Those ridges are too to three meters high and will offer us some protection . . . not much, but enough."

"A good idea," agreed Camellion. He unsnapped the buckles of his backpack. "We are in some luck. There aren't any high spots close by. The Chinese won't be able to fire down on us."

"*Nyeda ko,*"[17] said Sidkeong, with a smile. "I feel that position is the best we can do under the circumstances."

Within an hour the camp was set up: the tents erected and their end flaps fastened together so that there was one long structure of wind-and-waterproof cloth, one end facing north, the other south. Helena Banya's tent was a few feet north of the north end, Major Sidkeong's situated south of the south end. On either side of the main tent

[17] The Bhutanese equivalent of "That's good."

54

structure, to the east and the west, were the tents of the four Bhutanese soldiers, two on each side.

There was a long hummock eighteen to twenty meters to the northwest, its east end almost connected to the west end of a smaller hummock to the northeast. Southeast of the camp was another rough, twisting ridge, this one shaped somewhat like a crescent, with its ends turned away from the tents. The fourth, and largest, ridge, to the southwest, reminded the Death Merchant of one of the Indian burial mounds in Honduras, only this mound was longer, not quite as high, and shaped more irregularly.

There was a fifth ridge—the smallest of all—situated between the hummock to the northeast, and the ridge to the southeast, at a distance of perhaps twenty-two meters from the encampment.

Once more Camellion and West planted Model-4 Emergency Alarm stations around the entire perimeter of the camp, placing them a good thirty meters, or a hundred feet, from the outer sides of the hummocks, the sides to the outside of the camp. And while the Death Merchant and West went about their work, Captain Degenhardt and his three men busied themselves burying ten-ounce packets of HBX-1 in the outer sides of the ridges. Each pack of HBX-1 was very special, but not because it was a high explosive. Each square had a transducer connected to a button-sized relay-trigger transmitter, a miniaturized but highly sophisticated system that could very efficiently detonate the HBX-1.

After the work had been completed, the Death Merchant and Vallie West had placed a dozen M-4 E.A. stations, and Degenhardt and his boys had buried fourteen packets of HBX-1.

As West and Camellion reached the long tent, Vallie looked all around the landscape, at the snow and the rocks and the scattered *findop* shrubs, all of which were now tinged an eerie red-orange by the setting sun.

"Dammit! I've seen better defensive terrain in the Sahara Desert," the big man mumbled and put his gloved hands on his hips. "You've got to be right, Rick. If the riceballs don't hit us tonight, they're either stupid or were never around to begin with."

"We might as well be realistic," Camellion suavely intervened. He glanced in the direction of Red Degenhardt and Loren Eaton, both of whom were coming toward him and West. "Think of it this way: out here there's only a little more danger than exists in the average American home.[18] Only a riot or a battlefield is more violent."

West shifted the lollipop in his mouth and gave Camellion a reproachful look. "And what do you think this place is going to be before the night's over, if not a battle-ground?"

"True, but with a difference," Camellion said. "We're the ones in control of the situation—hopefully!" He looked at Red Degenhardt, who had ambled up. "You have the stuff in place, Red?"

The Black Beret chief grinned slyly. "We buried each one about a foot under loose rock. You know what that means? HBX-1 is about forty percent RDX and about thirty-eight percent TNT. When all that power goes off, it will tear apart the rocks and turn them into natural shrap-nel."

"Let's go feed our faces," the Death Merchant said.

Over supper, further plans were made. It was decided that guards would be posted on four of the ridges, each man lying partially on top of each hummock and watching the terrain through a nightsight device, although in the bright moonlight it would not be all that difficult to see any approaching figures. The three regular Black Berets would trade off every half hour with the four Bhutanese Army men. At the first sight of anything unusual, one of the men would signal by radio.

The minutes crawled into hours. By nine-forty the moon was full, bright, and high in the sky, the entire area, except for the low moaning of the wind, as quiet as a tomb.

Protected by the walls of the tents, the Death Merchant

---

18 Camellion is not wrong. A national study of violence in American families reveals that, in 1977, more than 1.8 million wives had been severely beaten by their husbands; 2.3 million children had used a knife or gun on a brother or sister; and 1.2 million children, aged three to seventeen, had been attacked by parents using lethal weapons. As things stack up, you are more likely to be killed by a relative than by a stranger.

and the others sat grouped around a Primus propane stove, the only light a Primus double-mantle lantern . . . a soft glow that could not be seen outside the long tent structure.

They waited, sipping *solja*, tea heavily flavored with salt and yak butter, the Death Merchant keeping an eye on the E.A. alarm box. Next to him was an AN/PRC radio.

Convinced that the Death Merchant's plan would not work, Paul Gemz was not adverse to stating his opinion. "We could have tried the same scheme nights ago," he said, frowning at Camellion. "It would have saved us all the work of breaking camp and going down the hillside before dawn. I am opposed to the entire plan."

"Big winds often issue from small caves," Major Kor Sidkeong said calmly.

Gemz, who disliked Sidkeong with an equal intensity, ignored the Bhutanese Army officer and the amused smiles of Vallie West and Red Degenhardt.

Camellion put down the collapsible metal cup from which he had been drinking. "That's right. We could have used the same tactics nights ago," he said, feeling that he did owe Gemz an explanation. "But you don't understand the Chinese mentality, Gemz. They expected us to be on guard the first night. They knew that we'd take all the precautions possible on succeeding nights. Tonight's different. There aren't any high hills to climb. We're practically out in the open. The Chinese must conclude that this is the best we can do, which it is!"

Helena Banya, the other dissenting voice, spoke up. "According to your theory, Comrade Camellion, the Chinese have had us under constant surveillance. If such is the case, they will have seen you and the others place the explosive and the security devices. The Chinese are not fools. They are no more anxious to commit suicide than we are."

"Yes, that could be a problem," Camellion said pleasantly. "I'm hoping the Chinese will assume that all we have done is ring the area with alarms. They couldn't see all that clearly from the distance, but at least they could see well enough to know that the objects weren't land mines."

"They didn't see us play out any wire on a reel," interposed Red Degenhardt, crushing out a cigarette. "I don't think they'll get the idea we're going to use this little gadget on them." He tapped one corner of a metal box in front of him. About the size of a cigar box. the detonating station had a panel with one large red button and many smaller orange ones. Each orange button detonated a single package of explosive. Press the red button and everything would blow simultaneously.

Vallie West made amused noises deep within the well of his throat. "It's a full moon tonight, so maybe the rice-balls will be irrational—more so than usual."

"I've heard about the full-moon crazies," mused Red Degenhardt. "I've always considered it a lot of nonsense, like UFOs or voodoo." He turned slightly and looked at the Death Merchant. "What's your opinion, Camellion?"

Camellion shrugged. "What we believe will happen influences what *will* happen," he said. "Most people don't focus on the full moon. But people can be frightened to death by voodoo, simply because they believe it works. In short, legends like the full moon can be self-fulfilling."

"It might not be a legend." Professor Lauterjung continued to wipe his glasses with a piece of toilet paper. "Human beings consist of eighty percent water. It's possible that the gravitational influence of the moon, which moves oceans, may also influence the 'biological tides' of humans." He smiled at Helena Banya, who was quietly smoking a cigarette. "I'd be interested in knowing how Soviet scientists view the theory."

"I wouldn't know, Professor," she answered in a soft, vibrant voice. "In my section of the KGB, I didn't associate with Soviet scientists. However, the KGB has made numerous studies about other strange factors in human existence. For example, one extensive series of studies disclosed that the time of death for an individual can be narrowed down. Half the people who die do so within ninety days of their last birthday. Nearly eight in ten deaths occur within the first six months of a person's last birthday."

"Interesting, most interesting." Lauterjung nodded studiously, as the Russian continued.

"As I recall, very few people die in the three months before their birthdays, making this an unusual 'grace period.' I suppose that this is when you could apply your American expression 'Death takes a holiday.'"

"Oh boy!" Degenhardt sounded disgusted. "I had a birthday six weeks ago!"

"That still is not a valid reason to worry," the Russian girl said quickly. "The theory cannot be applied to any given individual."

Richard Camellion changed the subject by turning to Paul Gemz. "By the way," he said casually, "it occurs to me that I know little about your work, archaeoastronomy."

Gemz rubbed a finger across his salt-and-pepper mustache and blinked very rapidly. "Archaeoastronomy is simply the discipline that combines the methods of archaeology and astronomy, to discover what primitive civilizations saw in the skies and how they interpreted their sightings."

Vallie West said thoughtfully, "It has been established that between 600 and 300 B.C., the Babylonians computed solar and lunar motions that compare favorably with modern tables."

Gemz drew back slightly in surprise. "Yes, and shortly afterward, Greek astronomers made equally astute calculations of the Earth's circumference, as well as the distances to the sun and the moon. Five hundred years later, the Maya of Mexico and Central America produced a calendar that was accurate to within one second per year, and predicted eclipses of the sun eight hundred fifty years ahead."

Professor Lauterjung joined in. "We must not forget that the Plains Indians of North America were diligent observers of the skies, this fact explaining many puzzling facets of their civilization. This is how we know that Indian towns and ceremonial centers were laid out in reference to the summer solstice, when the sun is at its northernmost point."

Red Degenhardt, sitting cross-legged, leaned forward slightly and peered closely at Professor Gemz. "I still don't understand what all that has to do with this mission? Okay, so maybe this or that ancient civilization made some hotshot math calculations in reference to the stars. How does all that tie in with this nutty search for Shambhala?"

Tapping ahe side of his nose, Gemz regarded Degenhardt solemnly for a long moment. "I'm considered an authority on ancient civilizations and unexplained factors connected with those civilizations."

"Myth! You mean myth," Vallie West said amiably.

"Yes . . . and no," Gemz said slowly. "Let me explain. Some things are considered myth only because science can't—or won't—explain them."

"Or in some cases even refuse to acknowledge that they exist!" inserted Professor Lauterjung with a vehemence that surprised everyone. "The trouble is that most scientists tend to pay heed only to what can be mechanically registered."

"For example," Gemz continued, "The Siddhanta-Ciromani, which is a Brahmin book, subdivides time until it reaches a final unit, *truti*, which is 0.33750 of a second. Sanskrit scholars are puzzled as to why such a small unit of time was used in antiquity, or how that unit could have been measured without instrumentation."

"Did you ever check with Brahmin scholars regarding the matter?" Camellion asked in a quiet voice.

Gemz nodded enthusiastically. "I met Pundit Karith Yogi in Madras, in 1974, and he explained that the original time measurement of the Brahmins was sexagesimal, and he quoted Brihath Sakatha and other Sanskrit sources."

"What did Pundit Yogi think about it?" Helena Banya asked, in a small voice.

"He told me that the learned Brahmins were obliged to preserve this tradition from antiquity too distant to recall. He said that they themselves did not understand why."

The Death Merchant wore an amused expression. "The time unit of *kashta*—1/300 millionth of a second—is meaningless without the proper instrumentation to register it. More important, a *kashta* is close to the life span of certain hyperons and mesons—atomic particles!"

All eyes turned to Camellion. The two academics in particular regarded the Death Merchant with wonderment.

"Odd that you should say that," remarked Paul Gemz. "Because it coincides with the Varahamira Table, which is dated 550 A.D. and which gives a mathematical figure that compares closely with the size of the hydrogen atom."

Red Degenhardt opened his mouth as if to speak, then

closed it again. Secretly, he wondered if any of them knew what they were talking about.[19]

At the southern end of the long tent, the flaps parted and Loren Eaton and Foster Cross quickly stepped inside, bent over because of the low height of the supporting framework.

"How's the weather out there?" called out Degenhardt.

"It's colder." Eaton removed the M14 automatic rifle from his shoulder and unzipped his parka.

"It figures. The barometer is falling," Degenhardt said.

Vallie West shook his head. "You can't always go on that, Red. Hell, the last totally accurate weather forecast was when God told old Noah that there would be a hundred percent chance of rain."

Foster Cross slipped out of his parka. "If the chinnies are out there, they're invisible. I wish those Red fatherless sons would attack and get it over with—if they're going to!"

As if to answer Cross, a voice, speaking calmly in Bhutanese, came from the AN/PRC Electro-5 radio.

"That was Gom Shinje on the northeast ridge," Major Sidkeong said, getting to his feet. "He's sighted the Chinese. They're more than one hundred twenty meters from his position."

A deeper voice came from the Electro-5, and more singsong Bhutanese. But no one hesitated as weapons were grabbed.

"Tolung Terskug, on the southwest ridge!" Getting his Bakhu, Sidkeong gave Camellion a quick look. "He estimates the enemy on his side are slightly more than a hundred meters from him."

"We should be hearing from Shireling," Degenhardt said. "He's—which side is he on?" He swung to Cross and Eaton, who were checking their A-Rs.

"Sweet Jesus, help us all!" muttered Professor Lauterjung. He had slipped into his parka and had a stunned, panicky look on his round face.

"The only way he can help is if he can fire a rifle or a

19 None of this is fiction. These writings do exist, and they relate what we have written.

61

sub-gun," laughed Vallie West, cocking a 9mm sub-machine gun.

Norbert Shireling's rather high voice crackled over the Electro-5: "I'm on the northwest ridge. The Reds—they're all in white—are creeping in low, maybe several hundred feet from me. They'll begin to run shortly. I'm going to back off and get the hell down."

The Death Merchant, already in his parka, twisted his mouth into a huge grin. "So! It's cemetery time!" He turned to Vallie West and Red Degenhardt, but gave the order to Major Sidkeong, "Major, tell your men to get down and take positions on the inner sides of the ridges. Tell them to keep their mouths open and to jab the tips of their fingers into their ears. The fireworks are about to begin."

While Sidkeong bent and jabbered into the Electro-5, Camellion got down on one knee and looked at the E.A. receiver.

"Red, once the chopstick chaps reach the sensors, they'll certainly be coming in on the run. Give them seventeen seconds then to reach the sides of the ridges. Even if they are still ten feet away, or have begun to climb, we'll still blow them halfway back to Peking."

Degenhardt, his finger close to the red button of the remote control detonating box, almost beamed with anticipation. "I never did like those Commie SOBs," he said savagely. "Too bad there aren't any windows around. I just love to hear the tinkle of glass!"

"You're going to have to settle for the sound of falling rocks," said Camellion. Smiling, he kept his eyes on the E.A. receiver as he talked like a teletype machine, in a strident, detached, steady rhythm of sentences. "Major, get to your men. Val, take everyone outside and get them flat on the ground. If something goes wrong and the Chinese get through, you know what to do and how to do it. Professor Lauterjung, don't panic or you'll lose your best friend—your very own brain. Gemz, watch yourself!"

"I can shoot better than most men," Helena Banya said, an angry note in her voice, "and that includes the use of a submachine gun. I didn't ask to be here. I was forced. It's about time I'm permitted to at least protect my own life! I'm speaking to you, Camellion!"

"Val, get her an Ingram," Camellion said. "We can use her firepower."

Moments later, as West and Banya, the last of the group, left the tent, the Death Merchant and Captain Degenhardt were alone with only hope and experience.

Then the red light on the E.A. receiver began flashing, and Camellion began counting, *"One . . . two . . . three."* Finally, *"Fifteen . . . sixteen . . . seventeen."*

"Here's a present for you Commie dog-eaters!" Degenhardt said grimly, and pushed down on the big red button of the detonating box.

The fourteen packets of HBX-1 exploded as one giant bomb, the sound of the explosion so thunderous that, for a microsecond, Camellion and Degenhardt had the feeling that giant hands had reached into their skulls and had squeezed their brains, the way one would squeeze dry a wet sponge.

Within half a blink of an eye the actual explosion was over, the sound of concussion slamming back and forth across the countryside. Camellion and Degenhardt could only imagine what the fourteen coordinated blasts had done to the attacking Red Chinese. The Chinese, having surrounded the entire areas, had advanced in unison; yet, because the ridges were set at different angles, not all the Communist soldiers had been in the same position when the HBX-1 had exploded. Scores had just started to climb the outer sides of the ridges; others had been ten, twenty, thirty feet, and even farther away from the outer sides of the ridges.

And then the HBX-1 had exploded!

The fourteen blasts couldn't have caught the advancing Chinese at a lesser advantage. Not only did scores of them die from the proximity of the concussions, but thousands of rocks, crushed into smaller, jagged pieces and acting as shrapnel, ripped into many, many more of the enemy. Bodies, some headless, others without arms or legs, were thrown high into the air. The unlucky ones were the Chinese who had not been killed outright, the Red soldiers who had lost a hand or a foot, or who had been blinded or had suffered broken limbs. Their screams of fear and pain mingled with the dying echo of the explosions and with the shouts of the remaining Red Army soldiers, who now charged toward the ridges and toward the narrow openings between the ridges—straight into the vicious sub-machine-gun fire of the Black Berets and the Bhutanese soldiers, all of whom, an instant after the explosion, had scrambled up the inner sides of the ridges.

Flat on their stomachs, West, Banya, Gemz, and Lauterjung fired at the spaces between the ridges, each person concentrating on a different area. To West, with his years of experience, the very short battle was not even a turkey shoot; it was pure slaughter, with Chinese being chopped down before most of them could even fire a shot.

Inside the tent, immediately after the enormous blast, Camellion and Degenhardt grabbed submachine guns and bags of spare magazines, left the tent, and dodged like rabbits to positions not far from where Vallie West and Helena Banya were lying. Just as quickly, they began firing, their high velocity 9mm bullets cutting into the advancing Chinese.

The tops of the ridges were alive with the high *duldulduldulduldul* of deadly Ingrams. Camellion could also hear explosions on the outside slopes as the Chinese, desperate to reach the tops, began tossing stick grenades. Another mistake! The throwing was not coordinated! Neither the Black Berets nor the Bhutanese had any intention of letting the Reds get close enough to throw grenades that could be effective. The grenades exploded harmlessly at the bottom of the slopes, throwing the majority of the shrapnel back into the faces of those Chinese who had not seen their Comrades do the tossing.

Other Chinese attempted to use the same ridiculous tactic in efforts to charge between the ridges, their efforts quickly reduced to total failure by the streams of slugs from the Death Merchant and the five persons lying on the ground with him.

Another disadvantage for the luckless Communists was that the Reds, trying to charge between the ends of the ridges, were slowed by the bodies of comrades already cut down, this delay making it easier for the defenders to send them to their most honorable ancestors. Not a few of the Chinese pulled pins, then died from 9mm slugs before they could throw the grenades, succeeding only in blowing themselves and their comrades to bits.

Suddenly there was no longer any steady firing. There were a few short blasts from the tops of the ridges. West cut down several riceballs with a short burst; at the same time, Camellion stitched three white-clad figures who were trying to climb over twisted corpses piled between the southeast ridge and the southwest mound. There followed a strange silence, an ominous, oppressive kind of quiet that made Camellion think of the stillness that exists just before a tornado strikes.

The Black Berets and the Bhutanese Army men had more sense than to rear up and look around. Emil Lauterjung started to get to his feet, but quickly dropped when Vallie West snarled, "Stay down, you idiot! Stay put until we tell you it's safe!"

Soaked with sweat, Lauterjung lay there, reflecting on how easy it is to kill. Strangely, he had not been terrified during the actual firing time. He thought of American soldiers during World War II, thousands and thousands of men in the Pacific, or in the invasion of Europe, wading ashore, disciplined to obey orders under fire. They too must have been full of the kind of savagery that comes from fear, their emotions so knotted that fear became indistinguishable from the emotion of trying to suppress that fear . . . each man driven by animal instinct to survive, each man overcoming that fear by destroying the source of the fear. *And that's what we did! We destroyed the source of that fear. We killed the Chinese. . . .*

An hour later, the Death Merchant and the other experienced men decided that there were no more Chinese in the vicinity, at least none that were alive. Another decision was made: the Black Berets and the Bhutanese would rotate on guard duty for the remainder of the night. Camellion, West, and Major Sidkeong would trade off with them. Each member of the expedition would get as much sleep as was possible.

Vallie West looked up at the moon. It was like a huge white-yellow lantern . . . the stars as bright as blue diamonds. West turned to the Death Merchant, who was fitting a nightsight infrared scope to a NATO M14 automatic rifle. The rifle had a Sionic silencer attached to the barrel. A nice weapon. A fine, quiet killer.

"Rick, you've thought about the riceballs using a mortar," Vallie said. "They can be pretty damned good with a 60mm job. We wouldn't be able to fight back."

"We don't have to worry about a mortar," Camellion said boldly. "If the chopstick-charlies had had a mortar, they would have used it in advance of their charge."

"We're not out of the woods yet. There's tomorrow and the day after." Vallie sighed nervously. "And we're low on ammo. We used three-fourths of our supply."

"We should reach the twin peaks by tomorrow afternoon," Camellion said firmly. "The Reds didn't expect a defeat. They'll have to regroup and they'll have to come from China. You know how the Red Chinese are, Val. They're cautious; they don't do things on the spur of the moment."

"We can use Commie machine guns," Vallie suggested. "There are plenty lying around and a lot of ammo. I guess I don't have to tell you that some of the 'corpses' out there could be playing possum?"

"I know. We'll have to be very careful when we move out in the morning. Before we're out in the open, we'll put a single bullet into each one, just to make sure." Camellion tightened the last screw of the clamp, closed the utility knife, and dropped it into one compartment of the ten-pocket Deschutes fishing vest he wore underneath the parka.

"Okay, Val. I'm going up and have a look. Keep an eye on things down here."

"Are we going to collect the E.A. stations in the morning?"

"We must. We'll need them on the return trip. The Chinese don't want us as prisoners. They want us dead; and I don't expect them to quit trying."

Camellion turned and started toward the northeast ridge. Vallie stood watching for a time. He then turned his romanesque head on the turret of his thick neck and looked suspiciously at Helena Banya, who had walked up and was watching the Death Merchant climb the side of the ridge. The moonlight gave her face a quiet kind of beauty. Well, she was good with a chopper, and coldly efficient under fire. The KGB trained its women agents well. Too damn well.

"I don't think your friend Camellion has much respect for human life," the Russian girl said. She sounded disappointed.

Vallie stabbed her with a fierce glare. "What did you expect him to do—invite the Chinese to tea?"

"Hardly! I meant the way he goes about planning; his complete ruthlessness. However, I realize the necessity of it all."

"You're wrong about Camellion," Vallie said impersonally. "Actually, he has more respect for life than the average man. That's why he's so damned good at what he does."

Lying flat, looking out between two headsized stones, the Death Merchant studied the moonlit landscape dotted with tiny, crumpled mounds of white. He had counted thirty-two of the little mounds. Thirty-two corpses on this side indicated that—figuring as many on the other sides—more than 150 of the enemy had been killed.

A slight smile crossed his mouth. He looked over the corpses. *Here lie the killer and the lover, the father and the brother. All common members in the Kingdom of Death.*

Old friend, we've done a good night's work. But the paradox is still there. Life feeds on death just as Death is constantly being nourished by life.

Chapter Five

General Hsun Chin, one of the youngest generals in the P.L.A., the People's Liberation Army, picked up the yellow sheet from the folding table and again stared at the radio message that had arrived the previous night. Chin still found it difficult to accept the fact that 172 soldiers had been lost in the attack on the tiny Occidental expedition. Incredible! If for no other reason than he had planned the attack, basing his strategy on the principle of *ku-lii*, of isolation. Mao himself had stressed that isolation should precede the disintegratian of a foreign enemy. Very well! The small enemy force had been totally isolated. Yet, it was the enemy that had won, in spite of Chin's unity of command and concentration of superior firepower. The defeat should not have happened. But it had. Only ten regular soldiers and three officers had survived. Captain Ts'ao Yu-Ling had immediately radioed news of the terrible defeat to the main camp at Lhakang. Intelligence had reported that the enemy leader was named Camellion. That white-faced devil! He was a true *wang-pa-tan*.[20]

Cognizant that Major Fu Siu-ch'un and Major Yang She-Tung, the two other officers at the conference table, were watching him with patient but curious eyes, Chin thought of how he had been forced to *t'u k'u-shui*, to "vomit bitter water," by having to report the defeat, by radio, to the Military Affairs Commission in Peking. He had not given a definite reason. He had, however, made it clear that Major Siu-ch'un, and Major She-Tung, had helped formulate the plan. He had also inserted an element from Chairman Mao's "On Protracted War"—*Owing to factors not clearly understood, it sometimes will happen*

[20] Chinese for "bastard."

*that a superior force will lose a battle. When this happens,
let us not place blame, but learn from the error and apply
what we have learned to the general principle of encircle-
ment and suppression, so that we might make use of this
contradiction of defeat, and thereby win over the many,
oppose the few, and crush the enemies of the revolution,
one by one.*

Tall, with square, angular features and deep-set, eyes
Hsun Chin recalled another of Mao's sayings: *Whoever
relaxes vigilance will disarm himself politically and place
himself in a passive, dangerous position.* Maybe so, but
Chin figured that he was safe from political retribution
. . . very safe. Major Fu-Siu-ch'un was a well-placed
member of the Social Affairs Department and a favorite of
Chan K'o-nung, the powerful head of the Ministry of
Public Affairs. Chan K'o-nung would protect Fu Siu-ch'un.
In order to do so, he would also have to protect General
Chin. But Chin couldn't be sure, not until a reply came
from Peking. The Military Affairs Commission would either recall him or give him orders to proceed into the tunnel. It would be either one or the other.

Chin reached for the bottle of *huang chiu*, filled his
glass, recorked the bottle, then looked first at Major Siu-
ch'un, then at Major She-Tung. "Have either of you estimated how long it will take Captain Yu-ling and the
survivors of the force to reach our base here?"

"By late this afternoon," Major Fu-Siu-ch'un said
promptly. He folded his hands and put them on the table.
"What difference does it make? He reported what happened. Practically the entire force was killed. By the time
he and the others got here, we should be well inside the
tunnel and on our way to Shambhala."

A Cantonese, and half a head shorter than either General Chin or Major She-Tung, Fu Siu-ch'un had steely
eyes and a tough expression. But when he was viewed
from a side angle, his rather flat nose took away most of

---

21 The first-level imperial examination degree, which qualifies
    the recipient as a candidate for the higher degrees of *chu-
    jen* and *chin-shih*. The *sheng-yuan* is roughly equivalent to
    a bachelor's degree in the West.

the fierceness. He held a *sheng-yuan*,[21] but had completed his education in the Soviet Union.

Taking a sip of the sweet yellow wine, General Chin made some rapid calculations. The base was just outside Lhakang, a village on the border between Tibet and Bhutan. The entrance to the tunnel was under the stone floor of an ancient, now-unused Buddhist temple several miles to the west. It was now almost ten o'clock in the morning. If the force left the base by noon, it could be well inside the tunnel by nightfall.

Chin set the glass on the table. "The American Camellion and his imperialist lackeys should reach the entrance on the Bhutan side this afternoon. We have no way of knowing if we can intercept him. In fact, we don't even know if his tunnel—if it exists—will lead north. It might very well move in another direction. Our own tunnel could be a decoy; it could come to a dead end. Or the enemy might enter a blind tunnel."

"I think it would be premature to make any predictions at this time," Major Yang She-Tung said fatalistically.

"I disagree." Chin was firm. "Our scouts have been inside the tunnel, on this side of the border, as far back as a mile. We know that the tunnel was not made by modern man and modern science. On this basis alone, once we're inside there are any number of possibilities."

Yang She-Tung, not making any kind of reply, looked down at the table, his face without expression. Like the two other men, he was dressed in a baggy green uniform that bore no insignia of rank, all insignia[22] having been abolished in 1965, except for a single red star on caps.

A tough but cheerful man, Yang She-Tung was the youngest of the three men; he was also the best-looking, his handsome face decorated with a small, neatly trimmed mustache, and topped with a head of thick, shoepolish-black hair. She-Tung was also *chung-kuo ku-tai she-hui yen-chiu*—an authority on ancient Chinese society.

[22] Navy men wear blue-gray. Air force men wear blue trousers with green jacket. Curiously, police uniforms are the same as those of the Air Force—with one variation. The policemen's cap has a red circle, not a red star like the cap of the three services.

Major Fu Siu-ch'un did not avoid General Chin's eyes the way She-Tung had, but his voice was low and cautious. "Comrade General, we must face the possibility that the enemy could reach Shambhala ahead of us—based on the premise that such a place exists."

"We know the tunnel is there; it had to be built for a purpose." Chin kept his eyes on Siu-ch'un, and his voice businesslike. "The shining blue walls and ceiling are not figments of the imagination."

Major Siu-ch'un tilted the bottle of *huang chiu* and filled a glass with the sweet wine, knowing that he was annoying General Chin by not making an immediate reply. Good. Let him be irritated. It was a disgrace the way the People's Party promoted uneducated, country clods like Hsun Chin, who had started his career in a *T'ien-ming*, a Party cadre, and whose first job of any importance had been that of a *Kuo Te-yu*, a puppet village head. Later, he had become a violent *chi-chi-fen-tzu* with the old Red Guard. As a violent activist, he had risen rapidly through the ranks. For several years, Chin had been a full general, with the reputation of being a *t'u-hao*, a "tiger beater."

Siu-ch'un's hand—the one holding the cork—paused over the bottle and let his eyes swing back to General Chin, who was hoping he would mention what was uppermost in Chin's mind: the Military Affairs Commission, and how those old fools would consider last night's defeat.

"All that is true, Comrade General," Siu-ch'un said calmly. "But nothing you have said gives evidence of an underground city. Granted that the glowing walls and ceiling of the tunnel should be investigated by scientists. However, that is not proof of an underground city. That is only proof of strange walls and ceilings that glow blue in the dark."

He recorked the bottle of wine, picked up the glass, and studied the amber-colored liquid. "I think also that for the moment there is another, more pressing matter."

"Comrade," began Major Yang She-Tung, his tone on the edge of anger, "have you forgotten the writings contained in the *Fengshen-yen-I?*" She-Tung frowned at Major Siu-ch'un. "It is quite obvious to me that we must face the prospects of readjustment to a new reality involving a scientific discovery of enormous importance, one

71

that can be used for the advancement of the People's Party, the advancement of the people, and the advancement of the proletariat the world over. The *Fengshen-yen-I* speaks of—"

"And you, Comrade She-Tung, speak the way a Party poster reads!" General Chin waved a hand impatiently. "I am well aware of the implications such a discovery would have on *Chung-Hua Jen-Min Kung-Ho Kuo*.[23] First we must find the city. We cannot do that by depending on ancient fairy tales written by believers in gods and demons and mythical worlds."

"I am in agreement, Comrade General," Major Siu-ch'un said, fingering the stem of the wine glass. "No matter the area of the world in which they originate, religious writings are always similar, always involving gods coming to earth, and other ridiculous trivia."

"Major Siu-ch'un, you mentioned a matter of greater importance," General Chin said icily. "I suggest you get on with it."

"The Military Affairs Commission will give a great deal of thought to last night's failure," Major Siu-ch'un said stoically. He cleared his throat. "We didn't give any particular reason for the disaster. We know what the Commission will do: it will wonder why the army was defeated last night when in 1975 it was possible to make a Russian force—one much larger than the present American expedition—turn back!"

Major She-Tung frowned slightly. "Captain Yu-Ling attributed the defeat to remote-controlled explosives." His eyes narrowed with cunning. "No doubt a new kind of powerful American explosive."

General Chin tapped the tip of a finger against his lower lip. Ah yes. A new type of explosive.

Major Siu-ch'un raised an eyebrow in disagreement. "We should have mentioned the explosives in the report—with all due respect, Comrade General."

"It is better to mention explicits in a face-to-face report," Chin said earnestly. "Let's not fool ourselves. We'll have to report directly to the Commission when we return to Peking. I'm sure of that. I'm also sure that the

[23] The People's Republic of China.

Commission will order us to proceed. To cancel the mission at this point would not be logical. The enemy force is too close to the tunnel entrance in Bhutan. The Commission has no choice but to let us go into the tunnel on this side of the border. Why cancel out when we're here? Suppose the Russians decided to return?"

"A reasonable deduction," responded Major She-Tung, feeling that General Chin sounded as if he were trying to convince himself as much as the two other men. "We do have more to fear from the bear than from the eagle."

Major Siu-ch'un smiled broadly, then became very alert when a soldier in padded uniform entered the command tent, zipped up the flaps against the cold wind, came forward, saluted, and handed General Chin a folded square of yellow paper. The soldier, an ordinary private, remained at attention, eyes straight ahead.

With careful, curious eyes, Fu Siu-ch'un and Yang She-Tung watched General Chin unfold the message and read it.

General Hsun Chin's face remained as expressionless as the rocks that surrounded the huge encampment.

"Have the operator radio Peking that we shall leave at once," he said, looking up at the soldier, who again saluted and left the tent.

General Chin shoved the radio message across the table and smiled at Fu Siu-ch'un and Yang She-Tung. "The Commission has ordered us to proceed with all possible speed," he said, his eyes glittering as he got up from the table. "We'll be well on our way toward Shambhala before dark. This time there will be no defeats at the hands of a *wang-pa-tan* named Camellion. . . ."

Chapter Six

"You're certain, Helena?" Camellion sounded like an inquisitor. "You're absolutely positive that those are the two peaks you saw in the photographs?"

Her eyes flashing in anger, Helena Banya glared at the Death Merchant. "That's the fourth time you've asked me!" she said in exasperation. "I'll tell you for the fourth time. Yes! Those are the two peaks I saw in the photographs. I have a good memory, and I remember other landmarks that were in the photographs." She pointed to the north. "There! That odd-looking mountain between the peaks, miles back from them. The mountain with the streaks in it. It was in the photographs, too!" She glared again at the Death Merchant. "Now, are you satisfied! If I'm wrong, then your American Intelligence is wrong. It was the CIA that checked map after map and estimated that this was the area."

Camellion nodded slowly, the birth of a smile on his mouth. He had been confident the first time he had asked her, certain the second time, and positive the third time. He had only been triple-checking the fourth time. *Yeah, baby! I'm satisfied. . . .*

Vallie West lowered his Zeiss binoculars and swung to Camellion.

"Those have to be the two babies, Rick. There aren't any other needlelike peaks in the area."

Major Kor Sidkeong pulled binoculars from his own eyes, and for the first time he sounded halfway excited. "We can get there within the next few hours. The area is only partially covered with snow, and there don't seem to be any large ravines to obstruct us."

"I still maintain we're making fools of ourselves," insisted Red Degenhardt, a firmness to his voice. "This 'underground city' business is a lot of pure-dee bunk!"

Helena Banya turned on him with all the ferocity of a cornered animal. "Those are the two peaks I saw in the photographs!" She spat out the words at the Black Beret officer. "I don't like you calling me a liar!"

"Go to hell, you Russian slut!" snapped Degenhardt, thrusting out his stubble-covered jaw. "You're not fooling anyone. You're nothing but an 'agent in place,' and I suspect the CIA knows it."

"*Bylo kroviyu boyakh-fevral!*"[24] screamed Helena, and moved toward Degenhardt, her pretty face twisted with hellish fury.

While the other Black Beret and the Bhutanese soldiers grinned, Camellion stepped between her and an astonished Degenhardt, grabbed her right wrist, and prevented her from giving the hard-faced man a stinging slap across the face.

"I'm doing you a favor, doll," Richard said patiently. "He'd turn you upside down and spank your pretty fanny. Think how silly you'd feel."

"Children, children!" mocked Vallie West. "All this violence is hard on my nerves."

The Russian girl's KGB training took over. She regained her composure and, staring malevolently at the Death Merchant, relaxed.

"Tell him not to call me a woman of loose morals," she said quietly. "I will not stand for it."

Not over his surprise, Degenhardt opened his mouth, which the Death Merchant instantly closed with a knife-like stare. "Red, it's over," he warned. "Don't start it again. And that includes tomorrow and the day after, and the week after next."

A tough man who feared only an inactive old age, Degenhardt didn't flinch before Camellion's warning demeanor. He merely turned away, a grim smile fixed on his mouth. What the hell! Coming to blows over the Russian whore wasn't worth it.

---

[24] Translated, this means "son of a low dog." The Russian equivalent of "sonofabitch."

Paul Gemz, a disgusted look on his face, jerked off his sunglasses.

"Gentlemen, standing here exchanging insults is not very intelligent," he said in a tired voice. "We are here to do a job. I suggest we move out."

The Death Merchant felt like laughing. Gemz was short on ears and long on mouth, but, for a change, he had suggested something that made sense.

Two and a half hours later, Camellion and his party closed in on the two peaks which, instead of being peaks or even parts of mountains, were two huge chimney rocks, so enormous they were almost in the monadnock class—an isolated straight-up mountain, rising above a peneplain. Sculpted over the centuries by wind and water, the left pinnacle, the one to the west, was a good seven hundred feet tall. The right column of rock—five hundred feet to the east—was about the same height, give or take fifty feet.

Now that they were near the needlelike rock on the right, they had a clearer view of Mount Kora, which the Bhutanese called the Mountain of Blood. Seven miles to the north of the two chimney rocks, fossil-layered Mount Kora—once beneath a primeval sea, as were most of the Himalayas—had contorted cliffs laced with quartz, the south side being one tremendous unconformity of cross-bedding arched up in folds, of a type geologists called anticlines. Running perpendicularly through this cross-bedding were long, wide streaks of red, this unusual color due to large deposits of oligoclase, a plagioclase feldspar.

"*Nyedo ko, yul-iha-hphreng!*"—"To the sun and the moon and the gods of this place"—muttered the Bhutanese soldiers, glancing fearfully at the Mountain of Blood where dwelt insane demons and *shal ngo*, those unhappy souls of evil men who could not reincarnate—all of which Major Sidkeong explained to Camellion and West as the small force made its way across a wide expanse of talus rock, and headed for the long cliff wall of the plateau, east of the right pinnacle. At the base of the twisting cliff, was a sea of partially snow-covered boulders, some of granite, others of andesite and novaculite.

76

They paused and stared at the east-side chimney rock, now several feet due west of them, then turned and studied the mass of boulders at the base of the cliff.

"None of us have dropped dead yet!" commented Vallie West. "Don't we get brownie points for just being alive."

"No, and I don't think any Russians dropped dead!" Red Degenhardt said in a mild tone, glancing at Helena Banya.

"It's possible," Camellion said. "But it's more probable that they ran into a mess of Reds, and told the 'drop dead' lie to cover a defeat."

Helena Banya gave him a surprised look, for a moment acting as though she might speak. She didn't. She turned her head and looked at the cliff wall.

"And we're supposed to find an opening in all that mess," grumbled Loren Eaton, staring at the boulders ahead. "We might as well be looking for a microdot in the sorting room of some post office."

"We could find a microdot, too, if we knew exactly where to look," the Death Merchant reminded him. "In this case, we go up to the face of the cliff, turn east, and count off two thousand feet to the east of the east pinnacle. At the end of that distance, somewhere in the area we should find a big boulder shaped like an egg. So let's go do it."

They moved northeast, Foster Cross remarking that at least they had not been attacked by any bears, to which Major Sidkeong replied that a bear wasn't stupid enough to attack a group of people.

Surprisingly, just before they reached the wall, they came to a *Chod do*, a Buddhist prayer station—piled up rocks in the shape of a cairn, on the top of which was a four-foot-high brass *Lhakhang* tower. Scattered around the *Chod do* were hundreds of *mani*, flat prayer stones molded of clay, which had been placed over the years by passing nomads and herdsmen.

They reached the base of the cliff. Above was 250 feet of rough rock face; ahead were thousands of feet of boulders of various sizes. With Paul Gemz and Emil Lauterjung keeping track of the distance with special pedometers, the members of the force—the Death Merchant out front— began to pick their way through the boulders.

During the late morning the sky had choked itself with dark clouds, and now it began to sleet, the falling ice sounding like millions of talking insects as it struck the rocks.

They found the large egg-sized boulder—2,106 feet east of the pinnacle. The north side of the boulder was a scant three to four feet from the face of the cliff, the face hidden by a tangled *findop* bush on the west end and by rubble rock on the south. The Death Merchant and Vallie West climbed over the rubble rock and quickly found the opening in the face of the cliff.

"I'll be damned!" whispered West. "You call that an entrance?"

"What did you expect—floodlights and bronze gates?" Camellion turned on a 93,000-candle-power Dynalite flash and shone the bright beam through the aperture, which was shaped like a wedge. Not more than five feet high, the slot was a foot wide at the top and four feet wide at the base.

The Dynalite beam revealed that, beyond the opening, there was space enough for a man to stand and that the tunnel gradually widened and led downward in a gentle slope. Beyond the end of the beam was blackness.

"We've found the entrance to Shambhala," the Death Merchant said.

"You mean *an* entrance," Vallie West said, "and a tunnel. We don't know what's inside."

"So let's go find out."

The Death Merchant went into the tunnel first. One by one, the other members of the expedition followed, turned on their Dynalites, and inspected the walls, floor, and ceiling of the tunnel—all rock. There wasn't anything unusual about the tunnel—or was it really a huge cave?—which was obviously a natural formation. No one seemed excited. No one believed that the tunnel would lead to the fabled Shambhala.

"If there's a city at the end of this tunnel, I still won't

78

believe it!" Norbert Shireling said with a half-laugh. He didn't add anything when no one commented.

"Gemz! Lauterjung!" the Death Merchant called out. "Keep track of the distance. The rest of you be prepared for anything." Camellion glanced behind him to make sure everything was in order, and saw that the four Bhutanese soldiers looked as if they had been slapped in the face with wet socks filled with chunks of sharp concrete. Judging from their expressions, it was plain that they would rather have been someplace else, anyplace but here. Camellion knew why. To believers in Buddhism, it was an accepted fact that *chostimptas*—terrible devils that loved darkness—lived in tunnels and caves and considered such places their special domains. And this was darkness, a blackness pierced only by criss-crossing, bright beams of light.

Gradually, as time passed, the tunnel became larger, the ceiling getting higher, the walls farther and farther from each other. All the while the rock-strewn floor tilted at an incline. All the time there wasn't anything but pitch blackness beyond the beams of the Dynalites.

"This is impossible," Red Degenhardt said, swallowing in a somewhat strangulated fashion.

"Huh!" snorted Vallie West. "This place is no big deal. Mammoth Cave in Kentucky makes this place look like a clothes closet!"

"Yeah, but this isn't a cave," Loren Eaton said hollowly. He looked up at the ceiling, which was thirty feet above the floor. The uneven walls were fifty feet apart. "Whoever heard of a tunnel this damn long. We've come more than a thousand feet, and there seems to be no end to it."

"One thousand seven hundred and sixty-two feet," Paul Gemz said in a businesslike voice.

"The air is fresh." Norbert Shireling sounded dubious. "It has to be circulating. But how, in a tunnel this length; and the farther we travel, the farther we go underground."

"This is a very strange place, murmured Helena Banya, to no one in particular. "I agree with Comrade Eaton. This is not a cave. It is a tunnel. Whoever heard of a natural tunnel this long? How can it be real?"

"Reality is much more than what we might think ex-

79

ists," the Death Merchant said, his voice echoing oddly in the tunnel. "We know so little, and see even less. The entire electromagnetic spectrum ranges in wavelength from a billionth of a centimeter to millions of miles. Of all that, we can see only a hairline—between three hundred eighty and seven hundred sixty billionths of a meter. You might say that 'reality' is merely what we 'need.'"

"A very intelligent observation, Mr. Camellion." Professor Lauterjung didn't sound the least bit nervous. His baptism of fire the previous night had given him a new reality about life and living, dying, and being dead. "At present, the concept of reality is changing throughout the world of science. This is because the definition of what we need is changing."

There was a short silence; then Foster Cross said amiably, "All that sounds pretty good. The trouble with it is that it's only philosophy. Running into something we can't handle—that's reality. Getting killed and being dead—that's very real!"

"Hell, you sound like a damned atheist!" grunted Loren Eaton.

"I don't care what I sound like," Cross replied. "There are a lot of people who agree with me."[25] He called out in a slightly louder voice to the Death Merchant, who was ahead of him, "How about you, Camellion? As practical as you are, you can't be afraid of being dead—I mean really stone dead and shoved into a box, and planted in the ground!"

"The human body, mind, and consciousness are evolutionary products," Camellion said[26] pleasantly. He further surprised those around by adding, "I think you'll find that death is, in reality, God's greatest surprise for the human race—or 'human consciousness' if you prefer." He called back over his shoulder to Professors Gemz and Lauterjung. "How far have we come?"

"Almost three miles," Gemz answered promptly. "I esti-

---

[25] A lot of people do agree with this view, which is known as *epiphenomenalism.*

[26] The theory of metempsychosis.

mate—based on the angle of the ground—that we've gone downward more than three-fourths of a mile."

West, next to the Death Merchant, gave Camellion a look of resignation. "How long are we going to continue on this route zero?"

"Until we find out where the tunnel leads to," replied Camellion.

"It apparently leads to nowhere."

"If it does, we'll know it—eventually."

"Camping here for the night is not my idea of a picnic." The big CIA agent didn't sound cheerful. "Who knows what's really down here?"

The Death Merchant's chuckle sent shivers up and down Vallie's spine.

"Sooner or later, we will," Camellion said. He patted West on the shoulder. "Cheer up, old buddy. We've been through a lot worse. We'll come out of this bash in good shape."

West wasn't so sure. . . .

At four and a half miles they spotted a very faint blue glow in the distance, and paused to study the perplexing hint of light, shutting off their Dynalites in order to see the nubilous radiance in its full intensity.

"We're only seeing the glow, not whatever is causing it," Vallie whispered, as if an enemy might overhear him if he spoke in a normal voice. "The ground's too slanted for us to see the actual object."

"It has to be a light," Helena Banya offered.

"Not necessarily," Camellion said. He turned to Red Degenhardt and lowered the beam of the Dynalite to Red's feet. "Red, make certain your weapons are fully loaded, including the Chinese subs we picked up back yonder."

"Everything we have is ready to fire," Degenhardt said scornfully, "You should know that, from all the experience you've had. You've spilled more blood than Dracula."

The Death Merchant's eyes darted to Major Sidkeong, who, with the four Bhutanese soldiers, was on the other side of the Black Berets. Sidkeong answered the question before Camellion could ask it.

"As you can see, my men are afraid of the 'demons' down here. But they will fight, and fight well, should we

81

meet an enemy, and once they see that the enemy is not a part of the supernatural."

"They know how to use the Chinese types 54 and 55 machine guns?"

Major Sidkeong fixed his mouth in what was supposed to be a smile. "Of course. There is no problem in that area, none whatsoever."

"Let's go," Camellion said in a loud voice. "We'll proceed slowly and take our time."

Twenty minutes, and 1,247 feet later, Camellion, West, Degenhardt, and Sidkeong—looking ahead through M-G6 nightsight scopes—saw the origin of the faint blue glow. Five hundred feet away was an apparently solid barrier across the tunnel. Could it be a wall? Whatever its composition, it was this obstacle that emitted the blue glow.

The four Bhutanese soldiers started jabbering excitedly among themselves, Troju Gyud pointing at the blue light and jumping verbally all over Major Sidkeong, who took the nightscope from his eyes and laid out Gyud with an oral assault of his own.

Sidkeong handed the scope to Paul Gemz and said in disgust, "I explained to them that whatever the light might be, it is not the work of devils."

"Superstition has its hold on millions of men and women," Gemz said, sighing. "We can demythologize wonder out of sacred books, but we can't demythologize the hunger for the wonderful out of the human personality." He put the scope to his eyes and began adjusting the focus.

"Uh-huh," said Foster Cross in a low voice. "But what kind of human beings around here made whatever it is up ahead?" He continued to stare at the glow through a pair of Bausch & Lomb all-purpose U.S. Navy binoculars.

Vallie West handed his M-G6 nightscope to Professor Emil Lauterjung, and spoke to the Death Merchant, who was standing in a curiously immobile position, studying the azure shine in the distance.

"Well, the light proves our trolley is on the right track," he said carelessly. "If the wall is glass or plastic, we

82

should be able to blow it aside without any effort. I have a feeling, though, that it's metal."

"Bunk! Metal doesn't glow unless it's hot," Red Degenhardt said roughly. He took the nightscope from his eyes and, frowning, handed the device to Norbert Shireling. "Even hot liquid metal doesn't glow blue. No metal that I know of."

I know of a metal that does! The thought was a hot iron in the mind of the Death Merchant. Twice before, over the years, he had seen that peculiar kind of blue glow. The first time had been in the Rajmahal Mountains in India, in a vast underground chamber built by aliens from another planet, from a world that circled a yellow-white star in the Pleiades.[27] The second time had been in a lost world beneath the Arctic Ocean, in a monster cavern called Thulelandia.[28] The "sun" of Thulelandia had been a shining globe of blue. Was it possible that the legendary Shambhala was a base built by the same advanced technology of aliens who had come to Earth in the dim past? *The evidence indicates that it is!* Camellion's logic informed him. He had won in India, and he had been victorious in the cavern world underneath the frigid waters of the Arctic Ocean. Both times it had been the Russians who had fallen before his guns. Not the aliens! He had never fought them. He had never seen them, except in India—sleeping in suspended animation. *Now, suppose the "little people" are awake and active in Shambhala? There's no way we can fight them! Their weapons make ours less effective than stones!*

"Cold light!" exclaimed Emil Lauterjung, his voice barely audible. "Earth science can't make cold light. However, it does occur in nature, in the world of insects."

"We can't be positive that the light is cold," Gemz said defensively. "We're too far away." He lowered the nightscope, took several steps toward Camellion, who was carefully putting his nightsight device into its padded case, and announced in a serious voice, "I think it's time

[27] The reader is advised to see Death Merchant #20: *Hell In Hindu Land.*

[28] See Death Merchant #21: *The Pole Star Secret.*

we had a conference. We shouldn't rush up there without analyzing all the possible factors."

Vallie West shook his head from side to side in disbelief.

Camellion raked Gemz with a piercing stare, the blue pools of his eyes as mysterious as the blue light in the distance. "Analyze *what* factors?" His tone was brusque, his manner impatient. "We're here. The light is up there. We go up to it and find out what it is. We could talk until the end of this century, but we must still investigate it up close."

"We could try to shoot through it at a respectable distance!" insisted Gemz, the change in his tone—he was now demanding—perceptible. "Or we could use explosives, at a distance, against the wall. No matter the method employed, we must apply basic security measures."

"And I thought *I* loved to blow up things!" joked Degenhardt, touching the flame of his lighter to the cigarette in his mouth.

Professor Lauterjung cleared his throat nervously. "He could be right, Mr. Camellion." His voice was surprisingly gentle and courteous.

"You see. He agrees with me," Gemz said in satisfaction.

Camellion waved his hand in a gesture of curt dismissal. "I don't! We have no idea who constructed the wall. If the builders are in the vicinity, they don't have to be our enemies. They could mistake gunfire or explosives as signs of violence on our part. As yet, we have no reason to be unfriendly."

"Your actions are still a breach of security," Gemz said threateningly. "And when we return to the United States I intend to report them to the proper people. You know whom I mean!"

"Oh, my, my! So you'll report me!" Camellion sounded almost jovial. He looked that way, too, as he stepped toward Gemz and tapped the man on the chest with a finger. "I'll tell you what you can do. You can get on the red panic phone and report me to God for all I care. But while you're with me, when I say, 'Jump!' you'll ask, 'How high?' Don't you forget it!"

Gemz made a tight mouth, rage flashing in his eyes.

"Have it your way," he said boldly. "Nonetheless, I shall have a talk with the deputy director of plans when we get back."

"Yeah, you do that," Camellion said dryly. "I'm sure he'll be interested." For a moment he scrutinized the nervous faces of the others, then turned and began walking in the direction of the blue light. The rest of the party followed, keeping pace with the Death Merchant.

Loren Eaton whispered to Norbert Shireling, "Speaking of panic, I don't suppose that now would be a good time to become hysterical?"

"Oh, I dunno," smirked Eaton. "I'd say this is as good a time as any. Have you noticed the Bhutanese guys? They're almost trembling."

Closing in on the light, Camellion and the rest noticed that the walls and ceiling of the tunnel not only widened but became smoother and less striated. At length, the Death Merchant and his people found themselves within thirty feet of the light source. The origin of the glow was indeed a wall, apparently a wall of metal, the surface the same pale blue color as the light emitting from it. There weren't any rivet heads or doors, the surface as smooth as glass.

"By God, what is it?" demanded Red Degenhardt, exasperated from a sense of frustration.

"As you can see, it's a wall. But I don't know what kind of wall," Camellion conceded. He stared at the structure which, completely blocking the tunnel, was thirty feet high and seventy feet wide. Each end of the wall seemed to grow out of the rock sides of the tunnel, with the top and the bottom appearing to be in the rock of the ceiling and the ground.

Vallie West put his hands on his hips and surveyed the weird wall.

"Somehow, I don't think HBX would even scratch it," he said.

The Death Merchant moved closer to the shining barrier.

"Careful! The wall could be radioactive!" warned Professor Lauterjung.

85

"If it is, we've already received a fatal dose," Camellion called back. "In that case it won't make any difference."

Lauterjung and the rest of the force watched with fear and frozen fascination as the Death Merchant slowly approached the wall. They had turned out their Dynalites, and the glow from the wall bathed everything in pale blue. It was as if the rocks had turned blue, as if the clothes and very skin of Camellion and his people had turned blue.

The Death Merchant reached the wall, stopping so close he could reach out and touch it. And that's what he did, first with the tip of his finger, then with the palm of his right hand. He called out a moment later in a loud voice, "The wall's cold. It's as cold as ice."

Vallie West moved forward. Degenhardt followed him. Finally the others moved toward the wall, which somehow no longer seemed to be a threat. The wall was just there, shining with a cold blue light.

West had almost reached Camellion when a section of the wall in the center opened noiselessly. The Death Merchant and the others scanned the door-sized opening as though it were the portal to hell!

"I'll be damned," muttered Foster Cross, his voice shaking.

Do not be afraid. Come forward. You will not be harmed.

The Death Merchant jerked his head around and glanced in surprise at Vallie West, who stared at him for a moment, then jumped his gaze to Red Degenhardt.

"Don't look at me," Degenhardt said nervously. "I didn't say it."

"I heard the voice," Helena Banya said, looking all around her.

"I am certain that I did," said Gemz haughtily. "The voice sounded odd, and seemed to be on all sides of me."

Go through the opening and come forward. There is no reason for any of you to be afraid.

This time the Death Merchant knew why the "voice" sounded unnatural!

An actual voice had not spoken!

Richard Camellion was thunderstruck. *The words we*

heard were within our own minds. What we heard was pure thought!

Intelligently, Helena Banya guessed the truth a moment later.

"Mental radio!" Helena Banya sounded like a little girl. "It's mental radio!"

Red Degenhardt peered suspiciously at the Russian girl. "What's mental radio?"

It was the Death Merchant who explained. "We call it mental telepathy. The Russian parapsychologists refer to such communication as mental radio."

"Good Lord! What kind of people are we dealing with?" Lauterjung asked in a hoarse voice. He sucked in his breath. "Nothing about this is normal. Mental telepathy is only a theory."

"In this tunnel it seems to have established itself as a fact," Paul Gemz said pontifically. "Obviously we are dealing with superior beings." He turned his attention to Major Sidkeong, who was chattering away to the four terrified Bhutanese soldiers. All four gabbled back at once, Gom Shinje and Tolung Terskug tapping their skulls.

Visibly shaken, Major Sidkeong pivoted around to face Camellion.

"They also heard the command, in our own language. The order said, *'Go through the opening and come forward. There is no reason for any of you to be afraid.'* We have been the receivers of a telepathic sender."

Vallie West reached past his open parka, put a hand into a pocket of his Deschutes vest, and pulled out a pack of Carlton 100s.

"What's our next move, as if I didn't know!" He gave Camellion a lopsided grin and opened one top corner of the pack of cigarettes.

Camellion appraised the doorway with contemplative eyes. Beyond the doorway was more blue light.

"We could end up refereeing a cockroach fight!" he said mildly, his face expressionless.

"We could end up dead, too!" Loren Eaton said morosely.

"Going past that door could be a trap," Norbert Shireling said complainingly. "Once we're in and the opening closes, how do we get out? This tunnel could easily become our tomb."

Foster Cross nodded his head slowly. We couldn't even detect a hairline crack in that wall. Then all of a sudden there's a door! We're up against something pretty damned weird!" He blinked in disbelief, feeling stupid when he saw the Death Merchant turn and walk toward the doorway. Vallie West, pausing only long enough to light a cigarette, followed.

The Death Merchant walked leisurely through the doorway. . . .

Chapter Seven

Albert Einstein was right, Camellion reflected, *when he said that the most beautiful experience we can have is the mysterious. It is the fundamental emotion, which stands at the cradle of true art and true science. For all the good it will do us here! But there wasn't any door or panel!*

Beyond the doorway, beyond the wall, there was more rock, more tunnel. The moment the last person had moved through the doorway—Major Sidkeong, who had to threaten his four men with a Chinese T-54 submachine gun before they would step through the panel—the opening was blotted out. One moment, there had been an opening; the next instant, nothing but a solid wall—all as quickly as one would turn out an electric light.

"We sure stepped into a bucket of black buzzards," Loren Eaton said grimly. He glared at the solid wall. "Now how do we get out?"

"Don't worry about it," Red Degenhardt rebuked him. "Camellion has the right idea. Whoever built that wall and gave the mental command could have killed us on the other side if they had wanted to."

"He had better be right," Eaton said, keeping his face deadpan. "We can't turn back."

"I suppose we can always pray if worse comes to worst," Foster Cross said plaintively.

Richard Camellion said, "We came to find Shambhala. Let's get about the business of doing it." His eyes moved to Cross. "There isn't anything wrong with prayer, no matter where it's offered."

He turned and began moving in the direction of the length of the tunnel.

Five hundred feet north of the wall, they again turned on their Dynalites, the blue light from the wall having merged into the darkness to the north. The ground was smoother and less dust covered, and Camellion led his party at a faster pace.

There was little conversation. For one thing, there was nothing to say; for another, each person was too tense and too concerned with the surroundings to discuss what might or might not be.

At length, there was another bluish gleam in the distance.

"Oh hell, another one!" Red Degenhardt muttered. He glanced in interest at West, who was lighting another cigarette. "I thought you had beaten the habit?"

"Those damned lollipops were making me sick to my stomach," West admitted. "All that sugar, you know. And I got to thinking: we all die. To me, it's not the quantity of life that counts but the quality. I'd rather smoke and be happy and die ten years sooner than not smoke and be miserable and live ten years longer."

Walking briskly, the Death Merchant was a few steps ahead of West and the other members of the Posten Expedition. At six hundred feet from the glow, they saw the wall. When Camellion was a hundred feet from the glowing obstacle, a doorway suddenly appeared in the center of the metal structure.

Everyone pulled up short, including the Death Merchant, who turned and looked impatiently from face to face. "What did you expect—a wooden gate on rusty hinges?" His tone was reproving. "We're not in any danger, so all of you can quit acting like old maids looking for a rapist under the bed."

He spun on his heel, walked toward the doorway, and a minute later strode through the opening. The others didn't hesitate. The four Bhutanese soldiers were the exception. Chattering about demons, devils, and lost souls, they cringed like small children who are terrified of the mythical bogeyman, only there were no covers they could pull over their heads. They almost ran through the doorway when Major Sidkeong threatened to cut off their legs with a scalpel of Chinese machine-gun slugs.

Richard Camellion and the other thirteen people had stepped into another world, into a land that should not

90

have existed, but did. They could only stare in wonderment at the fantastic panorama stretching out before them, each member of the force too filled with a sense of amazement to notice that the wall behind them was again solid—except Camellion! He had seen a similar world in Thulelandia, the cavern world beneath the frigid waters of the Arctic Ocean.

They seemed to be standing on a small tableland of rock at the top of a mile-long rocky slope. Stretched out below, as far as they could see, were rock-covered hills and outlandish vegetation—tall plants whose wrist-thick stalks were milk-white, the huge leaves the same chalky color. Other plants, some as high as fifteen feet, resembled giant mushrooms. These too were the color of milk, their creaminess tinged faintly from the tremendous globe hanging suspended in space over the center of the valley.

The same kind of "sun" I saw in Thulelandia!

It was this shining blue globe that first captured the attention of the fourteen people and tinted the rocks and vegetation with a tincture of light blue.

"*Snarivu-zhivul*" whispered Helena Banya, her voice choked with awe.

"Unbelievable is the word for all this," admitted the Death Merchant. "It's real. It's there. We're here."

"It's more like a nightmare," Vallie West said hoarsely. "Whoever, whatever, made that shining globe hanging out there—we're not dealing with anything human."

And I can't tell you what I found in India and in the Arctic Ocean! Camellion thought. *I can't, because it's top secret. . . .*

The size of the underground world was of such gigantic dimension that none of them could see the northern end or the east and west sides of the cavern. Except for a one-mile length of rock wall on either side of the tablerock, the distant areas terminated into haze. The sight was similar to that which one sees when standing on the seashore and gazing out over the rolling ocean. One can see only so far; then there is only mistiness, as the eye cannot follow the curvature of the Earth.

They could see the top of the sky, which was the roof of the impossibly huge cavern. From the tablerock, on which Camellion and the others stood, the ceiling was a mere hundred feet above their heads. On all sides the ceiling stretched out ahead of them, until it too became infused into the haze. The entire cavern was the apotheosis of myth. Yet all this was very real. It *was*. It existed. . . .

"I think I can see the north wall!" Vallie West said. He sounded excited as he adjusted the focus knob of the binoculars. "I can't be sure. But the east and west ends—forget it. There's nothing but a lot of haze. I guess that proves this place is wider than it's long."

"It's a matter of relativity." The Death Merchant was also surveying the cavern through binoculars. "You might as well have said it's longer than wide. It depends on the directions to which you assign width and length."

Richard let the binoculars fall to his chest and hang by the strap around his neck. Helena Banya and the others lowered their binoculars and glanced nervously at one another, then at the Death Merchant, whom they considered a rock of security in a raging ocean.

"It doesn't seem like a cave, not to me!" Red Degenhardt observed. He looked up at the high ceiling, and went on, "For one thing, the roof's flat. There's no stalactites hanging down. Or is it stalagmites? I always get the two confused."

"Stalactites hang down," Vallie West said heavily. "You were right the first time." He let his gaze wander down the uneven slope. "Look at the size of this place. The height alone makes you want to pinch yourself to wake up."

"I estimate the length of the incline at 1,609.35 meters," Paul Gemz said in a precise voice. "That means—"

"Dammit, use feet!" blurted out Norbert Shireling. "Meters are too damned confusing."

Gemz gave him a condescending look. "All right. I calculate the length of the slope to be about a mile long, or almost 5,280 feet. Now, if the end of the slope is the lowest part of the valley below us, that means that the ceiling"—he glanced upward—is 5,280 feet above ground level."

"Beyond doubt, this is the largest natural cave in the world," voiced Emil Lauterjung. He removed his glasses, shifted from one foot to the other, and looked around in curious anticipation. "However, I fail to see any 'city.'"

"Whoever gave us the mental commands must be around," Loren Eaton said. "And that globe hanging up there all by itself! Somebody had to put it there. What's so strange about it is that it gives off plenty of light. Yet it's not so bright that it hurts your eyes when you look at it."

"Have you noticed, there's no wind!" Major Sidkeong said anxiously. He was not a religious man, and only gave lip service to Buddhism because of his position in the army. He had always considered the paranormal and the supernatural a lot of bunk. Now he wasn't so sure. Now he wasn't positive about anything. "Nothing is moving," he finished. "Those leaves down in the valley might as well be made of wax, or stone."

"There's no chlorophyll in the plants," Helena Banya said. "The plants are fungi. We can see that much."

The Death Merchant spoke as he walked close to that point ahead where the flat surface of the tablerock tilted downward to form the beginning of the hillside. "Have any of you considered that all this was a natural formation that was enlarged by an alien technology?"

For a long moment there was silence. Paul Gemz exchanged a thoughtful glance with Emil Lauterjung, who was wiping his glasses with several pieces of lens tissue. Gemz said, "The prodigious size of this cave, as well as the light globe suspended without wire of any kind, does indicate a nonhuman science at work. We were given a command by mental telepathy. Whoever gave that command must be in the vicinity—down in the valley, I'll wager."

"I'm almost positive I saw the north side," Vallie West reiterated. He gave Camellion a long, questioning look. The Death Merchant, staring down into the valley, seemed frozen, as stiff as a marble statue. "In clear air, on a flat desert, you can see about forty miles. It all depends on the purity of the air."

"Forty miles to the north side!" Degenhardt said. "It's hard to believe."

"We can't be sure." Vallie again glanced at the Death

Merchant. "In this blue light, who knows how far we can see?"

The "voice" in Camellion's mind spoke, the words loud and clear:

"No one can hear us but you, Richard Camellion. We know who you are and why you have come to this place. From us no harm will come to you or to those who are with you. Proceed down the hillside in front of you. We will meet you and your party at the bottom."

The thought was automatic on Camellion's part: *They know who I am. How could they know, whoever they are?*

"We know everything about you, Richard Joseph Camellion. We know that you were born in St. Louis, Missouri, in the country of the states that are united under a central government. We know that you have a bachelor of science degree from St. Louis University. We know that you possess a degree in engineering from Washington University in St. Louis. We know that you have studied the occult extensively, are an expert in electronics and know many things. We know that you are protected from the Lord of Light. We could tell you how we know these things, but not even you would understand. Believe us when we say that the file of your existence in this present space-time continuum, is open to us. We have access to the life file of every human being on this planet."

"Are you the blue aliens?" Camellion asked mentally. At the same time, segments of thought of what had occurred in India and in Thulelandia skipped through the crowded corridors of his mind.

"No. We are not those to whom you refer as Sandorians. We are the guardians of those who wait in slumber. Do not concern yourself. The Inelqu were not harmed in India. They still slumber in that place known as Thulelandia. Only the entrance to the underground world was sealed. There is no force on this planet that can destroy the domes. Both times you succeeded only in destroying those who would have destroyed the Inelqu."

"You have dealt with the Lord of Light?" inquired the Death Merchant.

"Come down the hillside, Richard Camellion. There is work for you to do." -

"The Lord of Light?" insisted Camellion.

"Come forward, Richard Camellion."

By some preternatural sense, the Death Merchant knew that the mind-voice had departed, had switched itself off, and that continued mental questioning would only have been a waste of time.

He relaxed and turned to face West and the others. "We might as well go down into the valley. There's no sense in standing around here getting old."

"What are we supposed to be looking for?" Vallie's eyes were two curious slits, and from the expression on the big man's hawklike face, Camellion realized that the big man *suspects that I know more than I've revealed to even him!*

A *dome—or domes!* But Camellion said, "Whoever contacted us is watching our every movement. They'll find us."

Red Degenhardt glanced up at the blue "sun." "Yeah, you're right about that, Camellion. I'll tell you something else: we're completely at their mercy."

They started down the hillside, their boots crunching against pebbly rocks and a kind of fine dirt that was intensely black, Dr. Lauterjung saying to Professor Gemz, "Actually, I don't find this place very strange, not when I consider the Uncertainty Principle. You know, Professor Gemz, when you involve that principle, anything becomes possible. The impossible of today becomes the reality of tomorrow."

Paul Gemz stumbled over a rock and then caught his balance. Then he said. "Nonsense. I disagree completely with the Uncertainty Principle. It isn't science. It's not even a theory. It's only a silly hypothesis, completely without foundation or substance."

"And what, if I may ask, is this 'Uncertainty Principle'?" Vallie West asked.

"It comes from a physicist named Weiner Heisenberg," explained Professor Lauterjung. "In 1927 Heisenberg upset a very big scientific apple cart when he advanced his Uncertainty Principle. Before Heisenberg arrived on the scene, the physicist's view of the universe was much the same as nonscientists today—either an object existed or it did not. Heisenberg destroyed this view by stating that any realistic description of the universe must describe it in all possible states at the same instant of time. In other words, a man, for example, could be simultaneously described as being alive, dead, and unborn, and every one of those descriptions would be true. It was a schizophrenic universe, and the physicists were rapidly becoming that way themselves. Heisenberg opened a can of long worms, and it took almost fifty years for a semblance of order to return to the universe."

"I agree with Gemz." West gave a low laugh. "It does sound like a rather nutty theory," he said frankly "To a timeless being, I might be alive and dead and unborn, all at the same time. Yet, within the normal frame of reference, right now I'm alive. There is a past, a present, and a future. Even the present universe—and I mean the entire universe, not just our galaxy—had a beginning."

"One is always free to believe where the mind leads," Professor Lauterjung remarked stiffly. "Intellectual curiosity is the foundation of all science."

"Unless one lives in a Commie country!" Vallie said. "Then you're free only to 'accept the truth'—the Communist brand of truth."

The farther the Death Merchant and his force moved down the slope, the more impressed they became with the vastness of the underground world. Now, three-fourths of the way down, they could see the true size of the vegetation. Some of the mushroom-shaped plants were thirty feet tall, their trunks ten feet or more in diameter. Many of the stalked plants with the large leaves were even taller.

Lower, as the slope neared the valley floor, there were patches of gray-brown grass growing among the rocks and loose argillite, a compact, massive sort of shale. In other places there were elongations of large pebbles, the result of intense pressure.

"A carbonifrous formation," Professor Lauterjung explained to Professor Gemz. "And notice, to the left there, those formations of magnetite. At one time that magnetite was iron carbonate or siderite."

"Yes, I agree," Gemz said. "In spite of its size, this place is a cave, and it's been here for millions of years. Amazing!"

The Death Merchant, ten feet ahead of the others, was thirty feet from the end of the slope when three beings stepped from behind one of the mushrooms. Camellion stopped and gazed at them. The other members of the force did likewise. All fourteen heard the words, each in his mind: *Yes, we are men. We are human beings. We are the Goros who watch over those who wait in slumber. Do not be afraid. We will not harm you.*

"If you ask me, that's not much of a welcome wagon!" whispered Loren Eaton.

The Death Merchant moved forward, his eyes devouring the three Goros. All three were tall, each one dressed in a pure white garment that resembled a Japanese *yukata*, a lightweight, informal kimono that Japanese men wear at home. As Camellion drew closer to the three Goros, he saw that they were oriental and obviously very old. Their flesh had drawn itself until it provided little more than a modest covering for the obdurate bones. The eyelids seemed sad, yet as fine and as fragile as a spider's web. Each face—hard with reality—its soft contours devoured by age, its aquiline nose as brittle as flint, its mouth a bloodless slit, as patient as the eyes. Each Goro was as bald as a cake of soap.

Camellion stopped within six feet of the three Goros. Knowing that his mind, his each and every thought, was an open book to the Goros, he felt naked and defenseless. The tallest of the three took several steps forward and spoke for the first time in a voice that, while normal-sounding, was melodious.

"I am Amdu." He indicated the man to his left with a movement of his hand. "He is Urba." He turned his head slightly to his right. "His name is Tilhut."

The faces of Urba and Tilhut did not reveal any expression. Only their highly intelligent eyes gave evidence that they were alive and not expertly devised mannequins.

"I'm Richard Camellion."

"We know," Amdu said pleasantly. "We know each of you and every detail of your lives."

Without warning, the voice was a shotgun blast in Camellion's mind: *"You are also the man of death, the Death Merchant. Your secret is safe. No one else can hear me."*

Looking at the curious, strained faces on each side of

97

Camellion, Amdu pointed a finger at Vallie West. "You are Vallie Edward West."

The Goro's finger moved from man to man as he named each individual. Finally he pointed to a silent and fearful Helena Banya, gave her name, then added the year and place of her birth—1952, in Zagorsk, a town a short distance north of Moscow. Amdu, continued, "For a goodly length of time, you have been concerned about Cerill, your brother in the Soviet Air Force, and Sveltima, your sister, who is a housewife; afraid that the KGB would imprison them because of your defection from the land of the bear to the land of the eagle. The Soviet authorities have not bothered your brother and your sister. They are safe. They do, however, consider you a disgrace to your family and a traitor to the Soviet Union. No, Helena Banya, your brother and your sister do not know the nature of the work you performed while in the KGB."

The Russian girl could only stand there with the other members of the expedition and gape in astonishment at Amdu and his two companions. Along with the other people, she knew that something overwhelming was happening and she was emotionally devastated by whatever was eating at her sense of humanness. The attempt to use logic was unsuccessful. It was impossible to form any mental images of what could be described as a Presence.

"Amdu, why at times do you converse telepathically with me but not with the others?" Camellion asked in thought.

Paul Gemz stared at Amdu. "It was the three of you who used mental telepathy?" Tension made his voice crack. He stepped forward so that he stood horizontal to Camellion. "How did you do it?"

"How can you be certain that we haven't conversed with the others?"

"Yes, it was we," Amdu answered Gemz. "There are many things we can do. Thought travels on electromagnetic waves, on wavelengths that are longer than one of your miles."

"I know," Camellion thought. *"I know that you. haven't. I feel it."* Whoever it would have been, he—or she—would have said so.

Tilhut stepped forward and spoke. "This place is

98

Shambhala, although to us it is nameless and ageless. It only *is*. Agharta does not exist. There is no Rigden-Jyo-Po, no *Brahytma* or *Metatron*, no 'King of the World.' All that is myth, the tales of Buddhist monks who amused themselves by telling fables to naïve people from the West; and by men from the West who, motivated by greed, deliberately added to the lies for purposes of self-aggrandizement, and to further their own evil plans."

The Death Merchant's voice was very calm. "What about the system of interconnecting caves under Tibet, Manchuria, and Afghanistan. We know this cave exists."

Stepping closer to the group, it was Urba who answered. "This is the only cavern. There were—and are—tunnels that terminate in this place you call Shambhala. At present. there are three tunnels. All of you came through one tunnel. Another tunnel begins in Tibet. The third tunnel begins in Sikkim."

Professor Lauterjung spoke up, his voice quivering from nervousness. "We do have thousands of questions. Please understand that we are friends, interested only in the advancement of science."

"None of you are friends," Amdu said bluntly. "And while you have not come to us as enemies, and while some of you are truly interested in the advancement of science, your main quest is for weapons, weapons you would use to kill millions, to use in worship at the altar of the Cosmic Lord of Death. None of you will leave this place with a knowledge of such devices."

All of them were trying to recover from the shock generated by Amdu's words, when Tilhut answered the question that had been swimming around in the minds of West and Camellion: "Yes, we had a reason for permitting your passage through the tunnel; otherwise we would have done nothing. You could not have passed the first wall. Explosives could not destroy it. Or we would have sealed the tunnel completely before you entered. By using rays, the nature of which is beyond your understanding, we would have fused the rock solid."

The Death Merchant and Vallie West were the only ones who didn't have the feeling that they had been volatilized back into an unknown pit of being from which there could be no return.

99

Camellion was too practical to ask what the reason was. Why bother? The three Goros, who could read minds, already knew that he and the others were being consumed with curiosity.

Instead, he asked, "If you could completely seal the tunnel by fusing the very rock, why bother to build the two walls? Why are they there?" For the first time he noticed the thin red scar that encircled the upper skull of each Goro, as if someone or something had sawed through the top of each skull. lifted it off, had done *something*, and then had replaced the "cap." Camellion also noticed that the fingers of the three Goros were very long—like the naked legs of some giant spider. He couldn't help but think, *Are they really human?*

A voice spoke in his mind: "*Yes, but very different from the rest of humanity.*"

He smiled at Amdu, whose thought-answer he had just received, and the Goro said, "The walls are there for only one reason: to frighten away the curious who might accidentally find the tunnel. Within the last few thousand years there have been many who have come as far as the first wall. They became very frightened and turned back. No one living on the surface believed their stories. Those who did attributed the wall to devils. Very often we implanted images of hideous creatures in the minds of those who stumbled into the tunnels, doing this telepathically."

Foster Cross nudged Norbert Shireling and whispered, "Maybe that is how 'Hell' got started."

Vallie West, who feared neither God nor man nor Satan, said boldly, "Amdu, I get the impression that you and your two assistants have been down here for quite a while." *Thousands of years? That's crazy!*

"Crazy, yes. But only by *your* standards." It was then that Amdu laughed, a pleasant laugh, and Urba and Tilhut smiled. "There are forty of us and we are all equal. There are no 'assistants.' We are almost eighteen thousand years old by your reckoning of time. In another sense, by that same method of calculating the seconds, we are only two hundred seven years of age."

There were gasps of disbelief and sheer incredulity, of a

100

Pyrrhonism,[29] which was very normal under the fantastic circumstances.

All this time, the four Bhutanese had understood every word spoken by Amdu and Urba and Tilhut. the words—very clear in their minds—spoken in Dzongkha, the Bhutanese language. The Goros had chosen to speak English because English was the home language of Camellion and the majority of his people. As the Goros spoke, they also transmitted their words telepathically to the four Bhutanese soldiers.

Paul Gemz turned to the Death Merchant, then swung back to stare at Amdu. "I don't believe it," he said, his voice firm with the conviction of his skepticism. "Granted, there are methods by which the life span can be extended, methods that medical science will discover in years to come, there has to be a limit. A few hundred years? Maybe. But eighteen thousand? It's absurd."

Neither Amdu, Urba, nor Tilhut appeared to be insulted, their expressions remaining tranquil and unperturbed.

Richard Camellion said in a soft tone, "Amdu, by explaining how it is possible, you could clarify the situation."

"The process of aging occurs in every person, beginning from the very moment one is born," Amdu said, speaking in a patient tone. "Aging begins when two molecules in a gene—which as you know is the basic unit of heredity—become hooked together by a process Earth scientists call *cross-linking*. As more and more molecules become linked together, the cells that contain them do not function as well. There are certain enzymes, which can be manufactured, that dissolve the bond linking the molecules; thus stopping the aging process. However—"

"Not for eighteen thousand years!" Gemz was adamant.

"Correct," Amdu promptly admitted. "The maximum length of extension is from four hundred fifty to five hundred years. Beyond five hundred years, the Cosmic Lord of Death must conquer the individual."

"Then why do you maintain that you and the other Go-

29 The doctrine taught by Pyrrho, a Greek skeptic—365?—275? B.C.—that all knowledge, including the testimony of the senses, is uncertain.

ros are almost eighteen thousand years old?" demanded Gemz.

Amdu went on in the same patient tone of voice. "Mr. Gemz, you assume too easily and too readily. You should remember that a bird does not fly because it has wings. It has wings because it flies."

Now it was Gemz who was not only insulted but mystified; yet he didn't interrupt as Amdu explained that 17,950 years ago . . . "only a few years before the great conflict, I and thirty-nine others were brought from the surface to this place you call Shambhala, brought here by the Inelqu."[30]

Instantly, words of explanation were heard in everyone's mind: *The Inelqu are not native to this planet. They come from a planet larger than Earth, from a planet revolving around a star in the constellation Taurus.*

In spoken words, Amdu expounded on how the Inelqu had instructed the forty young men in various arts and sciences—"for hundreds of years," keeping them from aging by some sort of chemical process that dissolved the cross-linking in genes. Gradually, then, the forty had begun to age and to grow old very rapidly.

"The Inelqu used cell extension rebirth to re-create us," Amdu said. "It is a process that present-day scientists on the surface refer to as cloning."

"But—!" Paul Gemz closed his mouth tightly and, frowning, looked down at the blue-tinged ground. Then he lifted his eyes and looked in puzzlement at Amdu, who smiled, then spoke.

"But you cannot understand why—since we are what you call 'clones'—we have all our original memories and our identical personalities, which we had when we were young men on the surface, inhabitants of Yulyudyd, the nation known as China."

Gemz said in a loud voice, "No. I can't understand it. And I don't believe it, not a single word of it."

"I do feel that your story is somewhat incredible, Mr. Amdu," Professor Lauterjung said timidly. He cleared his throat loudly and shifted from foot to foot, in the manner of an untrained three-year-old about to wet his diaper.

[30] Pronounced *inn-el-que.*

"Shut up and let him explain," Camellion ordered, without taking his eyes from Amdu, who continued in his tolerant tone, saying that in every human being the DNA molecule encodes not only the biological details of one's ancestors but their historic experiences as well. The complex genes that carry information about the shape of a man's nose to his great-grandson, also transmit a record of his memory to the great-grandson.

"Racial memory!" muttered Vallie West, looking reflectively at the unlit cigarette he had just removed from the pack. "By God, we're all a bunch of unread *Roots!*"

"Yeah! Then why don't I remember what my great-great-grandpappy did in Austria?" Degenhardt said smugly.

Amdu answered Degenhardt's remark by saying that in the average human being, racial memory is buried so deeply in the unconscious that it can surface only in weird dreams or nightmares. No person can readily recall the life experiences of any of his ancestors, although there are those times when one has that strong sense of something previously seen or experienced. Psychologists call this, "false memory," or *deja vu,*[31] although it is actually a spark from the life-fires of a long-dead ancestor.

"We recall our existence of thousands of years ago because the Inelqu, in the process of the cell extension re-birth technique, know how to transmit each tiny memory, no matter how insignificant, of every individual. The Inelqu know how to encode these conscious and unconscious memories on the genes of each successive clone, each time one of us is re-created anew. In mind, in memory, in emotions, we are the same human beings we were thousands and thousands of years ago. However, while our original personalities, the original egos, have remained the same while being passed down from clone-body to clone-body, we have been 'reborn' fifty-nine times. Every three hundred years we receive a new body."

"There is hypnosis," Tilhut said. He stood tall and straight, his arms at his side. "While hypnotized, a person may or may not remember in great detail the life of a long-dead ancestor."

[31] From the French, meaning "already seen."

103

"Is that the origin of reincarnation, this having the memories of a dead ancestor?"

Major Kor Sidkeong's question did not come as a surprise to Camellion and the other people, all of whom had been thinking along the same lines—all except the four Bhutanese soldiers, who were frantically praying to all the protective deities in Buddhism.

"Yes," answered Tilhut. "Racial memory accounts, in large part, for the belief in reincarnation. There are other reasons for the fallacious belief in rebirth in this space-time continuum. A hypnotized person enters into telepathic communication with other people and from them obtains information about their dead relatives and friends. Like an actor assuming a role, the hypnotized person adopts the identity of these dead people, usually one at a time, as his own. Those who 'will' themselves to the belief are then convinced that the hypnotized subject is reliving a previous existence."

The Death Merchant said, "There is another way a person might think that he or she has lived before. A person with psychic ability might gain details of a dead person's life by means of psychometry, that is, by touching something that the dead person owned."

Tilhut nodded once. "That is true. But psychometry is very rare. In very few cases does it result in memories that amount to much; in fact, so few memories that psychometry can be ignored."

"Amazing! Amazing! Amazing!"—from Emil Lauterjung, who looked like a man in the middle of a daze.

"I agree. I also know that there isn't any such thing as reincarnation!"—from Richard Camellion, who spoke unequivocally.

It was Urba who said in a soft, gentle voice, "Indeed, there isn't. The concept of reincarnation is only one of many, many myths that man has created in an effort to understand his place in the universe."

"See! I was dead right!" Foster Cross said triumphantly to Norbert Shireling. "It's all a big joke. It proves that when you're dead, you're dead. Right in this life, right now—this is the only reality."

"Wrong you are, Foster Derek Cross." It was Urba who had spoken. "Existence in this sphere, in this time-continuum, is only the tiny beginning of the soul's exploration of the universe."

The Death Merchant was amused at how Cross staggered back in total disbelief, his mouth open, his eyes round.

Vallie West dropped his cigarette, carefully ground out the butt with the heel of his boot, then looked at Amdu.

"Everything the three of you have told us is very interesting," the big man began. "On the other hand . . ."

The Death Merchant, keeping a straight face, tried to keep West out of his mind; yet he couldn't help but admire the big man, who, as one of the Agency's best case officers in Operations, was a brilliant manipulator of people.

He's a past master of the pitch, and now he's trying to home in on Amdu and make him a target,[32] *in an effort to get him to tell us why they let us through and why we are here—all of it without coming right out and asking him. Such a technique won't work with the Goros. I wonder what the word means?*

Camellion expected one of the Goros to speak in his mind, in response to thoughts he had not been able to stop. The answer came. It was not the one he expected.

"*Goro means 'guardian.' It is from a language that has not been spoken on this planet for eleven thousand years.*"

"On the other hand," West said lazily, "this existence, this cavern, is very real to us. It must be to you, too. Why else did you permit us to come through the passage?"

Amdu's thin lips changed miraculously into a large half-moon smile.

"It is important that all of you perform a task, one that, when accomplished, will be to our mutual benefit."

---

[32] In CIA terminology there are two types of targets. One refers to a subject who is to be "retired," "neutralized," "terminated"—killed. The second type of target is a man or woman who has been assessed by a CIA case officer as being a likely candidate for agent—i.e., a person who will work for the CIA and betray his nation's secrets. At the appropriate moment, the case officer makes his "pitch." This technique, of trying to recruit agents from the "other side," is basic with all intelligence services.

"In that case, I suggest you tell us what it is," Vallie said, a faint note of suspicion shadowing his words.

Amdu's sad eyes skipped from West to the Death Merchant.

"It is necessary that your force kill the Chinese Communist soldiers moving toward this place through a tunnel from Tibet."

"I'll be damned!" growled Red Degenhardt.

Chapter Eight

The great value in being a pessimist and a fatalist is that news of an adverse nature never can crack the foundations of confidence. While Camellion and West were not unduly surprised at Amdu's request, nor worried about the Chinese, the other members of the expedition were convinced that the Goro was asking them to commit suicide!

Red Degenhardt was the first to lash out at Amdu, fire in his eyes, savage anger in his voice.

"Why do we have to fight the Chinese?" he demanded, moving both hands in a gesture of defiance. "Don't try to make us believe that you don't have weapons. You can seal tunnels by fusing rock! You must have some sort of heat ray. Why do you expect us to risk our lives and do the dirty work?"

Paul Gemz jumped in with both feet. "Amdu, are the telepathic powers of the Goros helpless against the Chinese? I am sure you didn't lie when you explained how you caused apparitions of devils to appear to intruders."

"Doesn't the tunnel the Chinese are using have protective walls?" thought Camellion.

The reply came from Urba. *"Amdu will explain to all of you."*

Amdu replied to Paul Gemz, "It is you, Paul Gemz, who are speaking an untruth. It is you, because you do not believe the tiny part of history we have revealed."

"Which doesn't answer my question!" Gemz said, as unperturbed as Amdu. "We will not conquer the Chinese by experimenting with epistemology!"

"We cannot kill," Amdu said politely. "We are not permitted to take human life. It is forbidden by the Inelqu."

Red Degenhardt was incredulous. "Not even to save your own lives?" he thrust in.

From an angry Loren Eaton: "The chinnies are coming through a tunnel. They must be! How are they going to get past the shining walls?"

Vallie West was more practical. "Give us your weapons," he suggested to Amdu. "Or are they too complicated for us to use on short notice?"

"We can always turn around and leave," Foster Cross said to Red Degenhardt, who was almost trembling with rage. "We can return to the surface."

"How?" growled the Black Beret chief. "The doorways are closed." He turned and glared at Amdu. "And I don't think our friends are about to open them for us, not until we've 'performed' our 'task!' "

Amdu raised his right hand, palm outward, like an American Indian giving the sign of peace. The mutter of angry voices subsided and fourteen pairs of curious and resentful eyes stared at the tall, white-robed Guardian.

"We cannot kill even to save our own lives," Amdu said, "and we are not permitted to give any kind of weapon to outsiders." He then explained, in the same unruffled voice, that the tunnel the Chinese were using did not have protective walls of "Kkokro metal." The walls had never been needed. The tunnel—very large and only a thousand years old—twisted across the border to Tibet, the main entrance opening into a secret room beneath a second hidden chamber underneath the stone floor of the *dukhang*, ("assembly hall") of the main monastery in the Forbidden City of Lhasa. A second opening, a side tunnel, was underneath a Buddhist temple not far from the Tibetian-Bhutanese border. After the Communist Chinese takeover of Tibet, the Dalai Lama had fled to India. The Lamas and gelongs who had remained in Lhasa had destroyed the main entrance to the tunnel to prevent the Chinese from finding it. Much to the sorrow of the monks, who could not get to the second entrance, the Chinese discovered it "only a short time ago, four of your months."

Why were Kkokro walls not necessary in the tunnel that led to Tibet? The Goros had always been on good terms with the Buddhist monks. The Goros manufactured their food with a machine that rearranged the atoms and the molecules of the "chorrten" plants—those monstrosities that resembled gigantic mushrooms. Nevertheless, the Goros varied their diet with foodstuffs from the surface, grain, *kamlo*, barley beer, and other things that were brought by the lamas. In return for this service, and in payment, the Goros imparted knowledge of medicine and other arts to the lamas, including a limited use of telepathy.

In response to the thoughts of Helena Banya, Amdu said that the various tunnels had not been built as passageways to the surface world. The Goros were totally self-sufficient in their cavern world.

The startled Russian girl, realizing that Amdu had read her mind, asked aloud, "Why are the tunnels there? The one to Tibet is 'only' a thousand years old, in which case you Goros must have built it. No one else could have dug such a long hole in the rocks. So why did you?"

"The order to build that passage was given by the Inelqu nine thousand years ago," Amdu answered. "We do not know why we made it. The Sleepers did not tell us why it was necessary to make the tunnel. We do not know the purpose of any of the passages."

It was the stolid Tilhut who spoke in reaction to Vallie West's thoughts that the . . . *Goros are nothing more than slaves doing the bidding of the mysterious Inelqu. Who said that aliens from other worlds have to be "benovolent"? Nonsense! The Goros dig tunnels like blind moles and don't even know why they do it!*

"Mr. West, would you attempt to instruct a three-year-old child in the science of biostereometrics?[33] I do not think that you would try to succeed in such an impossibility." Tilhut regarded a stunned West with melancholy eyes, the barest hint of a smile on his slit of a mouth.

Vallie didn't know what to say. Tilhut did, his words giving Vallie and Camellion and the other twelve people another shock.

"The civilization of the Inelqu was very ancient when Neanderthal man was still amazed over the discovery of fire! The Inelqu are as far above humanity as we are

[33] Maps of human terrain are the results of the new science of biostereometrics—the three-dimensional measurement of living things, using techniques similar to aerial mapping.

above the ants. As superior as they are in intellect, why should they have to give a reason for anything they order? They should not and they do not."

Vallie West's verbal thrust was a quick shot-in-the-dark. "They may have been mental giants, these Inelqu, but they were pretty damned dumb to destroy each other in a war. They poisoned the surface of the Earth with radioactivity—didn't they?"

"There was a conflict on the surface, and on the surface of two other planets in this sun's system," Urba said, speaking mechanically. Of the three Guardians, he was the shortest. And the youngest—not a day over 125 years! "We do not know the nature of the conflict. We can tell you that the Inelqu, whose life processes are suspended in sleep here and in other parts of the world, did not start the war. They did succeed in sealing the hole in the fabric of the time-warp through which their enemies were coming."

"Coming from where?" asked Norbert Shireling.

"From a parallel universe. But I cannot tell you more."

The Death Merchant, moving his hand back and forth across his chin, cocked his head in the direction of Vallie West. "Our new friends seem to believe in the Graham Greene philosophy—they couldn't believe in a god they could understand. If they fully understood the Inelqu, they might not want to serve them."

If the three Goros were insulted, they didn't reveal it in any way, their ancient faces remaining as tranquil as a pool of water. Not a wrinkle moved. Only the eyes blinked.

Amdu's dark eyes shifted to the Death Merchant. "Richard Camellion, it is vital that the Chinese force be totally destroyed." The Guardian raised his right hand and motioned for Camellion and the others to walk ahead. "Come. We will provide you with refreshment. There is time enough before the Chinese arrive, in eleven of your hours."

"Which means early tomorrow morning," muttered Norbert Shireling.

"Amdu, how large is the Chinese force?" Camellion asked in a somber voice. "We are not the workers of miracles."

110

"The Chinese number four hundred sixty men," the Guardian said calmly. Just as placidly, he added, "Come. We go."

Without giving anyone a chance to make a comment, Amdu turned and started to walk away with Urba and Tilhut.

"We can't stand here," Camellion said, and began moving in the direction of the three Guardians. The others joined him.

"It's impossible!" Paul Gemz shouted after the Guardians. He raised a fist. "We can't fight a Chinese Army!"

The three Guardians kept right on walking.

Red Degenhardt's face was tinged a light blue from the "sun." Yet, if one looked closely, one could see that the true color of his face was now an ashen gray. "Half a battalion," he muttered. "We're up against half a battalion."

Vallie West began to cough. He had been inhaling from a cigarette when he had heard Red mention half a battalion, and the smoke had gone down the wrong way. Walking next to the Death Merchant, and following the three Guardians through the tall gray-brown grass, Vallie halfway decided that, even with their know-how, the odds were against them. He finally stopped coughing and, getting his breath, managed to gasp, "What did you say about our not being able to work miracles?"

"We're as good as dead," Degenhardt said. "All we're waiting for is for someone to shovel dirt in our faces!"

Camellion's voice was hard. "We have to pull it off. We might do it with another ambush and plenty of explosives.

"Crap!" West spit on the ground in disgust. "We have thirty-five million laws to enforce ten commandments. An ambush won't work any more than those laws have worked. The riceballs aren't going to fall twice for the same trick. In fact, they'll be expecting an ambush. You know it and I know it. We've been in this business too long to kid ourselves or each other."

"The Commies will also be on the lookout for us!" Degenhardt mentioned sternly. His voice lacked the nervous notes of fear; he was only stating his conclusion, which he knew to be cold fact.

The Death Merchant remained silent. *They're both right. These mushrooms might well become our head-*

111

stones. He wiped his face with an apricot-colored bandana while feeling the perspiration from his armpits trickle down his sides and flood the tightness around his waist. He had opened his heavy parka, but his entire body was awash with sweat, his thermal underwear were soaked, and his pants and shirt were sodden. The backpack and carryall bags didn't help.

West and Degenhardt and the rest of the Posten Expedition were in the same state of heated misery. Deep caverns are never cold. The deeper one goes, the higher the temperature becomes—and Shambhala—the granddaddy of all caves—was deep, far deeper than any salt mine, the temperature in the low eighties.

The three Guardians led Camellion and his thirteen companions past enormous mushroom plants and other outlandish vegetation. There was not the slightest hint of breeze, the air so dead that a feather floating to the ground would not have moved a millionth of millimeter off course.

Another contributing factor to the uncanny authenticity of the monstrous cavern was the solid rock "sky," dim and hazy, a *mile* overhead. All of it, every bit of it—impossible. But it *was;* it existed. It was very real. Another five minutes floated by on a sea of sweat. Presently the Guardians stopped in a large clearing in which were two platforms. Made of metal that looked like stainless steel, each platform was a foot thick and rested on four telescoping legs. At the end of each leg, a round metal ball—a foot in diameter—prevented the leg from burying itself in the ground, which in places was very spongy, almost mudlike.

One platform was not very large, each side eight feet long. The second platform, also a perfect square, had sides of twenty-two feet. Even an idiot would have known that the two platforms were vehicles of some sort.

A meshlike guardrail enclosed the upper surface of each platform. However, there was a three-foot-wide opening, at the bottom of which was a set of four steps. One side of each platform there was a control column a foot from the edge. Presumably this was the front of the craft. At the top of the three-foot-high column, a panel was tilted at an angle convenient to the operator. From this panel protruded two rods with a knob on each end. The panel also contained buttons in round cases that protruded an inch from the surface.

On the smaller platform, behind and on either side of the control column, were two three-foot-high metal rods set in a perpendicular position. At the top of each rod was a crossbar with grooves at each end. The larger platform had three dozen similar rods with crossbar handholds.

"I don't think they're used to deliver the mail," quipped Loren Eaton. "I wonder what makes them work."

Emil Lauterjung, who had a phobia about flying, turned two shades lighter blue. "I only hope there isn't any danger."

Amdu and Tilhut went straight to the small platform and walked up the steps. Tilhut took a position by the control column while Amdu got behind one of the rods and placed his hands on the crossbar. Tilhut pressed a button and the steps folded back into the space of the guardrail. Tilhut pressed another button and the craft be-gan to hum faintly. The Guardian moved one of the con-trol rods forward, and the Death Merchant and his companions saw the craft begin to rise, straight up, until it had reached an altitude of several hundred feet. A moment later the platform moved north, its speed—so everyone judged—an instant fifty miles per hour.

"How about that!" Foster Cross said in admiration. "What a way to travel."

"Oh, I dunno," murmured Loren Eaton. "Our Air Force has the same thing, only on a smaller scale."[34]

Urba stepped onto the larger platform, smiled, and motioned with his hand. Camellion was the first to climb the steps and take a position at handholds directly behind the control column. One by one the rest of the group fol-lowed him, Emil Lauterjung more frightened than the four Bhutanese soldiers.

"There isn't anything to fear," Urba said patiently. "We

[34] Here Eaton is referring to the flying disk built by Hiller Aircraft. The rotor is at the bottom of the disk, and it's controlled in horizontal flight by the pilot, who stands, shifting his weight to change direction.

cannot tilt in the air and there shall not be any air pressure against your bodies."

"Why not—no tilt and no pressure?" Camellion inquired. He glanced at Urba, then at a sullen-faced Vallie West, who had chosen a position on the other side of the Guardian. The big man was seething with anger, directed not against Camellion but against the unreasonableness of the situation, against their own helplessness, against the idea of a battle they could not win but had to win. Or die!

"What do you call this contraption?" Vallie growled. "And what's the source of power?"

"It cannot tilt because that is how it is made," explained the Guardian. "The name is from a very ancient language and would be meaningless to you; translated, the name would still be meaningless."

" 'Flying platform' is as good as any," Vallie said.

"The power is electromagnetic, a power that nullifies gravity. The same power projects a force field around the craft when it is in motion, preventing air from exerting pressure against the body?"

"What's the top speed?" asked the Death Merchant.

"In the terminology you use, the craft could move at thousands of miles per hour on the surface. In this place, we never move them very fast. There is no need to."

Camellion, noticing that everyone was in position at the handholds, asked another question. "Tell me, Urba, do you and the other Goros consider these flying platforms weapons?"

"We do not," the Guardian said. "These machines do not kill."

Camellion saw Vallie's eyes light up with interest. The CIA case officer's mouth opened slightly, then closed again. A moment later his face became a mask of rage at his own helplessness when Urba, reading his thoughts and Camellion's, said, "Yes, we will permit the use of these machines against the Chinese. We shall now go into the air."

The Guardian worked the necessary controls. The steps folded and closed the space in the guardrail. The platform lifted and was instantly moving north. A hundred feet below, the unearthly terrain flashed by, moving like a

114

scene from a silent film, but without the jerkiness of early motion pictures. Yet there was not a whisper of breeze blowing against the occupants of the platform, all of whom had the impression that it was they who were motionless and the ground below that was moving.

"Amazing! Amazing!" Lauterjung's voice was a jumble of awe and respect. "This fantastic mode of transportation could revolutionize the surface world. On the other hand, it would disrupt the economy."

More daring than the others who were holding on tightly to the horizontal rods, Red Degenhardt reached into his shirt pocket, tore off a piece of foil from a pack of cigarettes, held it out in front of him, then opened his finger and thumb. The tiny piece of foil fell straight to the metal floor. Red released his other hand from the bar. "Look!" he said, joking. "No hands!"

This was further proof that the platform was encased in an invisible wall of energy and was not creating any wind to distort spoken words; it was also another factor that increased the sense of isolation and added to the feeling that one was an "outsider" looking in, a part of reality, yet somehow removed from it.

"Urba, none of you ever answered why your telepathic powers are apparently useless against the Chinese," the Death Merchant said. "Why can't you and the other Guardians use long-range hypnotism to make the Chinese hallucinate?"

Urba's answer was prompt. "There is a limit to the use of mental connection between minds. Our combined powers of concentration are too weak to induce hallucinations in hundreds of people."

There was a sharp edge to West's voice. "I'd like to know what kind of defense system you Guardians have had all these thousands of years. Don't tell me this is the first time that you and the Inelqu have been threatened with a major catastrophe?"

"In an emergency, we are permitted to awaken one of the Inelqu. We have never had to do this. Until now, only small groups have found the tunnels."

Vallie's heavy voice rocketed upward in anger. "And four hundred sixty Commies coming this way isn't an

115

emergency! Just exactly what do the Guardians consider an emergency?"

"Should your group fail to stop the Chinese, we will then have an emergency," Urba replied. An instant later he almost staggered from the force of merged resentment that stabbed into his mind from the fourteen—bitter thoughts of wrath and virulence, quick flashes of naked hate, and the conviction that the small expedition was being sacrificed to save aliens from another world, to save the Goros—*Freak slaves*—this from the one called Emil Lauterjung—*who might as well be robots!*

"I am sorry," Urba said unemotionally. "One cannot change events that have already happened in the endless stream of time."

The sight of the dome in the distance, only a few miles away, effectively pulled everyone's attention from Amdu.

"Look at the size of it!" whispered Norbert Shireling.

"But where did it come from?" demanded Foster Cross ruefully. "As big as it is, we should have seen that dome the instant we stepped through the last doorway, as soon as we were in the cave. It's hundreds of feet over the tallest mushrooms!"

Cross had not exaggerated. The dome was so gigantic that it didn't seem possible that such a structure could exist. From ground level to center apex the height was close to nine hundred feet. The diameter of the base stretched three city blocks! Inside the dome were numerous smaller structures, some dome-shaped, others built in the form of a cube. None of the cubes were more than a hundred feet on all sides. Conversely, some of the domes were four hundred feet tall.

"Yes, Richard Camellion, you are correct," Urba said, having received the Death Merchant's thoughts. "The home of the Inelqu is totally invisible until one is very close to it. Yes, this is done by bending light rays. The dome then becomes part of the spectrum the human eye cannot see."

The pragmatic Paul Gemz intoned, "The building is not a true dome. It's shaped more like an oval!"

"It is glass, plastic, or what?" Camellion asked Urba.

"The structure is made of metal," Urba said.

The Death Merchant, as stunned as he was, did not reply. Gemz did: "Impossible! There is not any process that will enable metal to become transparent!"

Urba didn't have a chance to explain. Professor Lauterjung turned on Gemz and spoke with an indignation that surprised even the Death Merchant.

"Professor Gemz, you are a pompous ass! You're always taking the stand that if our own science can't do something, it can't be done. You sound like a fool!"

Gemz snapped back his head in amazement, surprised that Lauterjung had such iron in his backbone. He let Lauterjung have a whiplike look, then tightened his mouth, his cheek muscles quivering.

"Once we land," said Norbert Shrieling, "the first thing I'm going to do is take off my parka and thermal underwear. I'm roasted."

"You mean if we don't crash into the side of the dome!" Foster Cross said nervously.

By now the flying platform was so close to the dome that the south side of the fantastic structure filled the sky ahead. When it seemed that the platform must surely strike the dome, Urba brought the vehicle to an instant stop. There was neither momentum nor a feeling of motion. To the occupants standing on the platform, there wasn't any true movement, because the craft carried its own field of gravity with it. The vehicle might as well have been going ten thousand miles per hour. There still would not have been any sensation of movement. No one would have been pushed forward when the craft came to an instant stop.

Urba touched a control rod and the platform rose. When it was fifty feet higher than the highest point of the dome, Urba worked another control. Once more the platform moved north. A few minutes more of travel, then the Guardian brought the platform to a stop and again moved one of the controls. The platform began to descend though a round opening in the center of the dome. Soon it was on the metal floor and Camellion and his people were getting off.

Before them, on all sides, were domes and cubes, many of which were opaque. Other domes and cubes were transparent, so much so that one had to look twice to make sure that the machinery wasn't just resting unprotected on the metal floor. Nowhere, including on the flying platform, was there a single rivet head or a weld seam. The strange-looking machinery and other objects were incomprehensible to the powers of reason and analysis.

Camellion and Company looked around. There was no sign of Amdu and Tilhut and their small flying platform, although white-robed Guardians could be seen in the distance, to the south and to the west, strolling along as if they didn't have a care in the world. The large group of Chinese, about to invade the cavern, might as well have been in China.

Except for the Death Merchant, everyone felt very uncomfortable, the sense of dread overpowering, the distance between the buildings and their hugeness, as well as the unbelievable size of the main dome, instilling a deeper feeling of vulnerability, increasing their sense of frustration over the Chinese approaching from the north, and stirring their anger against the Guardians and the Inelqu.

"All this power, all this incredible force around us, and we still have to do their fighting for them!" grumbled Vallie West.

"We'd have a better chance at unraveling a bunch of rubber bands inside a smashed golf ball!" said Red Degenhardt bitterly.

"Please follow me," Urba said.

He began to walk south.

Chapter Nine

Think like a man of action, but act like a man of thought. And that is the rule Camellion used as the minutes hurried into an hour, during which, in one rounded ceiling room of an opaque cube, the Death Merchant and his men divested themselves of their parkas, backpacks, equipment bags, and thermal underwear. After redressing in pants, shirts, and boots, they put on their sidearms, then turned their backs while a nervous Helena Banya removed her insulated clothing and redressed.

Per Urba's instructions, they waited in the windowless room whose temperature was a pleasant seventy degrees and whose furnishings were made of some clear material that resembled lightweight plastic. In the U.S. the furniture would have been called ultramodern, none of it following any standard shape, but flowing in curves that were unrelated to the circles, ovals, and spheres with which Camellion and the others from the West were familiar. Soft illumination flowed from the ceiling.

Degenhardt sat down in a curvilinear, molded chair and looked up at the Death Merchant who was testing the weight of a large square table made of translucent material, the same substance of which the other furniture was made. The table was as light as a large feather.

"Camellion, are we just going to sit here?" Red blinked very rapidly. "In another nine or ten hours, the riceballs are going to show up, all four hundred and sixty of them! How do we scratch them?"

"For now, we're going to wait," Camellion said warily. "I'll tell you something else"—he settled in one of the curved chairs. "We're a long long way from being dead. Personally, I have never considered myself a victim. I'm always the victor." He would have said more but at that moment, Tilhut and two other Goros, or Guardians, entered the room, all three carrying large trays filled with plates, glasses, decanters, and oval-covered casseroles. The cream-colored plates and glasses could have been plastic, the trays, decanters, and casseroles stainless steel.

The three Guardians placed the large trays on the table, and Tilhut introduced his two companions as Pel and Odox, both of whom were tall, bald, and as wrinkled in the face as he was. Similar to Tilhut, Urba, and Amdu, Odox, and Pel wore peaceful expressions and were just as unemotional and unfeeling.

Tilhut waved a hand toward the table. "Eat. Drink. Take in nourishment."

Suddenly, Loren Eaton, who had moved closer to the trays, gave a startled gasp. "I'll be a suck-egg mule! Look at that—knives and forks! There's knives and forks on the trays!"

The three Guardians smiled in apparent amusement as everyone stared at the trays. "Did you expect us to eat with our fingers?" Tilhut actually laughed—low and very lightly, but nevertheless a laugh.

Odox—locking his thoughts with those of the amazed Eaton—spoke in a gentle voice. "No. We have never used chopsticks. We are not Chinese. Before the Inelqu brought us to this place, many, many thousands of years ago, we lived in a nation whose inhabitants were the ancestors of the Chinese. China and the true Chinese were still thousands of years in the future. We did use knives and forks and spoons in our country. Naturally, we called them by different names. The meanings, however, were the same."

"It's logical," Camellion said, turning to the table. He took off one of the oval-shaped coverings. "Eating utensils are designed not so much from culture as from a standpoint of practicability." He darted a look at a chicken-necked Emil Lauterjung. "You should know. Correct me if I'm wrong."

"You're correct as far as it goes," agreed Lauterjung. "I should like to point out that there are those times when culture can become so firmly ingrained that, even after an outside society introduces a more practical method, the old ways and customs are still retained. For example, the Chinese have used chopsticks for thousands of years to eat rice, though it's obvious that a spoon or fork would be more workable."

"Maybe it's the Chinese way of making sure that they don't eat too fast," cracked Vallie West, who had moved to the table with the others and was inspecting the food. One casserole was filled with a substance that looked like green Jello. The other casseroles contained steaming thick round pieces of what resembled filet mignon, minus the pork or bacon garnishings.

"All the food is made from the chorrten plant," Pel explained, sounding mechanical. "We can change the density and viscosity to any consistency we desire. We can make the chorrten hard or soft, and of any flavor we choose."

"Say, this is good," exclaimed Foster Cross, who had filled his plate and had taken a bite of the "meat." "This tastes exactly like well-cooked beef. And it's very tender."

"Try this green stuff," urged Helena Banya. She grew expansive. "I would swear it was vanilla ice-cream if it weren't for the color."

"The condemned had a final meal," Degenhardt observed dryly, then put a forkful of the green gel into his mouth.

Camellion had filled a glass from one of the decanters. Now he sipped the cool liquid, which had the thickness of buttermilk and tasted like pineapple juice mixed with coconut milk.

He put down the half-empty glass and cut off a forkful of "beef," saying lackadaisically, "Tilhut, Time never waits. The Chinese are getting closer with each passing second. As soon as my friends and I are finished eating, I want you to show me how to operate one of the flying platforms, one of the large ones. I trust you can instruct me without breaking one of the rules?"

"Or do we have to lose more time having a powwow with some 'high council'?" West's voice was as hard as his eyes. "Or whatever ruling body controls this place."

"As Amdu told you, we are all of equal rank," Tilhut said. "There isn't any ruling council." His dark eyes moved to the Death Merchant. "I will show you how to operate the machine. . . . Yes," he added, in reply to Camellion's mental question, "the metal is bulletproof. There is only one kind of power that can destroy Kkokro

121

metal. That power is nuclear power. It would require a hydrogen device of five hundred megatons—to use your system of measurement—to disrupt the flow of molecular arrangement in the Kkokro. Not even a Tris Ray, which will annihilate any substance, can destroy Kkokro."

"But you can't give us any of these Tris Rays to use?" asked Camellion.

"We could not," Tilhut said. "The Tris Ray weapons are under the direct control of the Inelqu."

"The shining walls in the tunnel are made of Kkokro metal." There was an added quality of mistrust to Degenhardt's voice. "I'm sure you can explain why the walls glow and the platforms don't."

"Not all Kkokro metal glows," Tilhut said simply, "only the very strongest, such as the protective walls across the tunnel through which you came. The passage through which the Chinese are moving is made of Kkokro metal."

Vallie West and Red Degenhardt locked glances. Paul Gemz wrinkled his nose. Helena Banya's pretty blue eyes grew more serious. In spite of the previous heat, she hadn't lost that combination of honey and iron.

His fork pausing over his plate, the Death Merchant turned his head and looked directly at Tilhut, his eyes glittering strangely.

"The tunnel itself—walls, floor, and ceiling—is made of Kkokro metal? How wide is the tunnel—in feet?"

"The type of rock strata made it necessary that the entire tunnel be constructed of Kkokro metal," Tilhut said. "The tunnel is a square, seventy of your feet high and seventy of your feet wide. The Chinese are approaching in vehicles that move over the surface on wheels."

"Damm it!" growled Foster Cross. "They have troop carriers and armored cars."

"Maybe even tanks," added Loren Eaton in a hollow voice.

The Death Merchant resumed eating. No one spoke. The three Guardians remained standing, giving the impression that they could remain stationary forever and not become tired or bored.

Camellion finally broke the short silence. "Red, how much HBX do we have?"

The Black Beret leader thought for a few moments. "I'd

say maybe a hundred fifty pounds in five-pound blocks. What do you have in mind?"

A child would not have found it difficult to operate one of the flying platforms, any child with a normal sense of balance and depth perception. One control rod raised and lowered the craft for vertical flight—either straight up or straight down. There could be no rise or descent at an angle, at a slant.

The other rod controlled the forward motion of the craft. Push the rod to the front and the flying platform moved forward. Push the rod to the left and the vehicle would move to the left; in the opposite direction, and the platform would move to the right. The operator turned the craft completely around by rotating the horizontal flight rod in a circular motion. To increase or decrease speed was a simple matter, momentum regulated by foot pressure on a large button set in the floor, in a manner identical to a motorist pressing down on the gas pedal.

The Death Merchant's only worry had been the force field around the platform. For all practical purposes the vehicle was like a letter inside an envelope, in this case an envelope of energy.

Nothing can get past a force field, from either direction, Camellion had thought. *Neither from the inside nor outside the craft!*

Knowing Camellion's thoughts the instant they were born in his brain, Tilhut had immediately informed him, in spoken language, that the force field around the platforms could be turned off when the conveyances were in motion.

"This is necessary when we build tunnels. With the force field on, we would not be able to lower material from the machines."

Tilhut, Pel, and Odox—their faces expressionless as usual, and their arms by their sides, as usual—stood watching Camellion, West, and Degenhardt attach electric detonation timers to fifteen five-pound blocks of HBX. Four other Guardians had joined Tilhut, Odox, and Pel, and they too stood quiescent, arms at their sides, gazing serenely at the Death Merchant and his force of thirteen.

Camellion said to West and Degenhardt, "Make sure the prongs of the timers are solidly in the stuff."

123

"Listen, don't tell me about explosives." Degenhardt was not angry, his tone being that of an expert who has total confidence because he knows he is one of the best in his chosen field. Nor was he shy about saying straight out what he thought. "The only thing that worries me is whether you can fly the damn thing. This isn't a craps shoot. There's no second chance."

"We'll be tied to the crossbars," West said, and pushed the pointed prongs of a timer through the oiled brown paper of an HBX block. "We couldn't fall off if we wanted to, and we'll be up high enough to prevent the riceballs from seeing us on the platform. If they can see us in the distance—so what? We'll be too far away for any good shots."

Degenhardt remained unconvinced. "Sure, if we don't crash!"

"We won't," Camellion said. "You saw me fly the thing—up, down, sideways, and through the hole in the ceiling. It's impossible to crash. The only way would be if I deliberately rammed us into the rock ceiling or the sides of the cavern."

"I admit that the idea is sound," Degenhardt allowed, "and that you're right about the Chinese. It's a matter of simple tactics. Scouts will be in advance of the main force. When the main force reaches the end of the tunnel that opens into the cave, scouts will fan out and move forward. They'll radio back that all is clear and the big force will advance. We blow hell out of them with HBX. It all sounds as fine as frog hair, if you can fly the platform, if we stay high enough, and if we don't misjudge the height, set the timers wrong, and the stuff explodes short."

"Screw the 'ifs'!" West grimaced and jerked his head to toss back a lock of hair from his forehead. "If my Aunt Charlotte had a bouncing pair of balls, she'd be my uncle. But she hasn't, and she isn't!"

Remembering then that Helena Banya was only a short distance away and had to have overheard him, Vallie looked up at the Russian girl, who had a titillating smile on her mouth. "Sorry, Banya. It slipped my mind that you were around."

"Don't let it trouble your tender sense of morality." Helena paused and her smile grew in size. "I found your biological impossibility most amusing. Not even *Pravda* has claimed that Soviet scientists have succeeded in transplanting the male testicles."

"There isn't anything entertaining about the Chinese," Camellion said reasonably, glancing up at the young woman. "In another six hours they'll be coming through the tunnel." He called over to Tilhut. "Old buddy, Tilhut, will it be the scouts or the main Chinese force who'll be popping out in six hours? You didn't say."

"The scouts will emerge from the tunnel in four and a half hours," Tilhut responded. "Please do not ask me again how we know. It would be very difficult to explain."

Norbert Shireling, who was down on his haunches, bracing himself with an Ingram submachine gun, said airily, "Let's keep in mind another bit of information friend Tilhut told us, that the end of the tunnel is only fifteen miles from the dome. Course, the gooks won't be able to see the dome until they're within a mile and a half of it. What a surprise they'll get!"

The Death Merchant let Shireling's words walk on by. He shoved a timer into the last block of HBX, checked the signal light to make sure the tiny battery was working, then placed the block in a large carryall bag with the other bars, and got up from his knees. Having finished with their work, West and Degenhardt stood up, picked up the two bags, and carried them to a large flying platform that was only a short distance away.

The Black Beret boy is dead wrong, Camellion thought. *The Chinese are never going to live to be "surprised" at the sight of the dome. That's another problem, or it could be: I wonder if the Electro-5s will work in this cavern world?*

"They will function in this place," Tilhut promptly answered. "I must tell you that the nature of the Kkokro metal, of which the master dome is constructed, and the activity of our machines, will render your Electro-5s useless within two miles of this dome. Not even static would you receive."

The Death Merchant nodded and, rolling up the sleeves of his black plaid shirt, made a test, deliberately thinking. *"Homo sum; humani nihil a me alienum puto. Suppose you tell me what I just thought?"*

Tilhut did, verbally. "Spoken language is only the sound of phonetics, as you know very well, Richard Camellion. It is the meaning of the individual sounds, the meaning of each 'word,' in the mind of the speaker, that gives reality. You said, 'I am a man, and I consider nothing alien to me.'"

Quick to discover what was taking place between Tilhut and Camellion, Paul Gemz asked a question of the Guardian.

"Tilhut, how deeply can the Guardians probe the mind?"

"We can read the thoughts of the conscious mind. With concentrated effort, the forty of us can read the conscious mind and the unconscious mind of any individual in any place on the surface world. We do need the aid of a certain machine to do this."

Gemz's eyes became calculating, but he didn't press on for information. Even if he had intended to, he would not have had the time. Red Degenhardt, who had returned from the platform with West, walked up to the Death Merchant.

"I figure we can fly the platform north of the dome," he said, looking at Camellion, "and spot the Commie scouts. We can stay within the invisibility limit. We'll be able to see them, but they won't know we're there."

"Exactly," Camellion said and glanced at his wristwatch out of habit. The watch had stopped running within the two-mile limit. So had their engineer's compasses. The needles could spin only in a circle. "Once the scouts think it's safe, they'll radio back to the main body. It shouldn't take more than an hour and a half for the main force to get out into the open. Maybe sooner, especially since it's a motorized column."

"They have to be far enough up front," Vallie West was quick to point out, "far enough that we can blast them before they can retreat to the tunnel."

"They will be," Camellion said. "They can't outrun a flying platform and we're not going to make any mistakes." *Or will we?* The Death Merchant began to wonder.

Seven hours and forty minutes later, while belted to the control column of the Flying Door (as Foster Cross had nicknamed the platform), Camellion was still not positive

126

that his scheme would work. It had so far. He had flown the machine to a position half a mile north of the main dome and had kept it motionless at a height of five hundred feet, while he and West and Degenhardt had scanned the northern section of the landscape through high-powered binoculars.

West and Degenhardt stood toward the center of the platform, heavy leather belts holding them to the crossbars. Wrapped once around the crossbars, the belts had then been wrapped one time around the perpendicular supporting rods, after which the ends buckled around the bodies of Degenhardt and West. It was a tight fit; yet the two men had their arms free. Furthermore, the belts could not slip from the crossbars any more than West and Degenhardt could fall off if they lost their balance. On each man's hip, outside his safety belt, was a carryall bag filled with HBX blocks.

From their position of five hundred feet overhead, they had not been able to see the mouth of the tunnel—indeed odd, since they could detect the side of the north wall. Very dimly, yes. Nonetheless, the wall was discernible.

It was West who had first spotted the two Chinese scouts. The two chopsticks had been decked out in camouflaged whites, which, in the light of the blue "sun," made them look like azurean shadows as they had darted from rock to rock and had zagged and zigged from mushroom to mushroom. Vallie had had to look half a dozen times to make sure his mind wasn't playing tricks on him.

"Hot damn! I see two of them!" Vallie had said. "They're coming in just like you said, Rick. With any luck, maybe we will save ourselves and the Guardians and their godlike bosses, the Inelqu—even if none of the smug bastards will fight."

"Every man's a god," Camellion had replied, "if he has a dog."

A few seconds later he had made out the second team, far to the east of where Vallie had pointed out the first pair. Then Degenhardt had seen the third team, a mile west of the first pair.

"Give them time," Camellion had said. "They can't see

127

us or the dome. We have one hundred percent advantage."

Within the next twenty minutes they had detected fourteen different teams of Chinese scouts spread out in a five-mile semicircle. They could not be certain, however, that they weren't counting some teams twice.

"We'll wait another hour," the Death Merchant had said. "By now the scouts should have reported to the main column that there isn't anything around but god-hideous vegetation."

Vallie had been impatient to get started. "The main force should be coming out into the open by now. But we had better be right, or it's bye-bye to life and 'Hello, Death.'" He had then placed his binoculars in their case and had closed the top of the leather container.

Degenhardt, putting away his own binoculars for the time being, had said, "In the long scheme of things, it might not be so bad if we do get scratched in this damn hell-world. Dying here would be better than being put out to pasture years from now. I prefer filet mignon all the way, every second. The hell with the hamburger of retirement."

Vallie had not been in the mood to make a reply to Red's philosophical opinion. The hell with the future. The hell with retirement. The hell with Degenhardt. Better to take care of the present.

"Rick," he had said, "the height we use will determine the number of seconds we click off on the timers. I suppose you know that for purposes of standardization, the acceleration due to gravity is g equals 998.665 cm/sec. to the second power?"

"I know, Val. It's also a matter of dynes.[35] Since the Earth rotates, the weight of a body is somewhat less than the Earth's attraction for it, because of the centrifugal force, and in general is not directed toward the Earth's center. You take a plumb line ten feet long in the latitude of New York. Okay, this line departs about a quarter inch

[35] The dyne is the unit of force in the C.G.S.—centimeter-gram-second system of physical units. It is such a great force that, under its influence, a body whose mass is one gram would experience an acceleration of one centimeter per second per second—yes, two "per seconds."

to the south, from a line in the direction of the Earth's geometrical center."

"Which adds up to what?" Vallie had asked.

"Well, this same influence accounts for the oblateness of the Earth, and these two facts together account for the variation of gravity from equator to poles—a fact few people realize. At the equator the weight of a gram mass is 977.99 dynes. At the poles it exceeds 983 dynes."

"A blast goes upward," Degenhardt had said. "We want to make sure each block makes contact with the surface below. I'd set each timer at eighteen seconds. After all, if the stuff hits the ground and there's a few seconds delay— so what? Who can shut 'em off?"

Never a man to put foolish pride before pragmatism, the Death Merchant had mulled over Degenhardt's suggestion. *I estimated sixteen seconds. His timing is much better. But he's wrong. So was I. We both forgot that he and Vallie are standing toward the center of the platform.*

Vallie and Red could just as easily have been belted to crossbars on each side of the platform; they couldn't have fallen off. They were positioned in the middle of the machine because of the twenty-two blocks of HBX they carried, 110 pounds of the deadly explosive. Standing in the middle as they were, there wasn't any possibility that a slug could accidentally touch off the explosive, which was not immune to the shock of a bullet. A .22 could have done the job.

Camellion had said, "Red, we both forgot that you and Val have to throw slightly up and out to clear the sides of this contraption. Better set each timer for twenty one seconds. We'll have more leeway."

He had continued to scan the north area. West and Degenhardt had joined him with their binoculars.

Not quite forty minutes later, they had spotted the Chinese column. And what a column! First, out in front, were several JS-3 heavy tanks. Behind the tanks were three armored cars, several open command vehicles, and a large truck pulling what appeared to be a 75mm field gun. No one could be sure; the distance had been too great. Then came a line of armored troop carriers, weaving in and out of the huge chorrten plants.

The flying platform was not a fighting machine, it's

129

chief flaw being that it did not permit a clear view of the ground close by. One could see only the distance straight ahead. As the craft would draw closer to any particular point, the edges of the platform would prevent the passengers from seeing the ground in the immediate vicinity, the blocked area of vision depending on the height of the craft. *By the time we're within firing range from the Chinese, we won't be able to see them from up here. My judgment of distance has to be accurate. Val and Red will be lucky if they can see two miles behind the last carrier of the column!*

Vallie had grinned mischievously and had shoved the binoculars into their case. "Blessed be the man who shares his neighbor's burden," he had said with a laugh. "About the only thing we don't have to worry about is the scouts. They'll run like chickens with their heads off when the big noises start."

"Let's do it, Camellion," Degenhardt had grunted. Already he had taken a block of HBX from the bag on his hip.

Camellion had begun working the controls of the platform. He had to be right over the column. He would have to fly straight ahead and, when he was a quarter of a mile in front of the enemy force, he would stop, fly east, stop again, then fly straight ahead.

"This is a poor way to travel, boys, but it beats going in on a hang glider—hang on!"

"What do you mean hang on?" Vallie had yelled. "We're *belted* to this damn thing!"

Now the Flying Door headed straight for the Chinese column, Camellion's hands on the controls, his right foot pressing down on the speed button. The Chinese were no longer advancing, having seen the craft the instant it had passed beyond the screen of invisibility. They were still slightly out of rang when the Chinese opened fire with automatic weapons, hundreds of shots ringing out from the ground ahead and five hundred feet below.

Staring at the ground below, Camellion slowed the craft to what he estimated to be not more than thirty miles per hour. He had only his talent for gauging speed. There was no speedometer. The catch was that he had never had to

130

do it while standing on a "Flying Door." By now—he began counting off the seconds—he could not see the Red Army column but judged that he was only half a minute away from the first tank.

"Get set! Remember: twenty-one seconds," he called back to Red and Val, ignoring the wind generated by the movement of the craft.

The gunfire below had become a crescendo of pounding sound, the hundreds of echoes crashing into each other, reverberating back and forth with all the persistence of devils screaming at souls in hell. By this time the platform was well within range of the hundreds of barrels pointed in its direction. Hundreds of slugs had to be striking the bottom of the craft. Maybe so, but where were the high whines of ricochets? *Some stuff, this Kkokro metal!* Camellion thought.

"Go!" he yelled to Red and Vallie. *I figure the column is a mile long. We won't get all of them!*

Immediately, Val and Red turned the pointers of the timers to 21-s, then threw the two blocks of explosive over the sides of the platform, Vallie to the right (to the east), Red to the left (to the west). Red and Vallie had turned the timers on the next two blocks and were tossing the HBX up and out when the first two five-pound blocks detonated with mountain-shaking roars.

The first block of HBX exploded only ten feet from the first tank. The concussion was not sufficient to actually damage the heavily armored tank, but the blast had been powerful enough to turn it over on its left side and spin the second JS-3 around so that the muzzle of its 75mm cannon was pointed west.

The second block of HBX, exploding, turned an armored car into scrap metal, and changed its four occupants into chunks of bloody flesh. The third explosion, a short distance from the two command vehicles, overturned the cars, spilling out the ten Chinese officers and their drivers, including General Hsun Chin, Major Fu Siu-ch'un, and Major Yang She-Tung. They were lucky; they had been in the first command car. There was a bright microsecond flash of red, another deafening explosion, and the cab of the truck pulling the field gun vanished in a maelstrom of twisted metal, smoke, bits of rubber and uniform cloth, flesh, great splashes of blood, and other debris that would forever remain in Shambhala.

A long sliver of windshield glass speared itself into the throat of a Chinese officer who had been thrown out of the second command car that had overturned, the glass slicing in with such force that an inch of the tip protruded through the back of his neck. Shaking, the man started to fall, the blood, spurting from around the glass in his throat, appearing almost black in the glint of the blue "sun."

More of the wreckage slammed into the faces of three other Chinese officers who had been in the second command car. One man died instantly from the bolt buried in his forehead. The second man, knocked unconscious by a chunk of metal, pitched forward. The third man screamed. He had been blinded in one eye and bits of sharp metal had ripped his cheeks away.

In another few moments, the fourth and the fifth blocks of TNT and RDX[86] detonated, sounding like two baby A-bombs going off. A troop carrier and several dozen Chinese soldiers vanished in a brief flash of fire and smoke as flesh and steel were tossed in all directions.

The more intelligent of the Chinese drivers attempted to swerve either to the left or the right, to avoid the flying platform that was moving in a straight line five hundred feet overhead. Hundreds of Chinese regulars in the open carriers, raised their rifles and submachine guns and fired at the strange square object, so high that it was only three times the size of a Mao Tse-tung postage stamp. But how could they miss? Out of thousands of slugs, hundreds had to be hitting the bottom of the metal square.

The thundering of death continued and so did the screams and shrieks of Chinese P.L.A. privates and their NCOs. Bolted and cross-welded armor plates were ripped apart with a violence that most of the Chinese had never before seen.

[86] RDX is cyclotrimethylenetrinitramine, better known as Cyclonite. It is always used in U.S. ordnance with a desensitizer. In explosives such as HBX, the RDX is cast with TNT, which is trinitrotoluene. Thirty percent TNT and seventy percent tetryl compose tetrytol.

A supply truck disappeared in a huge flash of flame and smoke, and when the air cleared there wasn't anything left but half the frame, the front left wheel and tire, and a fraction of the driver's end of the seat.

Some of the carriers had caught fire, torrents of flame and oily black smoke rolling upward toward the flat-rock sky, a mile above the ground. Other trucks burned only for a few seconds before they exploded, balls of burning metal shooting up as high as a hundred feet, only to crash back down on jets of scorchingly hot air. And while the blocks of HBX exploded, scores of P.L.A. soldiers shrieked in excruciating agony from the fire that had turned them into human torches, and would very quickly reduce them to blackened corpses. Now, their only destiny was to remain in Shambhala . . . their mouths drawn back over their teeth in hideously charred grins.

To withstand such a terrible bombardment, a man needed nerves of beryllium and blood vessels of tungsten. Or he had to be Richard Camellion! Every third or fourth vehicle was either destroyed, turned over, or knocked sideways off the twisting route that lay between giant mushrooms, the tall, stalky vegetation with huge chalk leaves, and other strange kinds of trees and shrubbery. Turned into blazing bundles of agony, men ran in circles, only to collapse from shock or die when they inhaled fire that ate their lungs the way a blowtorch burns tissue paper. Scores of Chinese, toward the rear of the disrupted column, stopped firing at the flying platform, jumped from the carriers, and sought sanctuary under the canopies of the mushroom plants.

The explosions did not lessen. More carriers were shattered, the twisted, burning metal and pieces of things that had once been human beings vomiting upward, much of it coming back down on top of the mushrooms. There was one final explosion at the end of the line. Men screamed and then were silent. Slowly, several giant mushrooms toppled over. . . .

Vallie West had thrown the twentieth and last block of HBX over the right side of the platform. Even so, the Death Merchant flew over the platform to within a mile of the cavern's north wall. To inspect the damage on the re-

133

turn trip, he needed—at this height—plenty of distance ahead. He stopped the machine. Rotating the horizontal flight rod, he then turned the craft completely around. There was some jerking but he got the job done. The front of the craft was pointed south. He pushed the direction-of-flight rod to the front and pressed down slightly on the speed button. The craft moved south, its speed a slow ten miles per hour. *Or maybe fifteen miles per hour! If I knew how to activate the force field, we could go in very low and have a nice look-see. Too bad the Guardians wouldn't tell me how.*

The Flying Door flew back over the blasted Chinese column, moving slowly through the upper reaches of black smoke that, untouched by any natural breeze, floated almost straight up. The smell was not pleasant. They inhaled the nauseating stink of burnt oil and the odor of leather and fire-blackened flesh. The latter could have been overdone pork. . . .

The Death Merchant quickly saw that he had not miscalculated. Far below, personnel carriers lay scattered like gray-blue toys on a rug of wild, crazy patterns. Some of the vehicles were burning. Others were overturned. Half a dozen carriers and a few supply trucks were parked at weird angles. The truck and field gun were blazing, the cannon from gasoline that had splashed over it when the hauler part of the vehicle had exploded. One tank was turned over. Camellion wanted to laugh. There wasn't anything more helpless than an overturned tank. Camellion sighed. *The second tank is intact—dammit! So are two of the armored cars—damn, damn!*

Joy locked horns with a deep sense of failure—the former because, while the three men had destroyed at least one-fourth of the Red Chinese armor—and how many men?—dozens of vehicles were still in prime fighting condition. How many men? Had the platform been at a much lower altitude, they might have been able to better evaluate Chinese casualties. Even so, considering the round tops of mushrooms and the general mess that was the terrain, any accurate evaluation would have been impossible.

"We could have neutralized half of them," Vallie offered hopefully, as some of the Reds again started firing at the craft. "I doubt it. But if we did, that leaves only two hundred thirty of the freaks we have to deal with. They could give up the whole business and go home. They won't. Those damned Chinese never quit. The only way to stop them is to kill every single one of them."

Degenhardt shifted his weight against the belt holding him fast to the crossbar. "We don't have to worry about the odds. The odds are pressing us in on all sides. Ten of us against a couple of hundred chopsticks!"

Vallie was perplexed. "Ten? I count fourteen! I suppose you're leaving out the four Bhutanese soldiers. I suppose I agree with you. They're so damned scared that if they started shooting, they'd either kill us or each other. We can count on the two eggheads and the Russian doll. They did pretty good when we ambushed the riceballs. I was surprised."

"We all were," Red said. He paused for a moment. "That Banya's got a lot of scars. They don't show, but she has them." He called out in a much louder voice, "Camellion, have you any ideas?"

"We have our health, and ten blocks of explosive in the dome," Camellion called back, turning his head slightly. "And I don't think the creek will rise and make things difficult for us."

"Neither will the dead Chinese!" joked Vallie. He cursed then, and gave up trying to light a cigarette against the stiff breeze.

"I don't think any of it is a joking matter," Degenhardt said loudly. "Fifty pounds of big stuff isn't anything against a force of that size. They still have a tank and armored cars and carriers. How are we going to do it? I'd like to know."

"We fight like we have never fought before—and do a lot of praying!"

Chapter Ten

The Chinese had taken off their heavily padded jackets but they weren't any more comfortable, not that they noticed the sweat soaking their uniforms; they had too many other things to think about. Everywhere was ruin of the first magnitude—burned-out personnel carriers—many were still smoking—and dead bodies, many that were smoldering burned-black obscenities.

"*Please wait!*" Major Yang She-Tung called out, running to catch up with General Hsun Chin and Major Fu Siu-ch'un, who were moving down the line, inspecting the destruction.

General Chin and Major Siu-ch'un stopped and turned around as Major She-Tung hurried up to them.

"How many dead?" General Chin asked hoarsely.

"It is not good, Comrade General." She-Tung used a finger to brush perspiration from his small mustache. "One hundred and ten of our brave soldiers are dead. Sixty are badly wounded. They will not be able to fight. In armor, we have one tank, two armored cars, and fourteen carriers. We have two supply trucks. Our water supply is intact and all of our ammunition for small arms."

"Counting the three of us, that leaves two hundred ninety men," Major Siu-ch'un said carefully. He turned his brutal eyes on General Chin, who was staring at the blue "sun." Siu-ch'un didn't offer any advice. The mission was already a shambles and he didn't intend to have any of the failure fall on his shoulders.

"What are your orders, Comrade General?" he asked tonelessly.

General Chin turned away from the "sun" and put a hand on top of the closed holster on his right side. A terrible expression on his smoke-smudged face, he glared up and down the line, at the soldiers and the noncoms who were doing their best to make their wounded comrades comfortable and to bring order out of disorder. Finally, General Chin's deep-set eyes jumped to Siu-ch'un.

"I should like to know your opinion," he said gruffly, his mouth vacillating between a smile and a grimace, "and the strategy you would employ."

"I think we are in agreement that we have found an advanced civilization," Siu-ch'un said patiently. "The globe, hanging suspended and giving off blue light, proves as much. I would return to the surface." He didn't use the word *retreat*. "It is my opinion that we should report this find to Peking. We can then return with much larger weapons, including missiles and antiaircraft guns."

"As defense against whatever it was that bombed us?" General Chin's eyes narrowed in doubt as he stared at Major Siu-ch'un and unconsciously inhaled on a cigarette.

"Attacked us with conventional explosives!" Major She-Tung inserted quickly. He leaned his back against the side of a troop carrier. "It strikes me as very peculiar that this 'advanced civilization' should use *ma-an-tun pi-pang*, or what the Caucasians call TNT. Both of you can smell it as well as I."

"Yes, Comrade General," replied Major Siu-ch'un, ignoring She-Tung. "As defense against the flat-bottomed object that attacked us. We need missiles and the cover that smoke will afford." He smiled faintly at She-Tung. "Comrade Major, an advanced culture doesn't have to have advanced weaponry. I think it was the American, Camellion, and some of his men who attacked us. Camellion and his expedition arrived before we did. They have either entered into an agreement with the people who made the square that flies, or else Camellion and his technicians found the machine and figured out how it works. For all we know, the craft might be thousands of years old. I feel that the source of its power lies in its ability to cancel out gravity."

General Hsun Chin stared at Siu-ch'un, his brow wrinkling in deep thought. Amusement flowed all over the handsome face of Major She-Tung. "Comrade, aren't you letting your imagination run wild and unchecked through

137

the rice paddies? Come now—a craft that frees itself from the gravitational pull of the earth itself?"

"Comrade, you saw the machine." Major Siu-ch'un refused to become angry. Why should he? She-Tung couldn't help it if his brain was as small as that of a jackass. "The craft was there. Furthermore, the use of *ma-antun pi-pang* by whoever was controlling the craft, proves that this civilization doesn't have any weapons we can't handle. Or Camellion would have used them."

Major Yang She-Tung had no choice but to agree to the logic of Siu-ch'un's reasoning. "Let us assume that what you say is true," he said. "How do we defend ourselves against the flying square should it return, or should we advance?"

General Chin made an angry gesture with his left hand. "Enough of this rubbish," he said, breathing heavily through his nose. "When we advance, we'll keep the carriers far apart. There is no other way we can protect ourselves against the craft. We'll move out in a few hours and push straight south."

"Comrade General, I suggest we go to either the left or right flank," suggested She-Tung hesitantly. "We should break the route in which we were headed."

"Don't be a fool!" General Chin said reproachfully. "We can't use conventional tactics in this damned place. I agree with Major Siu-ch'un. If he's right and it *is* the American, Camellion, we're fighting, he'll expect us to come in from either the east or west flank. For that reason, we'll strike straight to the south. We'll find the base of the creatures who built that flying square before Camellion and his men can launch another attack from the air."

"The wounded men?" Major Siu-ch'un said.

"We'll pick them up when we come back," General Chin explained. His voice became very annoyed and impatient. "Both of you, hurry and get the men organized. I want to move out as quickly as possible."

Both officers saluted General Chin, then moved off, Siu-ch'un going in one direction, She-Tung hurrying south, a deep feeling of dread boiling over in his mind. It was General Chin who was the fool, an idiot because he was assuming that the American, the dog named Camellion, was a man who could be tricked. In She-Tung's analysis, Camellion was an incredibly clever enemy. The failure of Captain Tien-Shong's strike force at the monastery was proof. The ambush of Captain Yu-Ling's attack force was further proof. The slopes had been littered with dead—Chinese dead! Now this attack from the air!

Major She-Tung began screaming orders at the noncoms, telling them to get the men in the personnel carriers.

She-Tung suddenly thought of an old Chinese proverb: *A man must kill his own tigers.*

She-Tung had the feeling that he was one of the tigers. . . .

Chapter Eleven

The rumbling sounds of the barely audible engines filled the Death Merchant, and the people strung out with him, with a feeling of deep exhilaration. *I was right. The Reds are coming in straight from the north.*

Even Vallie West had resisted the idea of center-of-the-slot positions, adamant in his conviction that no Chinese commander in his right mind would make a straight-to-the-south attack. The head riceball would employ a flanking movement. "Come in from the east or the west," Vallie had argued. "Or from both sides. He has the men needed to execute a pincer movement."

Major Kor Sidkeong had gotten in his two cents' worth, pointing out that the Chinese could move far to the east, or to the west, as far as they could go. They could then head south until they came to the south wall of the cavern. The Chinese wouldn't be able to see the dome because they would be miles outside the two-mile limit. Once they reached the south wall, they would then turn around and go north.

"Such a method would be the safest kind of sweep," Major Sidkeong had said. "The Chinese are a patient and practical people."

At the time, Camellion had readily admitted that both West and Sidkeong might be right. "I can't prove that you're not. But I think you are. I'm counting on the commander being practical, but not patient. I don't think he has the time. I'm convinced that he will employ an unorthodox tactic, one he believes will take us by surprise. Common sense dictates that we're supposed to think he'll now use either an east or west approach, which is why I think he'll attack straight from the north."

Red Degenhardt had agreed with West and Sidkeong.

The Black Beret leader had then proceeded to bump his gums about "circular attack at an offsetting angle," "the enemy's sphere of defense" and "predetermined zones of contact"—to which Camellion had replied that Red was speaking of individual defense, when one man was attacked by two or three of the enemy.

"Exactly!" Red had responded in a deadly voice. "What do you think we'll be facing out there in the intercept from the north positions? We're outnumbered ten to one—and that's at a minimum!"

"I'll go along with that," Camellion had agreed, "but the chopstick boys aren't going to get that close."

He had then proceeded to explain—much to their astonishment—his basic plan. They had ten five-pound blocks of HBX. Why couldn't they space the blocks out, bury them, and explode each block individually by remote control, when a personnel carrier, or whatever, was crossing over it? The only tiny flaw was that the electronic components of the detonating station wouldn't work within the two-mile invisibility zone of the dome.

"We'll get into positions just outside the two-mile limit," the Death Merchant had said. "We'll turn on a Dynalite. Nothing that's electrical will work within the limit. As soon as the light goes on, we'll know we're outside the range of interference. We'll then bury the HBX seven hundred eighty meters ahead of us, spacing them out thirty feet apart, in places wide enough to allow a carrier or tank to go through. We'll—"

"I agree with Shireling," West had interrupted. "Screw meters! Use feet!"

"Okay—half a mile. We'll bury the blocks half a mile in front of our positions. When a carrier or armored car comes along—*bang*! That's all there is to it."

Degenhardt's brow had furrowed in puzzlement. "Like hell it is! How are we supposed to know when a carrier is close to a block of explosive—sit on top of a toadstool and rubberneck with a pair of binnocs?"

Loren Eaton had said worriedly, "It's the tank and the ACs that worry me. Those goddamn things carry cannon!"

"We have a dozen or so M-4 E.A. stations left over," Camellion had said. "We didn't use them all when we ambushed the Chinese a few nights ago. We can bury the

141

stations a dozen feet in front of the blocks. All we have to do is make sure we don't get confused when we press any certain button on the central detonating panel. If E.A. number-five is buried in front of number-seven transducer, and is connected to the relay-trigger transmitter in the block, we must press number-seven button on the detonating panel when number-five E.A. lights up on the E.A. receiver. That's not a problem. We can make a chart."

West had rubbed his long chin. "It could work. With luck!"

Degenhardt had glanced at both West and Camellion, disagreement swimming in his eyes. "Camellion, you're talking like a man with a retarded wisdom tooth! What assurance will we have that the Commies—provided that they do come down from the north—will even come close to any of the stuff?"

"None!" the Death Merchant had said flat out. "We can only hope that the chinnie pig farmers take the path of least resistance. If you have a better plan—speak up." He had swung his eyes at all of them. "Any of you—and I'm including you three." He jabbed a finger at Helena Banya, then at Paul Gemz and Emil Lauterjung. "If you have any ideas, now is the time to speak up loud and clear."

The three only looked at him.

Vallie West made a pensive face and scratched the top of his head. "We're not going to have luxury accommodations out there." He jerked a thumb toward the weird landscape outside the dome. "Every time I get into a mess like this, I end up with a mass of chigger bites."

"Chiggers?" Loren Eaton was surprised. "I doubt if there are any insects out there."

The Death Merchant got to his feet. The metal floor of the dome was not a comfort to one's rear end. "My idea of luxury is a house with two empty closets. But we can't have everything." Pausing, he hopped his gaze from face to face. "Let's get our act together. We don't have time for a session of hand-wringing."

"Camellion, have you thought about the Commie scouts?" Degenhardt got to his feet and pulled the stub of a cigar from his mouth. "There are almost thirty of those pigs out there."

"Suppose you tell me what *you* think they will do," said Camellion.

"They'll stay down in the area where they were when we started bombing the column. They'll wait for orders from their officers."

"Then what's the problem? The scouts were almost six miles in front of the dome. We won't come in contact with them when we plant the E.As. and the HBX. We'll use all the caution necessary, naturally."

Smoking a cigarette, Helena Banya stood up and brushed hair out of her face. "How are we supposed to get out of here, on one of the flying platforms?" She looked at the platform twenty feet away, the one Camellion had used to HBX bomb the China column. The fact that she didn't as much as give Camellion a glance or even speak with a trace of contempt in her voice showed all too clearly what she thought of him and his scheme. As far as she was concerned, Richard Camellion was a walking death-wish.

Camellion, sitting in the grass with his back against the five-foot-thick trunk of a giant chorrten toadstool, listened to the engines of the approaching Chinese armor. An excellent judge of distance, he estimated that the enemy was more than a mile to the north. Now, there wasn't anything to do but wait. He stared at the E.A. alarm panel on the box in front of him and, thinking of Helena Banya, smiled in amusement. *That Russian female pig farmer!* He had revealed his plan to Pel and Odox, and had asked them if there was any way he and his force could leave the dome without using a flying platform. Or was there a hidden door somewhere?

The two Guardians had then informed him that he and his people could leave the same way they had come in: by walking through the doorways in the Kkokro walls now blocking the tunnel. "Tell us when you are ready to leave," Pel had said. "There will be a doorway."

"Can we get back in the same way—and in a hurry if we have to?"

"Yes. We will be watching."

Vallie West sat Indian-style across from Camellion, the remote-control detonating station in front of him on the

143

grass. To Vallie's left, in various positions the length of a hundred feet were Degenhardt and his three Black Berets. To Val's right, stretched out in a longer length, were Banya, the two professors, Major Kor Sidkeong, and the four terrified Bhutanese soldiers, all eight concealed by toadstools, the plants with hideous white leaves and other vegetation that shouldn't have existed but did, such as the orange-colored fauna resembling kohlrabi. There were freaks, on ten-foot-high stalks, whose tops could have been cauliflower—the size of a Pinto! All the stalks were as unyielding as steel. It was impossible to cut them even with a razor-sharp Gerber throat-cutter.

Vallie saw that Camellion was smiling. "What's the joke?" he asked, rubbing a forearm across his aching eyes, wiping off sweat.

"I was thinking of how surprised everyone looked when the doorway miraculously appeared in the side of the dome," Camellion said. "Any science that can instantly rearrange molecules has to be out of this world—pardon the pun, old buddy."

Vallie cocked his head slightly to one side. "Hear 'em? The engines are getting louder," he said earnestly. "It's that damned tank and the armored cars that make the inside of my spine dance a jig. We had better blast those babies!"

The big man's manner changed. He relaxed, gave a short, bitter laugh, and looked up from the detonating station. "Say, did I ever tell you about the yo-yo in Du Quoin who had two wooden legs?"

Camellion grinned. "You will!"

Vallie laughed again and said, "He caught fire and burned to the ground!" He looked down at the detonating panel, his expression icy. "I think that in a very short time we're going to have company." He placed both hands close to the detonating device.

Camellion watched the panel of the Emergency Alarm system. The rumbling of engines was much closer—those telltale sounds that signaled that the drivers were either slowing down or shifting gears. The sounds were much louder as the drivers increased speed on stretches between mushrooms or other huge stalks of plants. Faintly now

144

came the familiar clank-clank-clank of treads, the heavy track links of a JS-3 tank.

"Fun time is about over," West said tiredly. "At least this is more exciting than shacking up with some doll. We don't know how this deal will turn out."

His face a calculating mask, the Death Merchant, watching the tiny bulbs set in the E.A. panel, did not look up. "Yeah, in intercourse the pleasure is momentary, the position ridiculous, and the expense a total waste of money. I hope those superstitious Bhutanese don't shoot each other!"

Number 9 E.A. light began flashing on and off. Camellion glanced at the piece of paper wired to one side of the panel. A troop carrier or an armored car or the tank had crossed the dozen-foot line-limit in front of number 3 transducer attached to a block of HBX.

"Number three, Val," Camellion said. "Give it a few seconds, and all the rest that will follow."

"One, two," Vallie said, grinned, and pressed number 3 button on the panel of the detonating device.

WEERRRRRRROOOOOOMMMMMMMM!

The big blast, to the east, rang in their ears and boomeranged hollowly in their heads. The plants ahead, and the general condition of the terrain, made it impossible for Camellion and Vallie to see the damage inflicted by the HBX, but Major Sidkeong, from his position, had seen the whole smash. A gray troop carrier had been rumbling along like some voracious behemoth. It had happened in a split second. There had been a flash of flame and a lot of smoke. The front of the carrier jumped six feet off the ground. The armored sides and two wheels shot upward as if impelled by rocket power, accompanied by Chinese soldiers who had been in the rear. Their uniforms slashed and shredded, their mangled bodies spraying blood, the heroes of the Chinese People's Liberation Army were pitched skyward. The bodies tumbled back to the ground, along with arms and legs that had been ripped off by the explosion. The last bloody object to fall was a decapitated head. It fell into the wreckage, which had begun to burn. There was another big flash of fire and a lot of noise. A tongue of flame had reached the fuel tank. The flames crackled, growing larger with each second, giving off thick smoke the color of soot.

Major Sidkeong used a large green handkerchief to wipe his face. He would like to have contacted Camellion by radio and informed him of the first success, but he couldn't. Camellion's order was not to break radio silence.

Sidkeong shifted his body to a more comfortable position in the grass. He checked for the third time to make sure the noise suppressor was firmly attached to the barrel of the Ingram submachine gun, all the time wishing he could erase the thought from his head—one of the dead Chinese had fallen to the ground curled in a fetal position.

Hur-gspas kyang!

The Death Merchant watched the panel, a tentative smile of anticipation fixed on his face. Right now was the crucial period. *The Red commander will either order a withdrawal or he'll continue the attack. He won't retreat, or he would have done so after we attacked from the air. Whoever he is, he's more afraid of Peking than of us.*

Emergency Alarm light number 6 began winking on and off. *The dull blob will now turn into the Fun Kid!* Camellion looked at the chart.

"Number fourteen, Val. Let her rip.

One, two! Vallie pushed down on the number-fourteen button of the detonator.

The explosion, far to the west, was sweet but smashing music to their ears.

"Scouts!" Vallie said emphatically. "They're using some of their armored stuff as scout cars. I hope one of those blasts wrote the end to the JS. With our-type luck, we'll get everything but that goddamn tank."

"Yeah, scouts. That explains the length of time between explosions. Fu Man Chu will now send in the whole damned force—one big frontal assault." He paused and used his sleeve to wipe sweat from his forehead. "Our luck's not all that bad," he said briskly. "We've only ten blocks. We won't get all their armor. We'll have to beat it back inside the dome. The halfwits from Mao's anthill will follow."

"Great!" mocked Vallie. He looked at Camellion, his eyes hard. "Where does that leave us? We'll be inside and

146

unable to get out. The riceballs will be on the outside and won't be able to get in! Where does a Mexican-standoff leave us? Crap! You'll be telling me next that it's 'all in the hands of God!' "

"We'll be as well off as the Chinese, that's where," Camellion said reassuringly. "You and the others have forgotten what happens inside the two-mile zone surrounding the dome—haven't you?"

The big CIA case officer looked at Camellion, his expression one of rapid thought. "Of course!" He grinned from ear to ear. "The moment a carrier—any of their armor—gets inside the zone, the engine will quit. The ignitions won't work. Everything they've got will be permanently stalled!"

His smile vanished and was replaced with a dubious stare. "You have a hidden bee buzzing around in your bonnet, a scheme you haven't clued me in on."

Emergency Alarm number 7 began flashing. Camellion glanced at the chart. "Push number four, Val."

The explosion came from half a mile ahead and, by the time the echo had gotten off to a good start, a lot of Chinese were dead. Half a dozen others, blown from the carrier, were alive but dying, including the two who were still conscious. They lay crumpled on the ground, bleeding to death.

The Death Merchant had been correct. All the Chinese armor rolled ahead, each vehicle moving as fast as possible, every driver desperately hoping that his vehicle wouldn't be one of the unlucky ones.

Not all the carriers contained soldiers. Some were empty except for the drivers and the machine gunners standing in the turrets built behind the cabs. The P.L.A. soldiers, using the carriers as shields, followed, bunched together and keeping low—brainwashed robots carrying submachine guns, automatic rifles, carbines, and stick grenades. In addition, noncoms had 7.62mm Chinese Tokarev pistols—copies of the Soviet TT M1933 Tokarev.

Number 8 block of HBX ripped apart one of the Russian Vorshorsky L-type armored cars, the way a shotgun blast would tear apart a tin can. The terrific concussion was of such magnitude that it scattered hot steel, flesh and blood, and bones for a radius of a hundred feet and

147

tossed the heavy 76mm gun as though it were a straw—right into a group of Chinese who were behind a carrier forty feet to the left. Two privates and a noncom were crushed to death. Four more screamed in pain as the barrel swung around and raked them like a blunt sickle, snapping their leg and hip bones. The whole pack yelled in fear and confusion, their frantic shouts drowned in another *WWERRRROOOOMMMMMM* as another carrier—this one full of HBX fodder flew to pieces in a flash of fire and smoke. It was all over within half a microsecond. All that remained was blazing junk and a lot of mutilated corpses.

"Number eight," Camellion said, then yawned. West pressed number eight button on the panel of the detonator. The transducer sent out its electrical impulse. The relay-trigger transmitter did what it was supposed to do and the five-pound block of HBX completed the job. Another flash and another thunderous concussion. Another carrier and its cargo of Red Chinese dummies became twisted steel and mangled flesh.

Within the next four minutes, West pressed buttons 9, 6, 12, and 24, all the while singing (off key), "The toe bone's connected to the foot bone, the foot bone's connected to the shin bone, the shin bone's connected . . ."

Four more carriers became scrap metal and eighty-three Chinese joined the ranks of the dead, the entire mess adding to the stink of burning rubber and paint, of cloth and leather.

Number 19 E.A. light went on. "Number five," the Death Merchant said lightly. Vallie rammed the tip of his finger down on number 5 button in the detonating panel. Once more there was a crashing explosion, one that seemed to stab directly into West and Camellion's mind. This time they could hear, very clearly, screams of agony, metal crashing against metal, and metal smashing into metal. Every now and then there were smaller explosions and series of loud poppings. The explosions were the 76mm shells going off in the wreckage of the armored car. *The pop-pop-pop-popping* wasn't the sound of popcorn but that of 7.65mm machine-gun cartridges exploding from heat.

"We have one block left." Vallie looked at Camellion, a

nervous, impatient glint in his eyes. "Then we're going to need a lot of luck."

"There goes number-four light," Camellion said savagely. "Hit eleven, fellow sufferer."

As West pushed his finger down on the button, the Death Merchant dropped the now-useless E.A. central station, picked up the Ingram submachine gun lying in the grass, turned around, and lay flat, keeping most of his long frame behind the trunk of the chorrten plant.

Vallie picked up his Ingram, to which was attached a noise suppressor, duck-walked to the other side of the mushroom trunk, then stretched out in a position similar to Camellion's.

The Death Merchant had given one order to the members of his force: don't let the Chinese get close enough to use hand grenades. The strategy of the Chinese was not unpredictable. Once the HBX explosions had stopped, the Chinese Reds would feel that Camellion had given them his best shot. The Chinese would then, in theory, charge forward with renewed vigor and confidence, more than anxious for revenge. The danger to the Death Merchant was the Chinese armor that was intact, particularly the tank.

"Let's hope the Commie commander gets overconfident and has the foot boys make a mass-wave charge ahead of the armor," Vallie said. "I guess I might as well wish for the moon."

"As well as the rest of the solar system," Camellion said. "He'll send scouts ahead. That's why I gave orders for everyone to stay well hidden and not fire until the scouts are right on top of us. By that time, the rest of the Chinese might be ahead of the armored stuff, provided the scouts have given the all-clear."

"Hey! I think I see one!" Vallie whispered.

"I know. I saw three to the west, about twenty-seven meters—approximately ninety feet—away." Camellion chuckled softly. "Those idiots think they're being clever."

The Death Merchant and his thirteen people were spread out in a 250-foot-long line, and soon all of them were catching sight of gray-green blobs darting first one way and then the other, moving like zigzagging road-

149

runners from mushroom to mushroom, from "kohlrabi" to "cauliflower."

Red Degenhardt and his Black Berets, all four almost holding their breath, watched as a dozen Chinese regulars dropped down in the grass less than sixty feet away. That did it! Degenhardt told himself that he would open fire if the enemy moved as much as ten feet closer.

Once more, the Death Merchant had been proved correct. He and his men could now see scores of Chinese soldiers running forward, a hundred yards behind the scouts. It was not possible to estimate their number because of the giant plants and the rough terrain. Half a mile ahead there were, in various places, huge megalithic blocks of stone. Toward the area in which Camellion and his force were waiting, the stones were much smaller, yet here and there were jagged chunks of flint-hard micrite and small slabs of granite.

Any moment now! Camellion switched off the Ingram's safety, thumbed the selector switch to full automatic, and pulled three spare magazines of 9mm ammo from the bag nestled against his left hip. The last Chinese scouts that he and West had seen were down in the thick grass forty feet away. *Will the scouts wait for the main body? Yeah, I think so.*

A few moments later, he saw three of the scouts up front begin to dodge and weave forward. *So I was wrong—dammit!*

"Let's do it, Val." A split second before Camellion's finger pulled the Ingram's trigger, he heard high-pitched screams of agony to the west. Chinese scouts were too close to Red and his boys. *Degenhardt's started the show.*

The Chinese in front of Camellion and West, hearing the cries of pain, tried to drop and bury themselves in the rocks and the grass. They were too slow. Camellion and West fired, the famous WerBell noise suppressors making loud buzzing sounds. On Camellion's side of the mushroom-toadstool chorrten plant, three Chinese Reds jerked wildly from the impact of 9mm slugs stabbing through their uniforms, into their bodies. Ten feet to the left of the three instant corpses, four more P.L.A. fighters jumped and twisted hideously from West's fatal burst of hollow-point projectiles.

By this time Camellion's entire force was firing, and Commie scouts and soldiers from the main body were being killed faster than a fruit jar full of moonshine at a Kentucky hoedown.

Knowing they had walked into a cleverly laid trap, the Chinese threw away caution and began a running, massed charge, pausing now and then to fire short bursts and yelling at the top of their lungs, supposedly to terrify the enemy. Yet the yelling and the short blasts from their weapons were very necessary, so the Chinese thought. It was the only defense they had against an enemy they could not see, against automatic weapons equipped with silencers.

The Death Merchant shoved another magazine into the Ingram, pulled back the cocking knob, then zeroed in on a broken wall of gray-green moving toward the line 150 feet away. His first projectiles popped one noodle-nasty, who fell sideways against another soldier, who was already dead and sagging from several 9mm bullets in his chest. Another Chinaman tried to dart to one side, but caught three slugs—one in the hip, one in the left side, and the third in his neck. The stinking air, filled with smoke and junk-yard odors, was alive with 9mm Ingram slugs. It didn't matter in which direction the Chinese ran; sooner or later, they charged right into HP Ingram slugs.

The Chinese soldiers tried another tactic. They began lobbing fragmentation grenades, throwing them as far ahead as they could. The explosions generated a lot of crushed rock, grass, and shredded leaves, but every grenade exploded short, a good hundred feet in front of the Death Merchant's line of defense. Steadily, however, in spite of the furious fighting of the Death Merchant and his men, the explosions grew closer as the Chinese gained ground in their advance.

Fortunately for Camellion and Company, neither the armored car nor the tank could lay down a short-distance barrage because the shells would have fallen into the midst of the charging soldiers; and although the Chinese gunners didn't know where the silent enemy was positioned, they could lob shells far ahead of the soldiers, in the hope that some of them might demoralize Camellion and crew. They could, and they did.

The first shell, from the armored car's 76mm gun, exploded a full mile behind Camellion's defense line. The second big blast—this one from the tank's cannon—was farther to the west but only a half mile or so to the rear of the line. The only damage it did was to the flora of the monstrous cavern, blowing apart one of the large chorrten plants.

"Like shadows do in poems," Vallie West called out, to make himself heard above screaming Chinese and bursting grenades. "They silently steal away. That's what we'd better do. That last grenade was only fifty feet away."

He swung the muzzle of the WerBell noise suppressor in a four-foot sweep and kept his finger on the trigger. A dozen slugs stabbed into nine Chinese, who jerked back as if they had collided with an invisible wall.

"Reload and hold the fort," the Death Merchant called back. "I'll give the word."

He wriggled himself behind the trunk of the chorrten plant, picked up the Electro-5 from the grass, flipped the Ext-Off-Int switch, put the set close to his mouth, and pushed the push-to-talk button.

"Apple cider," was all he said. He repeated the phrase three more times in quick succession, then switched off the radio, shoved it into its bulky case on his belt, stood up, and yelled at West, "Let's get the hell out of here."

"Apple cider" meant only one thing to Degenhardt, Gemz, and Sidkeong, the three of whom had kept the channels of their Electro-5s open—*Get back to the dome with all possible speed.* They in turn would give the "go" sign to the people around them.

It wasn't a stroll down memory lane! Camellion, and the thirteen people with him, ran over the rough ground, all of them doing their best to keep the mushroomlike chorrten plants between them and the Chinese, who were definitely on the offensive, having deduced that Camellion was in full retreat. Screaming and yelling, the Chinese fired burst after burst with submachine guns and assault rifles. Only occasionally did the riceballs catch a quick glimpse of a fleeting figure. But they hoped that some of their 7.62mm slugs would find the flesh of the enemy. So far none had, although many had come dangerously close.

152

It wasn't at all difficult for Camellion and his people to keep the huge plants between them and the Chinese—there were so many plants. On the other hand, there wasn't any barrier between them and the arrowhead shells whistling in from the armored car and the sabot-shot[37] crashing in from the tank. There were big bangs and brief, bright flashes to the left and the right of the fleeing members of the small force. Shells exploded ahead, others only a short distance behind. It was apparent to Camellion that the Chinese noncoms, charging in behind him and his men, were in radio contact with the tank and the armored car and were giving the estimated yardage to the gunners—a very dangerous practice, because a shell could always fall in the midst of the attacking soldiers.

On the other side of the coin, the Death Merchant's force did have one factor on their side: the fact that the shells weren't of the artillery variety. Not only did Howitzer shells burst over a much larger area than the antitank shells the Chinese were using, but they were jammed full of shrapnel which arrowhead shot and sabot-shot didn't have.

Slightly behind the others, Camellion and West, who had paused several times to rake the riceballs with Ingram fire, tore in the direction of the north side of the dome, their long legs eating up the ground, foot by foot. Chinese slugs burned the smoky air around them and shells exploded in front, slightly behind, and on each side of them. One explosion was so close to West and Camellion that the concussion almost knocked them off their feet. They staggered and kept going. A hundred feet to their right, the burst of a sabot-shell did slam Loren Eaton and Red Degenhardt to the ground, face down. Pros that they were, Red and Loren stumbled to their feet and again moved forward. Ahead lay safety. Behind was certain death.

The shelling stopped. Apparently it had occurred to the Chinese that it was rather silly to lob shells into such an

[37] Sabot-shot: the tank-killer supreme. Called that because in the barrel it is a full-calibre, lightweight projectile. On leaving the barrel, everything except the tungsten subprojectile is discarded, giving the subshell a good staying power to penetrate at long ranges, then explode.

153

enormous area in an effort to kill so few people, particularly when one of the shells might kill P.L.A. soldiers.

Camellion and West could now see the dome through the forest of giant plants several hundred feet in front of them. Inhaling great gulps of air, they plunged onward, neither man amazed at the distance they and the others had covered in so short a time. They had run this same kind of race many times before, in other parts of the world. They knew how fear and determination could work to produce extra adrenalin and give the body extra strength. Camellion and West's only concern was Professor Lauterjung. With his emphysema, how could he have kept pace with the others?

Nearing the vast north side of the dome, West and Camellion saw that Professor Lauterjung hadn't kept up with the others. They saw that he was draped over the right shoulder of Foster Cross, who, with his burden, was only 125 feet from the dome. Cross wasn't as big as Degenhardt, just as Red weighed in at twenty pounds less than West, who was built like the Empire State Building. Yet Cross was wide and stocky and as strong as a baby ox.

Forty feet to the right of Cross was Degenhardt and the two other Black Berets. Coming in at an angle on the other side was Major Sidkeong and his small troop. Running next to them, not far away, was Paul Gemz. The big surprise of the day was Helena Banya. She was thirty feet in front of Cross!

"That Russian bitch!" panted Vallie West, sounding envious. "She must have invisible wings. She's outrun us all."

Helena Banya quickly closed the distance to the wall of the dome, leaping over rocks, streaking under the big round umbrellas of chorrtens. She couldn't have been fifty feet from the dome when, in a twinkling of an eye, a doorway appeared in the mysterious Kkokro metal.

Banya didn't slow down, not until she had sailed through the doorway. Only then did she stop, lean against the inside of the wall, and gasp for oxygen. Foster Cross and Lauterjung were next to gain entrance to the inside safety of the dome. They were followed by Degenhardt and the rest of the force, the Death Merchant and Vallie West being last.

The entrance vanished, shutting off the yells and shouts of the Chinese who were several hundred yards behind.

No one spoke. Everyone was too busy gulping air. In the distance, a block away, they saw Urba and four other Goros strolling leisurely toward them, as slowly as monks walking in a meditation garden.

Camellion glanced at Lauterjung, whom Cross had placed at his back. The scientist had regained consciousness but his lips were bluish and his face a pasty white.

"Rick, what's our next move?" Breathing heavily, West fumbled for his sweat-soggy cigarettes.

Degenhardt said, to no one in particular, "In spite of all the gooks we killed, there must be a hundred of them left out there."

The Death Merchant turned and coldly eyed the approaching Guardians. "They have to wake up one of the aliens! We must have a superior weapon."

"Suppose they won't?" Degenhardt asked, his tone neutral, his eyes watchful.

"Then we're as good as dead. . . ."

Chapter Twelve

Standing straight and tall in the center of the room, Urba did not reveal what he might be thinking, the wrinkled parchment of his face as immobile as a slab of shale. The faces of the other four Guardians had the same lackluster, the same lack of expression.

"All of you are safe inside this dome," Urba said after a short pause. "The Chinese cannot get in. There is not any need to awaken one of the Inelqu."

The Death Merchant, who was standing, couldn't help the anger and frustration from flashing in his eyes. Vallie West and the rest of the group stared at Urba in disbelief. The Guardians were intelligent? They were plain stupid! First class fools!

"And we can't get out!" Camellion said acidly. He glared at Urba and put his hands on his hips.

"All of you are welcome to stay with us," Urba said simply.

Red Degenhardt could no longer contain himself. "We don't intend to spend the rest of our lives in this creepy place!" he said, exploding with anger. His big body shot up from the molded chair and he glared defiantly at Urba. "Haven't you the sense God even gives to morons? Don't you know that our lives—and yours—won't be worth a cracked egg once the Reds get inside? Eventually they will, you damn fool!"

"With an H-bomb if they have to!" Camellion said. He raised a hand to silence Degenhardt and moved several steps closer to the group of Guardians. The rest of the group shifted uneasily in their chairs, all but Emil Lauterjung, who had been placed on a low, sofalike piece of furniture, and Troju Gyud and Tolung Terskug, two of the

Bhutanese soldiers, who were stuffing their mouths with green "Jello."

"Tilhut told us that nuclear power could destroy this dome," the Death Merchant went on doggedly, his voice soft but deadly. "The Chinese outside right now can't do us any harm, but they'll return to the surface and report their find. You can't stop them because you can't kill." He began shaking a long finger at Urba. "The Chinese will return with a much larger force and surround this dome. Scientists will come, and sooner or later, after all else fails, they'll resort to nuclear power. They'll blow up this entire cavern if they have to."

"You're supposed to be guarding the Inelqu," snapped Helena Banya from across the room. "I suggest you start doing so and start acting like Guardians."

The Russian girl was slightly flushed and was breathing heavily from pent-up tension, her ample bosom rising and falling. Her clothes were disordered, her hair dishevelled, and her face smoke-smudged.

"She's right and so is Camellion," cut in Vallie West, getting to his feet. "It's better to stop a few Chinese now than thousands later." Facing the Guardians, he made angry motions with his hands. Urba and his companions were so unemotional that Vallie had the impression he was talking to animated mannequins. "I'll tell you something else. Once the chinnies get back to their world and tell what they have discovered, the whole world will know about this dome. Your secret will be out. The Soviet Union has agents in Chinese Intelligence, and so have we, the United States. You can't fight the world, Urba."

Urba did not reply. He and the other four Guardians closed their eyes. They didn't move. West gave Camellion a long look. Were the Guardians communicating with each other or, possibly, with the Inelqu?

"God Almighty!" grumbled Norbert Shireling. "Who'd believe this back home?"

"The hell with them," Degenhardt said flippantly, then sat down heavily in the chair, his tough face twisting with unconcealed rage.

For a full two minutes Urba and the other Guardians stood with their eyes closed. About the time that even the phlegmatic Major Sidkeong was becoming impatient, the

Guardians opened their eyes and Urba said, "We will awaken one of the Inelqu."

The Death Merchant and his force followed Urba and the Guardians to the largest nontranslucent dome, located toward the "south" end of the main oval.

The entire group was only twenty feet from the dome when a doorway blinked into existence, the entrance remaining open until every single one of them was inside the giant circle-shaped chamber. As instantaneously as it had appeared, the doorway vanished. The wall was again solid.

"This is the sleeping place of the Inelqu," Urba said reverently.

In the soft blue glow radiating from the inside surface of the dome, Camellion and his party gazed at devices whose original concepts had not originated in the minds of human beings. Excluding the Death Merchant, none were prepared for the sensations generated by staring at the vast aggregation of cyclopean machines and alien architecture that embodied bizarre perversions of geometric laws.

"Sweet sad Jesus!" choked out Foster Cross, overcome with awe.

There wasn't any way to describe the reality of the moment; there was no language for such abysms of hideous impossibility, such grotesque contradictions of universal order. No words in existence to depict the broad impressions of colossal angles too great to belong to any earthly science. The Guardians and the master dome had been eerie enough, but at least the Goros were human beings. Here, inside this dome, it was different. All its contents belonged to something horribly remote and distinct from mankind, to something frightfully suggestive of ancient and unhallowed cycles of life in which Earth and human concepts had no part, no existence.

The fourteen human beings stared at machines that were truncated cones surmounted by tall cylinders capped with tiers of black scalloped disks; enormous metal constructions, suggesting piles of multitudinous rectangular slabs, or circular plates, with each one overlapping the one beneath. There were hundreds of composite cones pulsating with a greenish glow, the radiance throbbing from florid to pale, then back again to lambent, as if the shimmering were emanating from a beating heart; and pyramids—either alone or surmounting cylinders. There were pink cubes of various sizes, needlelike devices and double-pyramids that defied all laws of balance and gravity, in that the top pyramid rested upside down on the bottom pyramid, the apex of the top conoid supported by the utmost point of the bottom pyramid.

All of these alien structures were knitted together by more cones and cylinders, and smaller tubular bridges crossing from one to another at various dizzy heights—every bit of it terrifying in its sheer gigantic size, and, in the minds of Camellion's people, tainted with a latent malignity and infinite evil. But not to the Death Merchant, who refused to be drawn into the reality of another space, of another time, and stood mentally firm against the menacing symbolism of the alien machines.

It was the metal boxes—one hundred metal caskets stretched out in a row across the floor—that demanded the full attention of each person. Slightly longer than five feet, each casket, as shiny as polished chrome, rested on a glistening three-foot-high metal framework and had, for its full length, a curved transparent top. There were tubes and twisting conduits that led from the machines to the top metal section of each casket.

At a signal from Urba, the group timidly approached the caskets, walking slowly and solemnly, automatically exhibiting the same kind of veneration that jumps from simple Russian folk who, when visiting the tomb of Lenin in Red Square, gaze down in idolization at his mummified corpse.

There were exclamations of expected shock and some fear, and quick inhalations of surprise as the group looked down at the alien lying underneath the pellucid lid of the first casket.

Identical to what I saw in India! thought Camellion, his mind racing. *Here and in India! Underneath the Arctic Ocean. Where else on this planet—and why? Definitely, the creature is a Sandorian!*

The alien was dressed in a bright blue, skin-tight uniform without buttons or zippers. But it was the body inside the uniform that made everyone feel helpless and

159

guilty over having invaded the privacy of these creatures, of this "thing" beneath their eyes.

Not more than four feet tall, the alien had gray skin, the tiny mouth of a baby, and thin lips, a shade lighter than the skin. Where a human being would have a nose, there was a V-shaped slit.

The same eyes! screamed Camellion's thoughts. Enormous black eyes, but very, very different from the eyes of a human being. Without any visible irises or pupils, the eyes of the Sandorian looked like two gigantic black marbles—the size of a baby's fist—stuck on a face of putty-colored dough. The skull, in proportion to the heavy chest, was hairless and crisscrossed with a network of raised blood vessels that pulsed under the skin. The alien lacked earlobes, nor were there any openings in the side of his head, the skin being perfectly smooth.

Helena Banya broke the oppressive silence. "I think he's rather cute," she said nervously, glancing from Camellion to Paul Gemz. "He's shaped like a small man, almost. I mean except for his face. He doesn't have a nose and his eyes protrude. But he's not actually ugly. Do any of you think so?"

No, the Sandorian could not be described as ugly, not technically. Words that mean a lack of beauty stem from human concepts and can be applied to only the vegetable, the mineral, and the animal kingdoms of this world.

The alien was not repulsive. He was different. His body was humanoid, and although the creature was not deformed like a dwarf, by human standards of body ratio the creature's well-muscled arms and legs were too heavy for the rest of the body. The feet, encased in short, pale blue boots, were too large—bigger than those of an average-size man.

Degenhardt said, in that kind of voice that comes when the speaker has a dry mouth and throat, "I once read a book titled *We Are Not Alone*. I guess all this proves it!"

Commented Major Sidkeong, "I wonder how these beings, without meaning to, have contributed to the various mythologies of the world?"

No one commented, and Sidkeong did not elaborate. All were intrigued by the strange creature in the casket, and there were ninety-nine more of the aliens. None of the humans were actually afraid, none save the four Bhutanese soldiers. Scared stiff of ghosts, goblins, and of only Buddha knows what, they had taken out their prayer wheels and were frantically mumbling prayers to all the protective gods they could think of.

In a state of tense excitement, Paul Gemz was at the foot of the first casket, gaping in wonderment at the diminutive figure, whose utter strangeness and air of genuine abysmal antiquity offered the rare opportunity to pry open the door to another world, to another civilization, to another science.

"The greatest discovery in the history of the world," Gemz said, so ecstatic and overcome with emotion that his voice shook, "and poor Professor Lauterjung is not here."

He looked at Urba and pointed to the tubes that protruded from various machines and terminated in the top of the first casket. Similar networks of lines ended in the tops of the other ninety-nine caskets.

"I trust that is part of the apparatus that keeps the Inelqu in a state of suspended animation?" he asked.

"Yes, but with some qualification," Urba said. "It is not the kind of suspended life-function you are thinking about. The mind is functioning, but on a level of thought different from yours. Some of the tubes connected to the caskets are beaming information to the Inelqu, the data of radio and television broadcasts from all the stations of the world." Urba turned his head toward Camellion. "Yes, a form of sleep teaching, Richard Camellion, yet different, and ten thousand times more effective. We will not awaken this individual Inelqu. The decision to give you weapons must be his."

Urba and two other Guardians moved to a large cube on which rested a pyramid. Long tubes, pulsating with various colors, projected from the four triangular faces of the pyramid on whose point rested a large, glowing yellow ball. The Guardians took positions on three sides of the cube and began to move their hands—palms toward the cube, back and forth in the curving motion of a windshield wiper. Fingers pointed toward the cube, palms facing each other, the Guardians made horizontal movements, then vertical motions, then circles as well as other kinds of movements.

161

"Your answer is correct, Richard Camellion"—the voice said in the Death Merchant's mind. *"We are changing the wave-flow of pure energy."*

"Look!" shouted Foster Cross, pointing at the first casket.

The curved cover was swinging open and over to the right.

Fourteen pairs of eyes riveted themselves on the body of the alien, and their owners found themselves stepping back involuntarily, as though the creature in the casket might reach out and grab one of them.

The cover opened to maximum. The alien sat up in the casket and looked at the group. Helena Banya gasped loudly and put a hand to her mouth. The others—their quick, combined intakes of breath very audible—gasped in immovable fascination at the being from another world. Whether the Sandorian was staring at them was purely academic. The black doorknoblike eyes did not mirror emotion or expression. The alien, his hands on the rims of the open casket, sat motionless, and for the first time Camellion noticed that the six fingers and one thumb on each hand of the creature were very long. Fingernails and knuckles were not in evidence. On a human being the hands would have been grossly abnormal.

Now, all of them noticed that the alien did not possess a neck, the head attached squarely on the top of the torso; also that the center of each eye throbbed with a lighter color, a slit that was constantly changing width and length, fading from a light black to dark gray, then to shades of lighter gray, until the color was almost white. At other times the whiteness would shift, and both eyes would be ink-black. It was a process that reminded the Death Merchant of slow-moving shutters in the lens of a camera.

The wave of intense vertigo, striking each member of the force, was unexpected, excruciating to comprehend and impossible to control, an effect that was like a trillion voices stabbing inside the brain with nonsense and confusion. The alien was probing their minds. Vallie West, standing between Camellion and Helena Banya, swayed back and forth as if buffeted by a strong wind. Degenhardt, Eaton, and Sidkeong, their bodies weaving like tops

162

about to topple, put their hands to their temples. Eyes tightly closed, mouths open, they tried to blot out the billion voices bombarding their brains. Troju Gyud and Podku Kalimpong lost consciousness and slumped to the floor.

As quickly as it had begun, the feeling of physical giddiness and mental drainage passed. The alien turned his head to the Guardians, all of whom had closed their eyes. Plainly, the being was communicating telepathically with the Goros, a two-way communication that lasted almost five long minutes.

Trying to watch both the alien and the Guardians, Camellion and his comrades shifted about the small area, in an effort to compose themselves. Major Kor Sidkeong, Gom Shinje, and Tolung Terskug went about reviving Troju Gyud and Podku Kalimpong. The entire group was uncertain of the reality into which they had been thrust. They were frightened and repelled and angered, their humanness telling them that the alien and his kind were intruders. Earth was not their native planet. They had no right to be here. They were cosmic trespassers!

Once more the alien directed his attention to Camellion and his group and, much to their surprise, spoke in English.

"Fear caused the two on the floor to pass into unconsciousness. I will not do harm."

The voice was high and had an odd timbre, but not deep or throaty. None of that mechanical quality that tinged the voices of the Guardians. Each word had come out precise and very clear.

"Who—who are you?" Gemz spoke with heavy deliberation. He trembled from nervousness. "Why are you and your kind on Earth?"

"He's not going to tell you anything" Red Degenhardt said hoarsely, his wide unbelieving eyes on the alien, gaping at the extraterrestrial as though he were a demon that had just popped up from Hades.

"Do you have a name?" The Death Merchant moved closer to the casket. Just before he had taken the first step, Helena Banya had noticed that Camellion's face had somehow changed. Something subtly merciless had ingrained itself into his features. And his eyes! She found

163

it difficult to accept that his eyes had a peculiar blue sheen, a blue fire burning with hypnotic brilliance.

Words poured from the Sandorian, the tiny mouth moving rapidly, each syllable as polished as a diamond.

The alien did not have a name! He didn't need one. "We are One. We are minds, forces, wills. I am I. I am we. We are One. There are trillions of individual parts, and these parts comprise the whole. The whole is I. The whole is we. We are the Inelqu. *We* are, yet we are individuals with personalities."

The alien said that human beings would not be able to understand them as a concept. They could not conceive it or experience it. They were prisoners of a reality established at "this stage of human development," of modern psychology, which teaches that person and personality must be tied to psychophysical acts—thinking, desiring, willing, wanting, imagining, plus the exterior acts that are a result of these mental processes. "Person" is an individual self-awareness of being a self-contained entity. In this sense, based only on human logic and perception, "person" and "personality" are material, measurable, three-dimensional, and finally, perishable.

The Inelqu had passed beyond this stage of mental evolution "almost ten million of your Earth years ago."

The alien's words became even more incredible; fantastically monstrous, because they knew he was telling the truth. With some strange preternatural certainty, they knew that he was not lying.

The Inelqu had landed on Earth 1.9 million years ago, in search of metals vitally necessary to their advanced electronic civilization, metals that were electroconductive as well as metals that were light- and heat-resistant.

"We did not find man on Earth. We found apelike animals. These animals were your ancestors. Using a science you humans are only now beginning to understand, we changed the gene structure of these animals. To use terms familiar to your terminology—by artificial insemination of female ape-men, we created Homo sapiens—your 'modern man'—to work for us."

Stunned, Loren Eaton said sharply, "Slaves! You turned men into slaves!" Unconsciously, he knotted his fists.

"We changed animals into higher physical development.

164

We made it possible for their minds to think on a crude level. The word *slave* is a relative term. *Slavery* implies one part of a species forcing another part of the same species into total subjugation. Is the horse that pulls a wagon a slave? Or the cow that is held a prisoner for her milk?

"Men of this planet have confused thought-processes, and insist in arranging their lives based on concepts in which truth is not truth, but only conveniences needed to prove the validity of their own concepts of morality.

"Man, as man, is a danger to man. Men did make slaves of men. Men kill men, members of their own species. Man kills lower animals for food consumption, doing so in the belief that he is a special creation, and far above the animals he slaughters. Man *is* a special creation. He was created whole, and in the image of his god. But the god was not one being, but rather a part of a race who came from another planet. That race was we, the Inelqu. We, who are called the Sons of God in the religious book called the Bible. That is how we are remembered in racial memory."

The Death Merchant laughed deeply within the hollows of his throat.

"Your race is mentioned in the Bible in another manner, too," he said to the the alien, speaking as much to his companions as he was to the Sandorian. "The Book of Genesis, in the Bible, mentions the *nefilim*. In some languages, it translates to 'giants', but the ancient Hebrew word means 'those who descended from heaven.'"

The first artificially created men were neuter hybrids, like mules, incapable of reproducing themselves. The Inelqu intended it that way. Then, after many thousands of years, and much to the horror of the Inelqu, man developed the ability to procreate.

"I—I can't believe it!" Red Degenhardt shook his head from side to side, his voice weak with confusion, his consciousness a dead blanket of depression. "He's destroying all our beliefs."

"You mean you don't want to believe what he just said!" Camellion's tone was thick with contempt. "The truth is that the Inelqu has given us an explanation that solves the apparent discrepancies in the Bible and in the

165

books of other religions. It also clears up the impossible contradictions between the workings of Darwinian evolution and observed history of life on earth. The inexplicable, sudden appearance of Homo sapiens, in the shape of Cro-Magnon man some 1.8 million years ago, cannot be explained scientifically. There's no way."

"Yes," broke in Paul Gemz triumphantly. "I agree with you, Camellion. The Darwin explanation is all external and mechanistic. It's a species explanation that maintains that genetically separated races became sufficiently divergent so that when they came together again, they would not cross and would be separate species. But just the reverse is true. Whenever you find endemic species, species native to the area, you'll find forms living with them that are their closest relatives."

"Is there really any proof?" asked a wild-eyed Norbert Shireling.

"Plenty," replied Camellion. "But now is not the time to go into it."

"One time I explored caves of the Appalachians—mountains in the United States," he said to the Russian woman. "I discovered a whole new fauna of cave beetles. They were isolated, completely blind, and could not live outside the caves. Sunlight killed them. Then, two years later, I discovered that this fauna had counterparts in Europe, counterparts very closely related. It is impossible that these insects could have developed independently, as Darwin would have us accept. They must have been together at one time. I think they were together because the Atlantic Ocean was once part of a huge continent—Atlantis!"

The Death Merchant had to admit that, while Gemz had a way about him that would have driven Job insane, he was a very educated man.

Camellion said, "I have studied, at various times, the fauna of the Caribbean, the Bahama Plateau, the Azores, and the Canary Islands. They are all related to each other. And it's more than the theory of continental drift. To me, it's very good evidence of the breaking up of a huge continent between today's continents." He looked at the Inelqu, who sat motionless, mouth closed. "Was there such a continent?"

The alien did not answer the question. Instead, he said that artificially created man revolted against the Inelqu and "We had to expel these savage creatures from the various complexes we had established on this planet, which was then the fourth planet revolving around the star in this locked system."

"*The Fall of Adam and Evel*" whispered Helena Banya, interrupting without thinking. She blinked at the strange being. "How can you explain ancient legends that ascribe incredible life-spans to the rulers of Earth before the Flood. Soviet scientists have established that there was a Deluge. They also believe that there was a huge continent that sank into the ocean."

The alien stated that time on the giant home planet of the Inelqu was scaled in the same manner that it is determined on Earth. While it takes a year for Earth to orbit the sun, "it requires forty-three hundred of your Earth years for our planet to orbit its star in the group you call the Pleiades. We used our own time system on Earth. This system was the one first learned by primitive man-creatures, and was retained by the early race for thousands of years, until men had developed sufficiently to calculate the length of time required for their native planet to travel through its entire ecliptic."

A thousand years after the revolt of created man, 21,000 thousand years before the birth of Christ, war on a cosmic scale came to the Inelqu. Beings from another space-time continuum "crossed into this universe." The home planet of the Inelqu, and the planets in the galaxy on which they had established colonies, were attacked. In the solar system, some of the titanic struggle was fought on a few of the outer planets. One planet was completely blown apart, the debris forming the beautiful rings of Saturn and the almost invisible rings of Uranus and Neptune. But most of the war "in this system was fought on a planet between Venus and Earth, with weapons whose power sources have only recently been discovered by Earth's scientists. Earth possesses this power in only a very primitive way, The difference between our weapons, and the most advanced weapons possessed by the various nations of the world, is the same as the variance between a thrown spear and the explosion of a hydrogen bomb."

The surface of the third planet was completely destroyed. Its atmosphere drifted off into space. The very planet was knocked out of orbit, this interference with the order of celestial bodies causing havoc among the inner planets circling the Sun. Great chunks of Venus were pulled loose by the close proximity of the runaway planet, which turned in space and headed outward from the Sun, at an angle that did not bring it close to Earth, but caused it to intersect the orbit of Mars. The Red Planet was devastated. All life-forms were destroyed.

During this period, Earth suffered terrible earthquakes and tremendous storms. Thousand of volcanos erupted. Man, cowering in fear, believed his angry god was causing the destruction.

After many hundreds of years, the maverick planet that had destroyed Mars was captured by the gravitational field of Earth, and settled into orbit around the blue world.

"This planet is the satellite men call Moon," the alien said.

The Flimmms, the enemy of the Inelqu, promptly established bases on the Moon, in preparation for an attack against the Inelqu, on Earth and on Venus. During the following hundred years, terrible battles raged not only on the Moon but in space. It was during this period that the Inelqu went underground on Earth.

"We did so as protection against the Flimmms, as well as against the destruction approaching the Earth from space itself."

"During this period, wasn't the last Ice Age on Earth?" asked Vallie West. "Wasn't the Deluge caused by the melting of the ice?"

"Yes, this was during the last Ice Age on Earth. The melting of the ice did not cause the biblical flood."

Finally, the Inelqu and the Flimmms fought a terrible space battle that could be seen by men on Earth. With the help of a superior weapon, recently perfected by the Inelqu they finally won the struggle. The giant space vessel of the enemy—two hundred miles long and thirty-four miles wide—was destroyed only a thousand miles from Earth. And it was on Earth that the spaceship fell, blazing like a meteor.

"'I beheld Satan as lightning fall from heaven,'" the Death Merchant said. "St. Luke, chapter eleven, verse eighteen."

The alien said, "Your estimation of the origin of the myth is accurate, Richard Camellion. The Flimmms are the 'devils' of religious literature, of men. Even after the major catastrophe, when almost all of humankind was destroyed, the Flimmms were remembered in the minds of the survivors. It was these survivors that kept the myth alive, and incorporated the Flimmms-as-demons into the religious systems of the world. Men still use this myth of non-physical evil to mentally enslave millions of other men."

However, some of the Flimmms managed to escape from the Moon to Earth. A terrible war was fought between the Flimmms and the ten thousand Inelqu on Earth, with vast parts of the planet being turned into radioactive wasteland. Neither side won. The Flimmms—what was left of them—fled into space. Less than four hundred Inelqu survived. They retreated underground. There they remained throughout the long centuries, for thousands and thousands of years. However, the nuclear war between the Flimmms and the Inelqu was not the catastrophe the alien had mentioned previously. Then what was it?

"Your star, that which you have named Sun, moves as the other stars move, moves in a vast millions-of-years orbit around the center of the galaxy, carrying its planets with it. In pursuing this orbit, the solar system passes through the spiral arms of the galaxy. Clouds of dust and gas are particularly thick in the spiral arms of the galaxy. It was these clouds that caused all the ice ages on Earth, including the last one. The Ice Age was begun and did not cease until Earth had passed through the cloud.

"The planet had passed through the cloud, and the ice was receding, when your star and its planets entered into an area of gravitational disruption caused by a previously collapsed star. Due to its mass, the star partially touched into another reality, into another space-time continuum. Only recently have Earth astrophysicists discovered this strangeness in outer space, which they call Black Holes.

"It was this gravitational disturbance that knocked the inner planets—by reason of their small mass—off their axis.

The poles of Earth changed instantly. In less than four of your Earth hours, this continent and fourteen million of its inhabitants died.

"Such a disaster on a worldwide scale is normal. Earth will again pass through an arm of the galaxy, and again the poles will shift, and again the sun will rise in the west and set in the east. There have been many floods and many reversals of the poles during the history of this planet. It will happen again, and soon, and the civilization on the surface of your world will be destroyed."

The Death Merchant remembered. He thought of Dr. Raya Dubanova, the Russian climatologist, and her grim prediction.[38]

No one spoke. By some cryptic proxy, the members of Camellion's force felt the pains of an agony they could not escape, knowing in their hearts that they were part of an inescapable woe of billions of human beings whose fate was catastrophic disaster, unmitigated by any poignancy or any pity.

Paul Gemz was surprisingly calm. "The Pleiades," he said to the alien. "You said that the Inelqu came from the Pleiades. How was your craft powered? How can you travel around the galaxy as you do?"

"We travel in the entire universe," the alien said. "We are able to do this because we do not propel our vessels through space.[39] We travel in time. We travel in a continuum in which every point in space is not only connected with every other point in space but is also interconnected with every part of time—past, present, and future. This process gives us access to many space-time continuums, one of which is the universe containing the Flimmms. The Flimmms also use this mode of time-travel. The Inelqu from our own planet cannot come for us until

38 See Death Merchant No. 17: *The Zemlya Expedition.* The real Raya Dubanova died of subarachnoid hemorrhage on August 14, 1977—"somewhere in Canada."

39 Thus far, the best conceived by our scientists is a space craft that would accelerate without expelling *any* mass—called a "field drive," or "space drive," for lack of a better term. The name implies that propulsion is furnished by some kind of force field. The idea is only a concept.

the Flimmms have been totally destroyed. On Earth we do not have the means necessary to construct a time screen."

Abruptly the alien changed the subject. "The Chinese have tried to enter by means of explosives. They are afraid and do not know what to do. They cannot understand why their vehicles will not work. I will give you weapons to end the lives of these evil creatures."

"Why can't *you* kill the Chinese?" demanded Vallie West brusquely. "I don't doubt that you could probably wave your arms and kill them. Why must *we* risk our necks?"

"Life is part of the order of the universe. The Inelqu kill only in self defense. We are giving you weapons for only one reason: should the Chinese return to the surface and return in force, we would then have to kill to defend ourselves. Our weapons could destroy all life.

With a quick motion, the alien jumped from the casket to the metal floor. Helena Banya gasped. Excepting the Death Merchant and Vallie West, the others took a few steps back, staring at the being, who appeared comical with his short but muscular body and big feet. The Inelqu almost bounced as he led the group to a large cube a hundred feet from his casket.

"His native planet is much larger than Earth," Paul Gemz whispered to Helena Banya. "Earth, being smaller, has far less gravitational pull."

The alien, standing in front of the cube, made a series of motions with his hands. When a section of the cube opened, he reached through the opening with both hands, and removed two bright red devices that resembled two tubes attached to each other, the smaller tube fitted inside a section of the larger tube. Together, the tubes were several feet long, the largest tube several inches in diameter. At the end of the smaller tube was a needlelike projection an inch long.

Holding a device in each hand, the Alien turned and faced the group. "These are known as Tris Rays." He then explained that each weapon fired an invisible laser beam, but not the kind of laser beam known to scientists on Earth. Each Tris Ray was a concentrated wide-angle beam that shot from the needle projection point with the speed of a *picosecond*—that is, a million-millionth of a second, a span of time so brief that, by comparison, light (the fastest thing in the universe) can travel only the thickness of a piece of paper.

Equally incredible was the fact that, a foot from the weapon, the laser beam widened to five feet—not gradually but instantly—for a maximum distance of five hundred feet. The actual length was infinity; however, each weapon was currently set at a maximum range of five hundred feet. Operation was simple: Point the weapon, and press the gray button on the underside of the tube. A green button on top of the tube was the "safety." Press the green button once, and the weapon would not fire. Press the green button twice, and the weapon was active and ready.

Gemz and Degenhardt and the three other Black Berets felt both stupid and guilty when the alien, reading their thoughts, said that it would not be possible for them to leave the cavern with the Tris Ray weapons.

"The Guardians would prevent you from doing so," the alien said.

"We were under the impression that the Guardians weren't permitted to kill," Degenhardt said, eyeing the Inelqu suspiciously.

"The Goros are not allowed to kill," the alien said. "But there are states of existence in this three-dimensional world much worse than the state humans call death."

The alien handed one weapon to Camellion, the other to West. He looked up at them, the pulsations in the center of his eyes glowing light gray. "Go now. Do that which you must do, that which must be done."

Leaving the dome housing the hundred Inelqu, the Death Merchant heard the voice speaking in the inner sanctum of his mind: *We, the Inelqu, know. But the secret will remain ours. And yours. The creatures with you are not ready to enter the mystery of creation, nor that higher state of contact which would let them feel immortality. They do not understand that we are one with nature, one with the universe, and participants in the sacraments of its change, of Life and Death.*

The Death Merchant became aware that Degenhardt

was saying, "We're having more trouble down here than Stanley had when he searched for Livingston."

"Naturally!" mocked Loren Eaton. "They didn't have to slink around in a damned cave and fight Commie pig farmers. . . ."

Chapter Thirteen

In all of Asia, no man was more worried and frustrated than General Hsun Chin, who wondered what he had done to deserve such bitter failure at the hands of whatever fate controlled such matters. Nonsense. There wasn't any particular reason for the defeat. Or was there? But how could he have known that the column would be attacked by a machine that looked like a square platform from the bottom, a flying machine in—of all places—*a tremendous cavern*. Why should he lie to himself and minimize his position? Fool! Chin told himself. Peking would not accept such a report. The Military Affairs Commission would have no choice but to accept the report if Yang She-Tung, Siu-ch'un, and the surviving soldiers confirmed the existence of such a strange flying object.

They could also testify against him in the matter of the one-sided battle in which 230 men had been blown to bits, or killed by machine guns. From the original force of 460 men, only 43 remained alive. And one tank, one armored car, and five armored carriers! The tank, the armored car, and three of the carriers had been rendered useless by some mysterious power. If the other two carriers had not been kept back, they too would probably have stalled.

How could he explain the catastrophe? Could he tell the truth to the Commission, that he had taken a calculated risk and had sent in the full force on the very first all-clear of the advance reconnaissance group? He would be fortunate if the Commission didn't order him shot! In any type of totally unknown situation, tactics demanded that the commander exercise caution and hold back his armor and infantry until the scouts have acquired ample intelligence about the entire forward area. A basic rule that Chin, anxious for speed, had ignored. Even worse was the inescapable fact that all those men and most of the armor had been trapped in another ambush involving not only explosives but machine guns. The Commission would demand to know why he had not considered the possiblity of a second ambush, especially since 172 P.L.A. fighters had been ambushed by Camellion several days earlier, by a force of only 14 people. And one of them a *woman!* Oh, that *wang-pa-tan* Camellion. He was a devil!

"General Chin"—the worried voice of Major Fu Siu-ch'un pulled Chin reluctantly from his own fearful thoughts—"we must return to the surface. We should retreat right now, and with all the speed at our command." He glanced apprehensively at Major She-Tung, who was half-sitting on one of the front mud-shields of the now useless tank. "Comrade She-Tung agrees with me. So do the other officers."

General Chin found himself reacting by instinct. He didn't like being on the total defensive. For a moment he studied the pitiful survivors of the once-mighty force. They were clustered in little knots, talking in low, nervous tones. Thirty-eight were regular soldiers; the remaining two were officers—Captain Ts'ao Yu-ling and Lieutenant Wei Kuei. Eleven other officers and all of the noncoms had been killed.

General Chin's fierce gaze turned to Major Yang She-Tung. "Why should we retreat, when we have succeeded in chasing the running dog, Camellion, to the dome?" He made an angry face, and his voice was triumphant, resounding. "We have the pigs trapped in the pen. We saw them inside the dome; therefore there has to be an entrance."

The look of exasperation on She-Tung's grimy face deepened. "To be sure, there's an entrance, but we can't find it. We're not going to, especially if the white-robed men are helping the pig Americans. I think they are."

Major Fu Siu-ch'un quickly inforced She-Tung's conviction. "All of us saw those white-robed fossils; and some of the soldiers, who were close to the enemy, saw the doorway disappear," he said firmly. "Explosives are useless. It's clear that some kind of energy field killed our armor—disrupts anything electrical. We had to touch off the explosives by match-lighted fuses. It's not only useless to remain here, it's extremely dangerous. Counting the three of use, we number only forty-three."

"But there's only fourteen of them!" countered General Chin, spitting out the words. "They're outnumbered three to one. Look ahead! You know what the Commission will say when we report we ran with our tails between our legs before an enemy we outnumbered three to one."

Siu-ch'un stood his ground. "Comrade, we can't deny the evidence. We saw those robed monks, or whatever they are. We're fighting—"

"Nonsense!" raged Chin. "They're men, the same as us! As for your theory that Camellion is being helped by those silly old fools, that's paper-tiger talk. He's using only conventional weapons. We're not leaving."

"But, Comrade General—" began She-Tung.

"We're not leaving, and that's final!" stormed General Chin. "It's time we plan an ambush. When we leave this cave, the Americans are going with us—as prisoners!"

Chapter Fourteen

No one disagreed with Vallie West in his description of the mission. It was like boxing: a great sport but a dirty, dangerous business. Only worse. Boxers didn't have to fight; they could quit. The Death Merchant and his force didn't have any choice. They had to find and neutralize the Chinese, to keep the secret of the cavern intact; otherwise, the Commie rats would return with half of the Red ants in Mao's anthill. How to find the Chinese was the problem, a puzzle that was not unsolvable, once a foundation for analysis was established.

Degenhardt's thesis was that Orientals are unpredictable. The Death Merchant and West disagreed, their contention being that Degenhardt was only repeating a false belief of most non-Orientals. The actions of the Chinese *were* predictable. In matters of force and violence, the Chinese were more logical than Americans. They were more prone to consider long-range results. They were more prone to consider long-range results. They were willing to take greater risks, not because they were less cautious than Occidentals, but because their philosophy of life and death was different. Unlike Americans, who put life above everything else—even to the exclusion of their nation's honor—the Chinese weighed victory against defeat. Life and death didn't enter into it. People were always expendable.

The Death Merchant deduced that the Chinese would not retreat. In fact, they couldn't. Not only would the commander and his officers lose face but, on the basis of the way the military operated in Red China, they would surely suffer serious consequences. They might even be executed for exercising bad judgment.

The Chinese wouldn't hang around the dome either.

Comparing the Chinese to the Apache Indians of the old American Southwest, Camellion added up the possibilities and arrived at the only sensible answer. The Chinese would establish positions that would protect their escape route through the tunnel made of Kkokro metal, placements that would permit them to see Camellion, should he attempt to get to the tunnel. There was little chance that the Chinese would block the exit through which he and his force had entered the cavern. There was no exit. There was only a solid wall of glowing blue metal. The Chinese had no way of knowing that there was a tunnel behind the wall. Even if they suspected that there might be, their own open tunnel would surely take precedence.

The Death Merchant inserted other factors into the analyzer of his .44 Magnum mind: the fight at the monastery had been a disaster for the Red Chinese; on the slopes, north of the dwelling of the Dopka, the Chinese had been butchered by HBX and machine gun fire; the attack from the air had blasted men and armor all over the crazyquilt landscape; the last battle had been a massacre. By this time, the Commander of the Reds—even if he was a Peking pigfarmer—should have learned a lesson, should know that he wasn't fighting Boy Scouts.

I think he will try to make us believe he's given up. I think he will attempt an ambush. I don't shiv a git what he does. If he's there, I'll kill him.

Emil Lauterjung and Helena Banya remained in the dome. The Guardians conveniently provided a doorway in the north end of the oval, and the Death Merchant with his eleven men left the sanctuary and warily moved out. They proceeded south for a hundred feet, then stopped by a cluster of chorrten plants to test the Tris Ray tubes.

"You first," Vallie said, grinning at Camellion. "I want to get over this feeling that I'm either Buck Rogers or a refugee from *Star Wars.*"

The rest of the men hung back, their faces full of curiosity.

The Death Merchant looked around, then pointed to the south. "See that mess of stuff that looks like squash growing upside down? Let's try that."

178

Holding the Tris Ray tubes in both hands, he pressed the green button twice. He glanced around again, to make sure that all the men were not within the two-and-a-half-foot range on either side of the needle. Confidently, he pointed the needle end in the general direction of the "squash" and pressed the gray button.

There wasn't any sound, not even a faint hum. No one saw any ray, any light of any kind. They did see the squashlike vegetation and other strange plants vanish. For five hundred feet there was a square shaft of nothingness.

"Man, oh man!" whispered Norbert Shireling, his breath quickening. "It zapped everything. Look at that large mound. The sides of the square hole are as smooth as glass."

"I wonder what a *big* Tris Ray will do?" said Loren Eaton. "You could destroy entire armies."

"Go ahead, Val," the Death Merchant said.

Vallie nodded and stepped a few feet ahead of Camellion. "I'm going to dig a shaft in the ground, just for the hell of it."

He held the tube in front of him and slanted it downward. If the Tris Ray had been a hand gun, the bullet would have hit the ground fifteen feet away.

Vallie pressed the gray firing button. In an instant, the test was over.

There it was, the beginning of the shaft that slanted gapingly into the ground, the square opening six feet in front of West. Vallie pushed the green button once and, with Camellion and the other men, ambled over to the hole. Several feet inside the square opening, the bluish light from the blue-globe "sun" faded off into blackness. They rubbed the inside walls with the tips of their fingers. The stone was glass-slick and cold to the touch.

"The beam disintegrates everything it touches," Camellion said, his voice crackling like dry leaves. "It's like a CPB, a charged particle beam, only different. But the effects are the same."

"Yeah, how's it different?" West asked.

"A CPB is a stream of highly concentrated, high-velocity atomic or subatomic particles. When they hit the target they cause it to burn. We're working on it and so are the Russians. Camellion took a .44 AMP cartridge from his pocket. "Everybody—quiet. Let's see if this shaft is five hundred feet deep." He flipped the cartridge into the hole and listened. Far below, he and the men heard the cartridge hit one side of the shaft. They heard it roll, the sound gradually growing fainter.

"The riceballs won't have a chance against the Tris Rays," said Loren Eaton. "It almost seems unfair to use them on the dumb bastards."

The Death Merchant picked up his TR-tube, got up from one knee, and looked down at Eaton, his icy-blue eyes flashing a warning. "Don't become overconfident, Eaton. The Tris Rays are way ahead of our time. But they don't actually give us an edge over the Chinese. They only make us their equal."

"Camellion's right," Degenhardt said, He placed his hands on top of the Ingram submachine gun which, at waist level, was attached to a strap that went around his neck. The leather tightened as the weight of his hands and arms pushed the weapon downward. "We could walk into an ambush and be cut down before Camellion and West could use the tubes. So all of you"—he looked from Eaton to Cross to Shireling—"watch yourselves. This damned place isn't fit to be a marble orchard, not for any of us."

"This is as good a spot as any to split up," Camellion said, his eyes sweeping the areas all around the men. "Everyone knows the setup. Any questions?"

West, Degenhardt, and the three Black Berets moved toward the west. Camellion, Gemz, Kor Sidkeong, and the four Bhutanese regulars headed east. Earlier, Gemz had opposed dividing the force on the grounds that the split would weaken their firepower. He had continued to resist the move even after Camellion had explained that the two groups would link up and form a whole, once side-sweeps of the dome had been accomplished.

Camellion had to give the man credit. Although the Death Merchant didn't like the archaeoastronomist, whose imperious manner was a constant irritation, he respected the scientist. Gemz was an overbearing pest—*But he has intestinal fortitude. He could have remained in the dome.*

180

But as he put it, 'No man does my fighting. It's my life and I'll be the one who defends it.'

Camellion and the six men carefully went east, Gemz behind the Death Merchant, Major Kor Sidkeong and the four Bhutanese spread out on either side of Camellion in such a manner that the group formed a wedge, with Camellion as the point.

Their eyes darting about constantly, watching every gruesome plant and bush, Camellion and the men of his group turned, when they were several hundred feet east of the dome, and headed north. Camellion was no longer concerned about the Bhutanese regulars. Common sense had finally won, had finally shattered the iron curtain of superstition that had detached the wires of logic in the cognitive part of their brains. The four Bhutanese no longer feared Shambhala. The Guardians were no longer devils and the aliens weren't *Khadomas*, very evil demons who could use any kind of disguise. The only enemy was the Red Chinese, and the four soldiers knew it.

It was the unnatural stillness of the unnatural forest, that constantly reminded them that they were in a world far removed from ordinary men. The "sun," tinging everything, including their own bodies, was another constant reminder. And the lack of even a very faint breeze, of any wind movement. Nothing moved, not a leaf, not a single blade of grass. The air was as dead as the inside of a sealed jar. The only sound was their own breathing, and their feet making contact with the gray-green, light blue grass.

The risk they were taking was enormous. They weren't traveling in a jungle. They weren't in a rain forest in which small trees, vines, creepers, and bushes are often so matted and intertwined that a dozen men can hide and you won't spot them six feet in front of you. Even so, the chorrtens and other flora were dense in places. Here and there the tall growths with the huge chalky leaves—the Guardians called them Mekeketugze—grew very close together, their leaves forming a curving barrier of white that the eye couldn't penetrate. Not infrequently, the Mekeketugze were grouped close to chorrtens, an arrangement that offered choice concealment for any enemy.

The Death Merchant didn't believe in taking a risk if

181

the odds were not on his side. But sometimes there wasn't any choice—like now. Each time he spotted a conglomerate of growth in the distance, he used the Tris Ray tube. Point. Press the gray button. The masses of vegetation would vanish, leaving behind a five-foot square, five-hundred-foot-long tunnel! Hold down the firing button, sweep the weapon back and forth and a much larger "tunnel" would appear, with eight feet being the maximum on all four sides. This maximum was due to another safety feature built into the TR-tube. The shooter could not swing the weapon at a horizontal angle and accidentally touch himself with the edge of the ray projecting from either side of the needle. If the angle exceeded the margin of safety, the tube would not fire.

Camellion and his group of six had moved far enough to the south so that now, having travelled the length of the oval, they could see the end of the protective shield over the smaller domes of the alien station.

"I don't see West and his group," declared Paul Gemz. "We should be able to, but we don't."

"We don't, because he must have advanced at a slower rate," the Death Merchant said. "Don't borrow trouble. It will find us soon enough."

Troju Gyud jabbered in Bhutanese to Major Sidkeong, who replied in a singsong monotone, then said to Camellion, "He said if the Chinese were close by, they would be able to smell them. A foolish belief, of course."

"Common enough though," said Camellion. "We have morons in my country who think they have the same olfactory ability in regard to black people. Stupidity doesn't have any bounderies."

Camellion was about to start toward the west, when Gemz stepped between him and Major Sidkeong, his hand over his mouth, his fingers scratching his mustache. "I would advise you not to go ahead until we're sure West and his men are safe," he said. "We should stay here until we see him."

It would be a crime to smack the idiot!

"Gemz, you've got to break some eggs to make an omelet. Understand?"

Frowning, Gemz thought for a moment. "I fail to see

what cooking an omelet has to do with our present predicament?"

Camellion gave up in disgust. "Never mind," he sighed. "Come on."

"In my opinion," Gemz began, "we—"

Camellion's movement was so incredibly quick, that neither Gemz nor the Bhutanese saw his hand move. They only saw that suddenly the Death Merchant's right hand was full of Gemz's shirt front, twisting the heavy corduroy to the extent that the pressure forced Gemz's arms to move sideways an inch or so. His lower jaw going slack was due to his utter astonishment.

"My opinion is that you talk too much about things in which you have no experience!" The Death Merchant's every word had an enormous fang. "From now on, Super Chicken, keep your mouth zippered."

Much to Gemz's consternation and the amusement of the Bhutanese, Camellion released Gemz, then began stalking toward the west.

Major Sidkeong crooked a finger at the startled Gemz. "Come, Super Chicken."

They were halfway to the center of the oval's north end when they saw Vallie West and the four Black Berets come around from the dome's west side.

Breaking stride, Camellion turned to the sweaty-faced Gemz. "I hope you're satisfied," he said, a marked lack of cordiality in his voice. "All five are safe and sound."

Gemz assented with a casual air, tantamount almost to insolence—another condescending tact of his that infuriated the Death Merchant.

In short order, Camellion's group and West and the Black Berets had merged into one unit and were advancing north, this time in a T formation, an arrangement that allowed the death patrol to move in a tight group, with firepower to the front, and the men in the rear to react instantly to Camellion's orders—provided he had the time to give any. Degenhardt was in the center of the T's arm, Camellion ten feet to his left, West ten feet east of him. The rest of the men were behind Red, stretched out in single file.

The farther north they moved, the closer they came to

the end of the two-mile electrical disruption zone. Toward the outer edge of the zone, they encountered the Chinese dead, scores of bodies lying in grotesque positions, their baggy green uniforms caked with the peanut-butter-and-jelly stains of dirt and blood. The Berets sprayed the bodies with machine-gun slugs, using their silenced Ingrams; then the Ingrams were out of ammo. There weren't any extra 9mm magazines. The Ingrams were useless. The Death Merchant couldn't afford the risk. A "dead man" ambush was an old Chinese trick. He had the Black Berets and the Bhutanese finish the job with captured Chinese machine guns, after which they cut the ammo pouches from the bodies, to replenish their own supply of 7.62mm ammunition for both the Type 54 and Type 55 submachine guns they had taken from the dead Chinese three days earlier.

They found the armored car and the heavy tank just inside the electrical zone. The engines had quit a few seconds after the armor had plunged into the zone; their momentum had then carried them forward a short distance, except for the tank, which was only half inside the zone. A hundred feet west of the armored car were four personnel carriers. Camellion and West winked the armor out of existence with the TR-tubes.

Half an hour after passing the area where the armor had been, the Death Merchant signaled a halt with his hand and motioned the men to get down and stay down.

Several hundred feet in front of Camellion, was a natural formation known as a saddle, a large flat area surrounded by higher ground in two directions and lower ground in the other two directions. In this case, the higher ground was to the east and the west, with the lower ground stretching out to the north and the south. The low ground was composed of long, very gradual slopes. To the east and the west, the two inclines, much steeper and only half as long, moved upward to become part of two huge mounds, so that the "seat" of the saddle, between the east and the west mounds, would have been a deep ravine, *If* the two rises had been large hills and *if* the north and the south sides had been higher than the flat section.

"It's perfect for an ambush," West said bleakly. Flat on

184

his belly, he lay propped up on his elbows. "A hundred riceballs could be hidden up there."

"It's a waste of time to discuss it," Degenhardt said indignantly, staring at the saddle. "All of us know we're not going to take that kind of a chance. Either we go around or cut it all down to size with Tris Rays."

The Death Merchant noted every feature of the saddle. The east and the west sides were thick carpets of gray-green-blue grass, and dotted with monstrous chorrtens and Mekeketugzes. The tops of the mounds were similarly decorated. In comparison, the flat area had only sparse growth.

"Dammit, Camellion! Say something!" demanded Degenhardt in annoyance. He had scooted himself closer to Camellion, and had spoken almost into the Death Merchant's right ear.

Camellion smiled. "Patience is the reward of all virtue."

"I'm not blessed—or cursed—with either one," growled Degenhardt. "Let's do something!"

The Death Merchant did do something. He stood up, held the TR-tube out in front of him, pointed the needle toward the northwest, and pressed down on the firing button. The first area to vanish was the region fifty feet to the west of the long mound to Camellion's left. He intended to destroy any area where the Chinese might be hiding.

He moved the red tube slowly to the right, at times raising and lowering the needle slightly. The entire sweep lasted less than a minute, and when Camellion finally pressed down on the safety button, the saddle no longer existed. The vegetation that had been fifty feet to each side of the mounds had vanished. So had the mounds. There were no slopes. All that remained was a gigantic, almost totally flat area as smooth as a billiard ball and as bare as a brand-new baby's bottom.

"Can you imagine a regiment using Tris Rays?" suggested Degenhardt, who stood to his full height, an expression of longing on his face.

"I prefer to think of the Chinese who may have been hiding up there," Camellion said. "If any were there, now they're not even drifting molecules. They simply don't exist in any form of matter."

185

"We still shouldn't cross in the open," West said firmly. "Any kind of cover is to our advantage."

"We're not going to," Camellion said quickly. He turned and looked at the men strung out behind him, then said to West and Degenhardt, "We'll split up. The two of you and the Berets go to the east, or the west if you want. It doesn't make any difference. I'll go in the other direction. We'll skirt the open area and keep close to the plants at the edge on each side. We'll regroup once we're past the flat. Okay?"

"That's what I had in mind," West said.

"Same here," agreed Degenhardt.

West and Degenhardt moved off, West calling back, "See you at the Resurrection."

Both groups moved out, West and Degenhardt and the three Black Berets going to the east, the Death Merchant and his men to the west. At length, when they drew close to the barren area they noticed that the concentrated laser beam had cut through the rock with such force that the granite on top, at the cutoff point, had been fused. Half an inch . . . six feet? It was impossible to tell. The surface of the entire open space was now colorless and luster-less. *Like pure quartz*, thought Camellion.

The men in single file, the two groups quickly sought the scant security of the hideous vegetation at the sides of the bare, glass-topped area—the Mekeketugze and chorrtens that the wide-spread laser beam had not touched.

With the Tris Ray tube held out in front of him, his finger close to the gray button, Camellion led his group six feet inside the vegetation. A short distance to his right, the grass ended at bare rock, the top of which was quartz, the north-south joint between the two sections as straight as a line laid by surveyors. To the right of the Death Merchant, 150 feet away, were West, Degenhardt, and the Berets.

Three-fourths of the way across, Camellion realized that he had made a serious error in judgment.

We've walked into a trap!

Chapter Fifteen

There are those rare times when even ordinary people exhibit intuitive flashes of genius. General Hsun Chin's estimation of the Death Merchant's course of action was one of these times. Chin had posted scouts all around the dome, at such a distance that they had had to use binoculars to see the enemy, to see Camellion and his men test the two Tris Ray tubes. Highly excited runners had then reported the weapons to General Chin and his officers: the enemy had two strange looking weapons, long red tubes that made no noise, that gave off no light, but disintegrated the countryside, leaving only a square "tunnel."

General Chin had almost frothed at the mouth. Now, more than ever, he was determined to capture the twelve-man enemy force. Taking them and the two tubes back to Peking was the solution to all his problems, the mystic "medication" that would heal his deep wound of fear and uncertainty. Handing the Military Affairs Commission such prizes meant that the Commission would conveniently ignore the hundreds of men who had been slaughtered. What were the deaths of hundreds in comparison to weapons that dissolved solid objects? Why, with such weapons in numbers, the Red Chinese could conquer the world.

An ambush was the only way to trap Camellion and his men. Even Major Siu-ch'un and Major She-Tung agreed. Yes, an ambush was the only way. Captain Ts'ao Yu'ling was not so sure. Why not just machine gun the American running dogs and take the two weapons? General Chin, calling Yu-ling an idiot, pointed out that some of the enemy no doubt knew how the weapons worked. Naturally, they would fight. If some of them had to be killed, that would be unfortunate. Live Americans were certainly not as important as weapons that could vaporize objects.

It was agreed: an ambush was the only answer. Accordingly, General Chin chose the first place on the route that could be used for such a trap—a saddle formation. Next question! What would be Camellion's probable course of action when he saw the saddle? As clever as he was, he would suspect an ambush. He was a devil, that one. He could lead his force around the saddle, either to the east or the west.

"No. He will not go all the way around." General Chin was convinced Camellion would have to assume that "we are hiding on the slopes, or on top of the mounds, waiting. I ask all of you: why should he let us live? Why should he go by and give us a chance to come at him from the rear?"

On this basis, there was only one course left open to the American pig. He would blast the entire saddle formation with the tube weapons the white-robed creatures in the dome had given him. He would level the entire saddle.

"Including us!" major Fu Siu-ch'un said grimly. "Comrade General, I don't see how we can possibly plan an ambush from that position, or any other. Those tube things can make whole areas disappear!"

General Chin opened Fu Siu-ch'un's eyes by explaining the rest of his master plan. As a precautionary measure, Camellion would no doubt vaporize large areas to the east and the west of the hilly rises—"Probably as much as twenty-five or thirty feet," Chin said. "He will want to be certain that we are not in the area, that all is safe for him to proceed." He might even form two groups, as he had first done after leaving the dome. So, all the Chinese had to do was dig spider holes eighty feet from the slopes of his mound. Ideal for an ambush, spider holes were foxholes with lightweight camouflaged covers.

"This Camellion, this swine American dog will take his men around the edge of the area," smirked Chin. "They will keep inside the growth of plants for protection. We will be completely underground, as it were, covered with a surface layer of earth containing grass, but we will leave a slight space so that we can see when the enemy is lined out in front of us. At the appropriate time, we'll leap out and overpower all twelve of them."

"Comrade, suppose the force is split into two groups?" Major Siu-ch'un asked. "We can of course have men on both sides. We are forty-three against twelve."

"Exactly," said Chin. "There is a great deal of risk, but I ask you, do we have a choice?"

By this time, Chin, Siu-ch'un, and She-Tung had no doubts as to their fate if they didn't succeed in capturing Camellion and the two fantastic weapons. Peking always frowned on failure, and up to now this mission was more than unsuccessful. It was total disaster.

General Chin sent a runner to recall the scouts. Radio would not function inside the zone, close to the dome, and in nonstatic areas the enemy might pick up the transmissions.

Chin and his men hurried to the saddle-formation. He posted forward scouts and ordered the men to start work on both sides of the mounds. The soldiers first began cutting large rectangular slabs of grass from the hard gray soil.

Five hours and thirty-four minutes later, the Death Merchant had done everything General Chin predicted he would do. He arrived at the saddle. He disintegrated the entire suspect region, including an extra fifty feet on both sides of where the mounds had been. He split the patrol into two units, five men going to the east, seven men to the west. When the two groups came to the vast open space, they moved just inside the foliage and, in single file, the men proceeded to the north. Good! Exactly what General Chin wanted.

Peering out through a tiny slit under the covering of sod, General Chin, and the twenty-two men with him on the west side, waited. They were less than thirty feet from the Death Merchant. Major Fu Siu-ch'un, leading the Chinese on the east side, was about the same distance from West and the Berets.

General Chin sprung the trap. There were wild yells to demoralize the enemy: The Americans were imperialist fanatics! The Bhutanese were animals, too stupid to know fear! *I-sipman! Sin-un ku-ha-ji!*

The Chinese pushed aside the thin covers of sod, spat

189

out dirt, leaped out of the spider holes, and charged, the officers carrying Chinese Tokarev pistols, the ordinary foot soldiers using Type 54 and Type 55 submachine guns, which they had orders not to use. "I want them alive!" General Chin had said.

The face of the Death Merchant became one big snarl. The Chinese—too many of them for a quick count—were only twenty feet away and coming on like Oriental gangbusters. *Damn!* Camellion wasn't so much afraid as he was angry with himself, in a rage because—*The Commie commander outsmarted me. He guessed right down the line what I would do and "buried" his force out of range. If only I had zapped a hundred feet extra on each side. Bull excrement! Now I know why he didn't try to kill us! He wants us alive to drag back to Peking—us and the Tris Rays. He'll get them over my dead body!*

He had no time for regrets. *The hell with trying to swim upstream!* He didn't have time to turn around either. He didn't have to. He knew that Vallie and the Berets were under the same kind of attack. He pushed the Tris Ray tube out in front of him, caught a glimpse of terrified Chinese faces, and pressed the gray button. Instantly, a square tunnel appeared ahead in the mass of leaves. The wide-beam laser ray had also turned into nothingness five feet of a chorrten plant, and now the top part toppled slowly to the ground, the mushroom-top canopy crumbling. What had been inside the tunnel area no longer existed, including three unlucky members of the People's Liberation Army.

The Death Merchant had reflexes that were among the fastest on Earth, but he wasn't Superman! Instinct warned him that he didn't have time to swing the tube and fire a second time, not unless he wanted to help the riceballs pull him down—*I could get my clothes dirty!* He did the only thing he could do. He flung up his arms, one finger pressing the safety button of the tube, and pitched the tube backward over his head. He hoped it would land far out on the slick quartz area and distract the Chinese long enough for him to draw his Auto Mags.

He had only a half a second to see that the flood of Reds was about to inundate Paul Gemz, Major Sidkeong, and the four Bhutanese soldiers; then the Chinese tidal wave tried to roll all over him.

Go suck stale ding-dongs, you dumb dodos! He jumped slightly and used his rightfoot to deliver a devastating *Dachi Kogan Geri* lower kick to the left kneecap of a wonton weirdo about to swing the barrel of a Type 51 subgun at his head. The halfwit howled as the karate slam shattered his knee bone and smashed his leg out from under him. He shoved out his left arm, blocked an intended knife-hand strike to his temple by a square-faced rice eater in front of him, and wrapped his right hand around the barrel of a machine gun the P.L.A. punk was about to stab into his stomach. Shih Huang would have had more luck trying to chop a Brahma bull!

Camellion pushed up the barrel of the machine gun, the twisting motion pulling Huang's finger against the trigger. The T-54 roared, the barrel vibrating and becoming hot in Camellion's hands, a dozen deadly 7.62mm projectiles burning upward at an angle, only a foot and a half from his face. A second later, he had jerked the weapon from Huang's grasp and had slammed him between the eyes with a left handed *Tettsui* blow, the fist-hammer giving Huang's brain an earthquake, and switching him into instant unconsciousness—only an instant before Chiang Nik Po, who had managed to get behind the Death Merchant, slipped an arm around Camellion's throat, preparatory to jerking him back and putting a knee into the small of his back. Nik Po didn't have time to tighten the arm. Camellion half-turned to the right, and kicked backward with his right leg, measuring the distance in his mind, the *Kakato Geri* slam did what it was supposed to do: the heel of Camellion's foot flattened Nik Po's testicles.

The man with the broken kneecap was down on the ground and in agony, but he hadn't counted himself out. Gasping in pain, he tried to grab Camellion by the left ankle, his effort not going unnoticed by the Death Merchant who, as he grabbed Nik Po's wrist in his left hand and twisted the arm away from his throat, kicked Broken Kneecap full in the face, breaking his teeth and upper jaw. His mouth full of blood, his mind screaming in protest, the demolished Chinese sagged, unconscious.

Nik Po couldn't offer any resistance, the *Kakato Geri*

having put him in a state of shock from the pain. His eyes open as wide as his mouth, he was beginning to sag when Camellion swung him around and pitched him into Lieutanant Wei Kuei who was coming at him, with a 7.62mm Tokarev pistol in each hand.

As the two Chinese started to go down, Camellion stepped back, moved to the right and, with lightning speed, pulled the two .44 Alaskan AMPs from their long hip holsters. His eyes sweeping the area, he thumbed off the safeties. He saw only his failure.

Paul Gemz, either dead or unconscious, was stretched face down on the ground. Major Sidkeong and the Bhutanese soldiers, surrounded by Chinese, were fighting like madmen. Major Sidkeong stabbed one Chinese in the belly, wilted a gook behind him with a left *Empi* elbow smash to the solar plexus, and kneed a third soldier, in front of him, in the groin. Just as quickly, he pulled the knife from the belly of the gook he had stabbed, and plunged the blade into the right side of the man he had kneed.

All five Bhutanese were using *sipongs*, the broad-bladed double-edged knife carried by Dopkas and other mountain men in Bhutan, using the foot-long blades with a deadliness that the Chinese were finding difficult to counteract.

Troju Gyud had cut the throat of one Chinese, and was struggling with two other soldiers—one had grabbed his knife arm—while the man with the cut throat lay on the ground, the gaping wound spurting red blood tinged blue by the "sun." Only, the blood looked black. Gyud finally went down when another Red chopped him across the back of the neck.

Gom Shinje and Podku Kalimpong stood fighting back-to-back, the Chinese around them as thick as flies on a piece of candy. Shinje had managed to slice open the stomach of one soldier before another man grabbed his wrist with both hands and a third tried to smash him in the temple with the butt end of a T-55 submachine gun. Shinje ducked the blow and pushed the man back by placing his foot in the Red's stomach and shoving. But another riceball grabbed his leg and pulled. Shinje started to go down, another Chinese twisting his arm and forcing him to drop the sipong as he crashed to the ground.

Podku Kalimpong's back was now exposed. Kalimpong, a sipong in one hand and a British Mark-1 Enfield revolver in the other, pulled his left arm free, shoved the muzzle of the weapon under the man's chin, and pulled the trigger. The Enfield exploded, the .380mm bullet tearing through the Red's lower chin, boring through the roof of his mouth, and coming to rest in the upper part of his brain. It was the last shot Kalimpong would ever fire. Wuchang Hupei, the Red devil who had picked up Shinje's sipong, buried the blade to the hilt between Kalimpong's shoulder blades, the tip of the steel slicing into Kalimpong's heart.

The Chinese didn't consider it vital that the five Bhutanese should be captured alive. It was the Americans who were important, whom Peking would parade before the world as imperialist spies and the agents of Capitalist war mongers.

While several soldiers pounded Gom Shinje's face to a bloody pulp. Wuchang Hupei began to sneak up on Tolung Terskug, who had already killed two Chinese with his sipong, and was trying desperately to free himself from the Reds swarming over him. One soldier now met with some success; he succeeded in twisting the big knife from Terskug's weakening fingers. Another rice eater knocked the wind out of him by crashing the butt end of a T-55 machine gun into his chest. A mass of pain, barely able to hang onto consciousness, Terskug stumbled, his body turning to the left. He was now in a convenient position for Wuchang Hupei, who was coming up from the rear. Hupei didn't get to use the sipong. The riceball who had smashed Terskug in the chest turned the T-55 around, pushed off the safety, and fired at point-blank range, the flaming muzzle only a foot away from the unlucky Terskug. The burst of 7.62mm slugs made splinters of Terskug's breastbone, cut through his lungs and back, and then ripped into the stomach of Wuchang Hupei, who was on higher ground. Hupei looked very surprised, dropped the sipong, doubled over, and toppled to the ground with Terskug.

In the meantime, Major Sidkeong, who had killed another Red with his sipong, was going down under the weight of his attackers, much to the satisfaction of General Hsun Chin and Major Yang She-tung. They had left their spider holes but, not having taken part in the direct attack, were watching the battle from behind a clump of chalky Mekeketugze leaves.

The earth-shaking roars of the Death Merchant's Auto Mags wiped the smiles of victory from Chin and Yang She-Tung's faces.

Although Vallie West and the four Black Berets had not been caught off guard, Vallie didn't have time to activate the Tris Ray tube. Instead, he dropped the tube and pulled Smith & Wesson 9mm automatics from shoulder holsters. He didn't have time to unstrap the T-54 submachine gun on his back.

Degenhardt, Eaton, Cross, and Shireling, who had been moving with T-54s and T-55s already in their hands, swung toward the attacking Chinese and opened fire, killing the Reds with their own weapons. Submachine guns chattered out four streams of 7.62mm death, and Vallie's two Smith & Wessons cracked. Within half a minute, nine Chinese were cut to pieces, the ground around them thick with blood and bits of uniform cloth. Neither West nor the Berets noticed. By then, the rest of the riceballs were all over them, gook hands grabbing machine-gun barrels and reaching for Smith & Wesson pistols.

Vallie found his arms being jerked upward, and Red pigs trying to twist the Smith & Wessons from his big hands. Another chinnie creep was getting set to slam a fist into his gut. A fourth Peking pervert was trying to get behind him, to dent his head with the butt of a machine gun.

Damned Communist trash! West became enraged. Letting out a bellow, he raised his arms with a mighty effort and brought them inward. The startled Red on his right arm hung on. So did the creep whose hands were closed over Vallie's left wrist. With another burst of strength, West twisted his entire body to the left, at the same time holding his arms out straight and swinging them around to the left, faster than he was turning. Fearing the pistols in his hands, the two Chinese holding onto his arms didn't dare let go. Vallie was counting on their fear and stubbornness. As he swung around, the two soldiers were

194

yanked off their feet, their only support being Vallie's massive arms. The body of the astonished Chinaman, holding on to Vallie's right arm, smashed into the Red who was throwing a piston-powered punch aimed at Vallie's gut, while the gook on the left arm collided with the "ah-so" dummy trying to come in behind Vallie. The smash-up was too much for the China boys hanging on Vallie's arms. They released their holds and tumbled to the ground with the two other soldiers, arms and legs flying. Vallie's arms were now free, and he still had a Smith & Wesson in each hand.

"I'm going to kill every damned one of you!" he yelled. Jumping back, he began firing. But not at the four men down on the ground!

The four Black Berets were also having their troubles. They had dropped their submachine guns, preferring to fight at close quarters with both hands. Unlike the dandy little Ingrams, the Chinese sub-guns could not be fired with one hand.

Red Degenhardt, using a razor sharp tricorner push-dagger with a solid, contoured grip, stabbed one Red in the left lower chest and, with his left fist, let another one have a dynamite smash, square in the mouth. He used a *Shinto-Ryu* karate inside roundhouse kick to take out another Red, who doubled over in agony from the battering ram blow to his intestines.

Only ten feet away from Degenhardt, wiry Loren Eaton was using his favorite in-fighting weapons: two ice-picks with the aluminum tube handles filled with lead. "Stinking Commie pig!" muttered Eaton. A quick jab with the ice pick in his right hand, and one Red screamed, staggered back, and put his hands over his stomach, staring down in fear at the hot, sticky blood oozing between his fingers. Captain Ts'ao Yu-ling then grabbed Eaton's right wrist with his left and and, with his other hand, tried to spear him in the throat with a four-finger *Nukite* jab. Eaton couldn't use the ice pick in his left hand because another damned gook had grabbed his wrist and at the same time, was trying to knee him in the groin.

Eaton blocked the knee jab with his left leg, easily ducked Yu-ling's spear stab, and gave both men a surprise by doing the unexpected. He swung out his left leg and slammed it against the right ankle of the Red trying to twist the ice pick from his hand. At the same time, Eaton leaned forward and shoved his face into a surprised Captain Ts'ao Yu-ling's face. Yu-ling yelled in pain when Eaton clamped his teeth on his nose and bit down viciously.

The entire move had taken only a few seconds—and the ploy failed. The leg took down the Red holding onto Eaton's left wrist, but he didn't release his grip. Instead, he pulled Eaton down with him. In turn, Eaton, hanging on like a determined turtle to Yu-ling's nose, and Yu-ling, who didn't dare let go of the Black Beret's right wrist, went down as well.

But time had run out completely for Foster Cross and Norbert Shireling, who were not even given a chance to fight for their lives!

Cross, after dropping his sub-gun, pulled out his Smith & Wesson auto, and an "Odin's Claw" folding knife which had been opened and, with the blade locked, rested in a small leather holster strapped to the center of his chest. He could have dusted two of the gooks, but the firing pin hit on a faulty cartridge. Cross didn't have time to pull the slide back and extract the dud by hand. He didn't have time to do anything but die.

Norbert Shireling didn't even have time to get off a shot with his Smith & Wesson. He didn't, because Major Fu Siu-ch'un was not a man who took unnecessary chances. Siu-ch'un didn't know how many soldiers had been killed by the enemy's short burst of machine-gun slugs. He didn't have time to count. But he knew that seven or eight or more must have died within seconds. The hell with General Chin and his order to capture all the Americans alive. It was the strange weapon that was important. And if one or two of the enemy could divulge information about the device, why bother with the others?

Major Siu-ch'un had deliberately hung back from the rest of the Chinese, keeping the soldiers between himself and the enemy. Now he got down on one knee by the side of a thick chorrten trunk, raised his Tokarev automatic, and fired around the soldiers at the first two Americans at whom he had a clear shot. Shireling, raising his Smith & Wesson autoloader, stumbled back, then fell sideways, a savage pain in his chest, a loud roaring in his ears. Foster Cross jumped slightly when Siu-ch'un's bullet struck him, low in the right rib cage. Twisting halfway around, he dropped the pistol, his legs folded, and he fell, his thoughts a jumble of crossed-wires, a black blanket drifting slowly over his mind. He sank into an unconsciousness that would become death within minutes. The 7.62mm projectile had cut into his liver and had clipped the inferior vena cava artery. Internal hemorrhaging was the result.

Major Siu-ch'un stood up and moved closer, noting, with satisfaction, that his men were about to subdue the Americans. Or were they? He cursed and began to move his Tokarev back and forth, when he saw a huge white-faced American dog swing two P.L.A. soldiers around and slam them into two other men. All four soldiers crashed to the ground, acting as if they were stunned. Worse, the large man had a pistol in each hand.

Hate and rage guiding his hands, Major Siu-ch'un raised his Tokarev and took careful aim.

The four riceballs, thrown to the ground by Vallie West, were still tumbling into each other when Vallie spotted Siu-ch'un raising his pistol.

Screw you, creep! You're dead! Vallie dropped a split second before Siu-ch'un fired. Vallie's knees were only half an inch from the grass when Siu-ch'un's bullet passed a foot over his head. He snap-aimed and pulled both triggers of the 9mm autos. One bullet stabbed Major Siu-ch'un high in the stomach, narrowly missing his spinal column and zinging out his back. The second slug, smacking him in the left shoulder, broke the knob at the top of the humerus, the long bone of the upper arm. His mind whirling, Siu-ch'un found himself being kicked backward by the impact of the high-velocity Hornady projectiles, his feet moving as if on a treadmill as he instinctively tried to catch himself. He couldn't, and he didn't. Not until his back slammed against the trunk of the chorrten plant. Then he came to a stop. Slowly, he slid down the trunk, settling down on his rear end. He sat there, half-conscious, rockets of pain going off in his stomach, his left arm dangling like a useless piece of string. Dumbly, he looked at

197

the pistol in his right hand, wondering why he hadn't dropped it.

West continued to fire, the Smith & Wesson autoloaders roaring.

One Chopstick Charlie on the ground—he was only six feet from Vallie—was picking up a T-54 sub-gun. He died from a 9mm slug that tore through his throat. The three other Chinese followed him into hell, jerking and crying out as slugs ripped into their bodies.

Vallie turned his attention to the other Chinese who were struggling with Degenhardt and Eaton. Degenhardt didn't need any help. Indeed not. The Beret officer was doing more than holding his own; he was about to slaughter the meatball he had smacked in the mouth a few minute's earlier. The gook had stooped to pick up a machine gun. Degenhardt had grabbed him, jerked him off balance, and had kicked him in the stomach. Now Degenhardt had the riceball on the rim of infinity. As he plunged the push-dagger into the Chinaman's upper stomach, Vallie dropped the muzzle of one of the autoloaders to the P.L.A. fighter whom Degenhardt had taken out with a roundhouse kick. On his knees, the P.L.A. soldier was in agony, his lips foamy with blood; nonetheless, he had picked up a submachine gun, his hate having predominance over pain. The man was swinging the subgun into position when Vallie put a 9mm bullet through his left temple.

Degenhardt let the creep he had stabbed fall to the ground, glanced briefly at Vallie, whose lang legs were tearing across the grass, then rushed after the CIA case officer toward Loren Eaton, who was still struggling with Captain Ts'ao Yu-ling and Yang Ku Fi. Eaton had succeeded in applying a scissors leg-hold around the middle of Ku Fi's body. Ku Fi was gasping in pain, yet he hadn't let go of Eaton's left wrist. The dazed riceball knew that if he did, the deadly ice-pick in Eaton's hand would go to work, either on him or on Captain Yu-ling.

Eaton still had Yu-ling's nose clamped in the vise of his teeth, but he couldn't use the ice pick in his right hand which Yu-ling had pinned. With the thumb of his other hand, Yu-ling was digging into Eaton's left armpit.

Then the struggle ended. Vallie West calmly bent down and put a bullet into a Yang Ku Fi's terrified face, the hot slug ripping through the Red's nose and splattering the grass with chips of back skull bone.

Captain Yu-ling had only a moment to feel intense fear. Degenhardt grabbed him by his thick black hair, jerked his head back, and shoved the push-dagger into the back of his neck. Blood jumped out of Yu-ling's mouth and fell all over the front of Eaton, who released his nose and tried to push the gurgling half-corpse from him.

Degenhardt jerked out the push-dagger and stepped back to observe his work. Neither he nor Vallie West, who was looking around at the dead Chinese, noticed Major Fu Siu-ch'un, who was twenty feet to the north, his head slumped on his chest.

For the few minutes after he had been shot, Major Siu-ch'un had sat with his back against the trunk of the chorrten tree. For the first time in his life, Siu-ch'un was face to face with something he knew was far beyond his reach to categorize. No man can understand death, not even his own. He hated, with a burning fury, the big American who had shot him. But was it possible to kill him? Siu-ch'un could still raise his right arm, and he could still see, although dimly, the three Americans in front of him. He tested his right arm, flexing the fingers which were still around the grip of the automatic. If he missed the first time, he would not get a second chance. All he could do was try. As fast as he could, Siu-ch'un raised the Tokaarev and centered the front and back sights on Vallie's broad chest. During the next instant everything went wrong, not only for Major Siu-ch'un but for Red Degenhardt.

Vallie West saw the Chinese officer with the raised pistol, at the same time that Degenhardt stepped in front of him and Siu-ch'un pulled the trigger. The Tokarev cracked. The bullet struck Degenhardt in the back, and buried itself close to his heart.

Degenhardt's mouth went slack, his eyes rolled back in his head, and then fell forward, his corpse narrowly missing Vallie, who jumped to one side and began pumping 9mm slugs into Major Siu-ch'un—into a corpse. Siu-ch'un had died after firing the shot that had killed Degenhardt.

199

Muttering curses, Vallie knelt down, placed one of the Smith & Wesson loaders on the grass, rolled Degenhardt over, and saw that he was stone dead. He looked very peaceful, as though he were sleeping. *He is!* Vallie thought grimly. *The Big Sleep!*

Loren Eaton had picked up a machine gun and now walked over to Vallie and stared down at the corpse of Degenhardt.

"We're the only ones left," he said in a choked voice. "Cross and Shireling got it too."

West glared up at him. "Dammit, get down. Or don't you hear the firing across the way?"

Eaton got down and lay flat in the grass. "It sounds like Camellion's Auto Mags," he said.

The Alaskan Auto Mags in the Death Merchant's hands roared, the stainless steel weapons jumping only slightly as .44 JSP projectiles bored through the long, Mag-na-ported barrels. The first two slugs sliced into Lieutenant Wei Kuei and Nik Po, who were trying to straighten up and fly right.

Lieutenant Wei Kuei might as well have had chopsticks in his hands instead of Tokarev autos. A .44 Magnum bullet blessed him an inch above his nose, and exploded his head with a loud *pop*. A grapefruit dropped onto concrete from a height of a thousand feet, couldn't have come apart with greater force.

Nik Po, splattered with parts of Wei Kuei's head, cried out piteously, threw up his arms and had one final look at the world as the impact of the .44 slug pitched him backward, doubling him over in the process. The lead had hit him in the stomach, and had gone out his back with the power of a locomotive. Nik Po crashed to the grass on his back, six feet from the headless corpse of Wei Kuei.

A blur of motion, Camellion jerked himself to the left, his eyes devouring the surprised Chinese, his mind evaluating the gory situation. Three of the Bhutanese soldiers were obviously dead. Troju Gyud might be alive, although his face resembled tomato paste, and his head was the size of a pumpkin. Paul Gemz lay face down. Dead or unconscious?

It was apparent that only Kor Sidkeong was alive and

in good health, judging from the way he was struggling on the ground with two Chinese. The Bhutanese Army officer wouldn't be fighting very long. Other Chinese were rushing to aid their two comrades, entwined with Major Sidkeong.

Once more, the Death Merchant fired both AMPs, a moment before his body settled behind a tough gray trunk of a chorrten. He couldn't take the chance of firing into the body of the riceball who was on top of Kor Sidkeong. The .44 slug would go all the way through the fishhead-eater's body and take out Sidkeong at the same time. Camellion did the next best thing. He put a .44 JSP projectile into Liung Bin Ichow's left ankle. The .44 Jurras hollow point did more than break the ankle bone. It tore off the foot of Bin Ichow, who jumped and emitted a long wailing howl, much like that of a wild animal being disemboweled slowly, an embodiment in sound of infinite fear and pain. The foot fell several feet from the ankle which spurted and tossed blood the way water is flung in every direction from a hose whose nozzle is not being held in place.

Camellion didn't even try to put a bullet into the goon underneath Major Sidkeong. For one thing, he didn't have time; for another, he couldn't get a clear shot. Too, he was certain that the fierce Bhutanese army officer could handle the man.

The next .44 Magnum bullet smashed into the chest of one of the soldiers who had been rushing to help the two comrades fighting with Major Sidkeong. The big projectile, going in at a sharp angle, went all the way through Tai Wloon's body, made its exit through the left side of his back, then smacked into the right side of the chest of another soldier who was behind and to the left of Tai Wloon. The soldier yelled and spun around in unison with Tai Wloon, who was already dead and sinking to the ground, a big gaping hole in his chest, another one in his back.

The remaining Red Chinese were so terrified at the quick death rolling over them that they didn't notice that Kor Sidkeong had rolled over with the man underneath him, that both men were lying on their sides, and that Sidkeong had his arms locked around Nam Choyang's neck—one arm in front against the throat, the other arm against the back of the neck—and was choking him to death.

Neither did General Hsun Chin and Major Yang She-Tung. They had moved from the clump of Mekeketugze leaves to a safer position behind a chorrten trunk. Chin and She-Tung couldn't believe that the carefully prepared ambush had failed, at least it was a disaster on this side of the large clearing. They hadn't even been able to get off a blast of slugs at the tall American dog. He had moved too fast, with a speed that was incredible; and every time those shiny weapons of his roared, men died. Didn't the *wang-pa-tan* ever miss?

Now the American dog was behind a large trunk of one of the toadstool-shaped plants. Chin and She-Tung knew that they couldn't hurt him with slugs, but maybe a blast would distract him long enough to let the pitiful few men still alive drop to the ground among the dead and somehow escape.

"We must kill him," General Chin whispered urgently. "We must."

They didn't! Chin was on the left side of the trunk, She-Tung on the right, each man holding a T-54 submachine gun. Both men fired together, at the same time that the Death Merchant triggered his Auto Mags.

Two Red soldiers had been dropping to the ground but they had been too slow. One man died when a .44 slug tore through his throat and almost decapitated him. He jerked like a broken wire and fell sideways, blood leaping from his throat. The second Red caught a slug in the right side. The big bullet broke five ribs, turned his lungs into a sponge, and knocked him over on his left side. He was dead by the time his head struck the ground.

All General Chin and Major She-Tung had accomplished was to warn the Death Merchant of their presence. The couple of dozen 7.62mm slugs had only smacked the tough vegetable material of the toadstool trunk, going in only an inch or so.

Thirty feet to Camellion's left, Kor Sidkeong had killed his men, but wisely he lay still, fearing that if he moved or tried to get to another position, the two submachine guns would open up on him. He had only one worry: the gook

Camellion had hit in the mouth with a *Tettsui* blow. Shih Huang was making sounds as though he were regaining consciousness.

From his position behind the chorrten trunk, the Death Merchant also heard Shih Huang and he could see him. Dazed, Shih Huang pushed himself to a sitting position, blood caked on his mouth, only mushy gaps where his teeth had been. This time, Camellion put him to sleep forever. He exploded Huang's head with a .44 slug, not at all surprised when the big *wooommm* of the Auto Mag brought another twin burst of machine gun fire from General Chin and Major She-Tung.

On both knees, Camellion estimated that the machine guns were less than forty feet to the north of him. *Officers! They have to be officers! Ordinary soldiers would have taken part in the attack! They will not come to me. I will go to them.*

He reloaded his Auto Mags, then unstrapped the AMP ammo bag from his belt. He next removed the T-55 machine gun from his back and pulled the cross-strap of the spare T-55 ammo carryall bag from his shoulder. The last two pieces of equipment that he placed on the grass were the Electro-5 and the Deschutes vest. One should always travel light and unencumbered when using *Ninjitsu*, the most chilling art ever to be brought forth from all the vast reaches of Asia. The secret of stealth was only a part of *Ninjitsu*.

Camellion studied the thick Mekeketugze leaves to his right. His features had taken on an immobility that was unusual. His chin, nose, cheeks, and forehead seemed to have been sealed with an unearthly motionlessness, as if inner determination had resulted in a total hardening of his appearance, a setting of his face into one without expression.

An Auto Mag in each hand, Camellion began to crawl very quietly to his right.

General Chin and Major She-Tung didn't know what to do. Both feared the tall American and his deadly accuracy with firearms, but neither man wanted to reveal his dread to the other. Neither wanted to lose face. They lay flat in the tall grass, each man aiming his submachine gun at one

203

side of the chorrten trunk thirty feet in front of them, General Chin to the left, Major She-Tung to the right. They had agreed that the best offense would be to wait until the American became nervous and made a mistake. All he had to do was expose a small portion of his body; the machine guns would do the rest.

In their own minds, the two officers were positive that the American could not escape. On She-Tung's side of the trunk—to his right—there was only empty space. To the left of the trunk—to General Chin's right—there were thick masses of leaves; nothing human could move behind those leaves without making them move.

"Comrade General," She-Tung began. "It has been over half an hour. Could he have escaped by moving back and keeping the trunk between him and us?"

"Don't take your eyes off your side of the tree," hissed Chin, his low voice a deadly warning. "He has to be there. He would not leave without the tube weapon. And we can see it, lying there to our right. He's up there. Be patient, Comrade."

Several minutes passed, the stillness laughing at the two Chinese. The short silence was broken by two explosions behind General Chin and Major She-Tung. There were two loud thuds as projectiles struck the barrels of the sub-machine guns and almost tore the weapons from their hands. Both officers then saw, much to their horror, that the bullets had half-penetrated the steel, a part of the slugs protruding from the metal.

"Drop the machine guns, roll over on your backs, and stand up!" a voice spoke in perfect Chinese.

Shaking with fear, Hsun Chin and Yang She-Tung let go of the wrecked machine guns, turned over on their backs, then, staring up at the Death Merchant, stumbled to their feet. Without Camellion's having to tell them, they raised their hands above their heads.

"How did you get behind us?" General Chin asked in a weak voice. He felt sick to his stomach, as if he might have to vomit. He could feel the bile of defeat trying to crawl into his throat.

Major She-Tung found his voice, which sounded strange even to him. "We are your prisoners, American.

We demand that you abide by the rules laid down by the Geneva Convention."

A darkness spun in She-Tung's mind, tiny crow's feet of obscurity dimming reality.

"You 'demand'!" There was scorn in Camellion's voice. Yet in his face there was no hint of unpleasant emotion. No fear. No anger. No hatred. General Chin and Major She-Tung saw only the strange glow in his eyes, and the black muzzles of the Auto Mags staring at them.

"You should not have come to Shambhala," Camellion said, almost in a whisper. "Now you must pay the price."

General Chin and Major She-Tung gaped in horror at the Death Merchant, each man trembling in fear.

For the first time Camellion smiled.

"Dominus Lucis vobiscum!" he said, and pulled the triggers of the Auto Mags. General Hsun Chin and Major Yang She-Tung were knocked six feet back by the two .44 slugs. They lay in the grass, fist-sized holes in their chests and backs.

The voice of Tilhut spoke clearly within the inner reaches of Camellion's mind: *Return to the dome. Your work is finished.*

Chapter Sixteen

Tilhut and Pel had landed the flying platform a short distance from the long slope, and had accompanied Camellion and his party to the tableland of bare rock at the top of the incline. Fourteen people had walked through the doorway of the blue wall. But only seven would leave the cryptic world of Shambhala. One Black Beret was alive—Loren Eaton. The five Bhutanese had been whittled down to Major Kor Sidkeong. Paul Gemz had been very lucky. He couldn't have won against a sixteen-year old boy in a fist fight. Almost immediately, the Chinese had knocked him out; he had not been a threat to their lives and they had not killed him. Gemz's jaw still hurt; otherwise he was unharmed. Camellion, West, Lauterjung, and Helena Banya comprised the rest of the group, now standing not far from the blue wall, facing Pel and Tilhut.

"The Chinese will make another attempt," the Death Merchant said to the two Guardians. "How will you defend yourselves?"

"We will not have to defend ourselves," Tilhut said softly. "The tunnel, through which came the evil men from China, is at this very moment being put into a state of nonexistence. In a small space of time, where the passage existed there will be only solid rock."

"I suppose you'll do the same with the tunnel we used?" Camellion said.

Tilhut nodded. "Yes. After all of you are safe, the tunnel will cease to exist. We are self-sufficient and do not require anything from the world outside this place."

"There are other tunnels," Vallie West said darkly.

"They do not concern you," the plain-speaking Tilhut replied. "Nor should you bother to wonder, to speculate about the American government. Your Central Intelligence Agency will believe the story you tell. Your government will keep the secret well hidden, just as it has not revealed the truth about the interdimensional machines used by the enemies of the Inelqu. Your government knows that these vehicles exist. They have destroyed United States aircraft. However, your government does not know that what you call UFOs or flying saucers are vehicles from another space-time continuum and that they are searching this planet for the places where the Inelqu wait in slumber for rescue."

Pel, reading the thoughts of Paul Gemz, said in a louder voice, "Incorrect, Paul Gemz. No one will believe anything you will put into your book. Write what you will. Shambhala will remain a myth."

Added Tilhut, "The reputation of a man is like his shadow, which sometimes follows and sometimes goes before. Sometimes it is longer, and sometimes shorter than he. Your reputation in the scientific world, Paul Gemz, is not as such that what you will write will be accepted without question. You book will be considered fiction. You will be laughed at by your fellows."

Visibly embarrassed, Gemz frowned. He would have liked to continue the conversation.

"Go," Tilhut said firmly. "Walk to the wall. The doorway will appear."

"Lead the way, Vallie," Camellion said. "I'll go last."

West strode toward the shining blue wall, which appeared as solid as a mountain. He was only ten feet from the center of the wall when the doorway became reality. Beyond he could see the rocks and slag of the tunnel.

West walked through the doorway. One by one the others followed. Camellion, who was last, didn't look back until he was in the tunnel, on the other side of the wall.

The doorway was gone.

The seven switched on Dynalites and began moving forward, all of them anxious to leave the tunnel, the last connecting link with the enigmatic world of Shambhala.

There was little conversation. They were alive and that was enough. But not for Camellion, who had another matter weighing heavily on his mind. In Barasat he had been given a message by one of the CIA men who had helped make arrangements for the flight to Bhutan.

"It came in at the Calcutta Station only a few hours ago," the man had explained. "It's a TS-1 priority message."

The message had consisted of two words: OPERATION THUNDERBOLT.

"Operation" meant mission. "Thunderbolt" was a code word from a special cipher that Camellion used in long-range contacts with the Central Intelligence Agency.

"Thunderbolt" meant North Korea. . . .

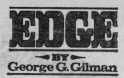

EDGE

◄BY►
George G. Gilman

Josiah Hedges is no ordinary man — he's a violent gunslinger.
Created out of fury, hardened by death and destruction, he's
rough, but not as rough as the fate of those who get in his way.

> Over 3.5 million copies sold!